MISGUIDED REVENGE

D. M. Bourgeois

Book Cover Layout © 2022 ebooklaunch.com

MISGUIDED REVENGE / D. M. BOURGEOIS. -- 1st ed.
ISBN 978-1-7357823-2-4

For my family
who have always been my safe haven.

*Family is supposed to be our safe haven. Very often,
it's the place where we find the deepest heartache.*

—Iyanla Vanzant

MISGUIDED REVENGE

CHAPTER 1

T he long winding road carried you deeper and deeper through the swamp, finally delivering you into a little fishing town surrounded by more swamps and bayous. The sun was still a few hours from making an appearance and the darkness brought on an unexplained feeling of isolation and uncertainty. The thick brush bordering the Bayou danced in the wind and threatened to reach out and grab you. Trying to stay focused on the task ahead, Evan Robert Cortez, E.R. for short, a local game warden, shook his head a few times, tightened his grip and continued to drive. He felt childish letting the night get to him. He had driven that road a million times and still found it to be unnerving in the dark.

When E.R. received the call from his coworker at 1:00 in the morning asking to meet, he didn't hesitate. Aside from being his coworker, Liam Barrios was a loyal friend who always had E.R.'s back. E.R. recalled their conversation and couldn't help but wonder why Liam called him instead of the local police. He still had a few more minutes to drive and his imagination continued to run rampant.

E.R. took the job as game warden for the Louisiana Wildlife and Fisheries and quickly discovered that the work satisfied his innate need to make a difference in the community. Now twenty-one, and two years at the job, he sometimes wondered if he should've pursued an engineering career. That was his goal for many years, but E.R.'s passion for the outdoors eventually drove him in a different direction. When the game warden position that included his hometown of Lafitte, Louisiana became available, he whole heartedly jumped in and never looked back. On a normal day, things were quiet, except for a few people who insisted on speeding through the park or the occasional fishermen who exceeded their limit of fish. As he drove to meet Liam, he looked around. *Man, I'm glad I work the dayshift.* All the local folklore flooded his thoughts and threatened to send him into a panic. The scariest one was "The Legend of Bayou Coquille", and the story goes that on that very road, always at midnight, a woman in a white wedding dress could be seen hanging from a big oak tree. E.R. made a mental note to learn more about the story. Thankfully, he could see the bridge ahead that would take him to the cemetery and was able to gain control of his thoughts. He prayed that he could help Liam with his problem and then get out of there quickly.

A light mist had begun to fall. When E.R. arrived at the cemetery, he turned off the engine and sat there for a while. Once he gathered up enough courage, he got out of his truck to search for Liam. He spotted a truck inside the gates but was too far away to make a positive identification. E.R. was never fond of cemeteries, especially the Fleming Cemetery in the town of Jean Lafitte. Hidden back on a dead-end street, flanked by Bayou Barataria, the darkness of the moonless night made it difficult to see. E.R. called Liam's name and waited for him to answer.

Fearing that he was too far away to hear anything, he made his way towards the entrance of the Cemetery. E.R. stopped there and took out his gun. His breath was shallow, and his body had begun to shake. He had never used his weapon before and he wanted to keep it that way, but at the same time he wanted to be prepared.

E.R. yelled, "Liam, where are you? Talk to me man. You're starting to worry me." He stood still again and listened. The only sounds he heard were those of chirping crickets and frogs. He wondered if he should turn around and call for help. He made the decision to keep going and find his friend because Liam was not the type of guy to ask for help unless he really needed it. He was vague on the phone when he called earlier but E.R. did recognize by the urgency in his voice that he needed help. As he moved towards the lights coming from the truck, he stayed alert. He took every step carefully and recognized the dangers around him. He thought he saw movement to his left and in haste picked up his pace. He jumped back when he realized he was about to step on a snake and lost sight of whatever it was he thought he saw. He waited for the snake to slither across the soggy ground to safety. He was amazed and frightened that at night the cemetery seemed to come alive. He chuckled at that thought. *Let's hope not everything comes alive.*

As he reached the truck inside the gates, he saw that it belonged to Liam. The door on the driver side was open, but no one was in the truck. Fearing that something had happened to Liam, his heart rate accelerated. Even with low visibility, he could clearly see the massive Live Oak tree perched high on the top of an old Indian Mound in the middle of the cemetery. The light mist was now coming down at a steady pace. He scanned the Cemetery and took note of all the graves and tombstones. Apart from being old and battered from natures elements, most were well cared for. He walked up to one of them and bent down to get a better look, but the engraving was too worn to read. *Where could you be?* E.R. started to wonder to himself as he looked around. *I'm in the right place because your truck's here.*

Being there alone at night was unsettling and caused E.R. to think of all the people that were spending eternity there. He looked around and noticed a grave close to the Bayou that looked freshly dug so he headed in that direction. Out of the corner of his eye, he saw movement again on his left side. Quickly, he ducked behind the nearest tombstone. It was one of the neglected ones, with years of wear causing the decayed stone to crumble from all sides. He was grateful that it was still tall enough to provide him with a place to take cover. He watched as it looked like someone was dragging something or someone, but he was too far away to tell for sure. He started to call out to Liam but thought better of it. E.R.'s thoughts raced as he tried to figure what his next step should be. E.R. was trained to handle a variety of situations, but nothing could've prepared him for this. He felt a sense of urgency to find out who it was and what they were dragging. *What if it's Liam and he's in trouble?*

Coming out from behind the tombstone with his gun raised, E.R. identified himself, and shouted for the person to stop. They didn't, but instead let go of what they were dragging and took off running. For a moment he stood, eyes scanning through the darkness, to see which direction he should take. He couldn't recall ever being that scared. There was still no answer from Liam, which confirmed that someone else was in the Cemetery with them and had possibly rendered him incapacitated. That thought horrified E.R. as he stood paralyzed with fear.

He was at a loss as he looked around the cemetery. He loudly called out "Liam" several times but heard no response. He remembered a quote that said, "Courage is not the absence of fear, but rather the judgment that something else is more important than fear." Liam was definitely in trouble and E.R. had to help him. He took off and as he ran, he said a quick prayer. It seemed appropriate at the time since he was in a Cemetery with only God listening. If it was Liam being dragged, he must be unconscious or worse, dead. E.R. was never a fan of horror flicks, but as he looked around, he felt like he was right in the middle of one.

He ran faster as he grew closer, stumbling through the high grass and weeds. Almost there, he felt a moment of relief. He was so focused on the object he was running towards, he failed to see the open grave site that awaited its new occupant and fell into it. It was so dark he could barely see his hands in front of his face. He felt around the dirt walls to see if he could find a way out. He found nothing but loose dirt and because the walls were being washed away with the rain, he was stranded. He became dizzy and disoriented and panic started to take over. He raised his hand to his forehead and felt the warmth of something wet running down his face - blood. He knew he had to stay calm but found it difficult to do. He reached into his pocket for his phone and attempted to make a call, but he didn't have service.

Think E.R.! You gotta get out of here. As he talked to himself, he got down on his knees and frantically started to feel around. He could still hear the crickets chirping, but now he heard a new sound. He strained to listen but with the rain it was almost impossible to determine what it was. He hoped that someone would come, but he knew the chances of that happening were slim. He was already really worried about Liam, and now he began to worry about himself. Dizziness took over and E.R. felt a calmness just before the darkness came.

E.R. jumped to his feet. He frantically patted his face, shirt, and pants. He reached for his forehead and searched for the source of the blood he felt drip down his face. There was nothing there.

"Where am I? How long was I out? What's going on?"

There was a light that illuminated in front of E.R. and as he looked up, he rubbed his eyes to get a better view. It was almost too bright to look at, but something drew him in and demanded his attention. He stumbled backwards when he realized that there was an image in the light.

"What do you want? Who are you?" E.R. looked around the dark space trying to find a way out. He wasn't sure what was going on but felt the need to be vigilant.

The figure was of a beautiful woman dressed in a long flowing dress. Her eyes were sullen and suggested deep sorrow. She was mysterious and eerie and at the same time tranquil and welcoming. She appeared to float above the ground ghost like. When she was sure that she had E.R.'s attention, she grew anxious. He watched her carefully as she tried to tell him something. She looked so familiar, but E.R. couldn't recall the connection.

"Do you know Liam? Where is he?" E.R. stood still and waited for some kind of answer.

She pointed towards the mound in the middle of the cemetery. The sadness in her eyes disappeared and was replaced with darkness. She continued to point and without moving her mouth, she urged E.R. to go.

CHAPTER 2

E.R. had always loved the outdoors. When he was a young boy, his grandfather introduced him to all the amazing things nature had to offer. Living in a small fishing town was a sportsmen's paradise providing them with great fishing, hunting, hiking, and more. Often, they would spend the night outdoors, make camp, and just watch the stars. When they went fishing or hunting, his grandfather would cook their catch of the day over an open fire. He felt blessed to have had all those experiences with his grandfather and wished that he had more time to spend with him now. Since he held a full-time job, E.R. had to manage his time, but spending it with his grandfather was still his favorite pastime.

E.R. sprang up and looked around the room. He seemed to be alone, so he sat back down on the bed. *Where am I? Where is Liam? How did I get here?* He looked at the clock and noticed that it was 9 am. With a splitting headache he was having trouble piecing together last night's events. He fumbled through his pockets for his phone and hit redial. Liam was the last person he spoke to the night before and E.R. hoped he could shed some light on what was happening. He remembered falling into a freshly dug grave and realized he was hurt and eventually passed out. He didn't think he would get out of Fleming Cemetery alive. He woke up alone in his own bed with a bandage on his head. He did recall that he had the strangest conversation with a ghost like woman trying to tell him something, but the whole thing was fuzzy, and he was confused. *I must've been dreaming.* E.R. was growing impatient for answers.

Liam picked up on the first ring and brought E.R. back to reality. "Hey Man, welcome back. I thought I was going to lose you last night."

"Liam! What happened man? Where are you? How did I get home last night?" E.R. kept firing question after question and wanted answers.

"Slow down man. I'm heading to your place now. I'll explain everything when I get there. Can I pick up anything for you? Coffee?"

"No. Just get over here. I'm gonna jump in the shower, so let yourself in." E.R., still in his muddy clothes, needed to clean up.

"See ya in about 15 minutes."

E.R. made his way to the bathroom and turned on the shower. His mind was still so foggy, and he felt weak. He stepped into the shower and allowed the hot water to wash away all the remnants of the night before. As he ran his fingers over the back of his head he flinched when he felt the egg sized lump. He remembered falling into the grave and feeling the blood running down his forehead but didn't remember hitting the back of his head. The hot water felt good but at the same time, E.R. started to feel lightheaded again. He turned off the shower and waited for his wobblily legs to steady. *I must have a concussion. Liam better get here with some answers soon.* He headed straight to his bed and waited. He was feeling vulnerable and that was not a familiar feeling for E.R. He was anxious and struggled to stay awake. He considered getting up and walking to keep alert but thought better of it. *What if I fall and can't get to a phone? Wait for Liam. He's gonna be here soon. Just don't go to sleep.* E.R. thought back to a time when he was young, when he fell off his bike and hit his head. His parents would not let him go to sleep in case he had a concussion.

E.R.'s mind drifted from one childhood memory to another. He and his childhood friend Conner were always getting into some mess and his parents were always there to clean it up. Their endless horseplay made E.R. the person he was today, and he wouldn't trade it for anything. He missed Conner but would never admit it because he knew he could ever forgive his best friend for betraying him. After being blindsided by someone so close to him, someone he thought he would always be able to rely on, E.R. learned to guard himself and keep people at a distance. Focusing back on the situation at hand, E.R. knew that he was better off staying in bed until Liam arrived. He didn't like it, but he understood that it was best. *He should be here soon.*

Again, E.R. was jolted out of sleep and this time by a loud cracking noise. He sat up and strained to listen for the noise that woke him. It was completely dark, so he took a few deep breaths trying to stay calm. *What time is it? Did I fall back asleep? Where's Liam?* E.R. reached for his gun on the nightstand and knocked over the clock sitting next to it. He listened as he heard footsteps, a door squeaking as it opened, then, crunch, crunch, crunch. It sounded like broken glass. E.R. ran towards the noise and found the back door wide open. *Was someone in here?* He walked slowly to the door and looked around. He didn't see anyone but the glass on the door was broken and all over the floor. He had a bad feeling which could be due to his injuries, but he didn't think so. It was his gut telling him danger was near and his gut was never wrong. E.R. dialed Liam's phone again and this time it went to voicemail. *Where are you man? This is getting old!*

Too weak to make it back to his bedroom, E.R. sat down on the kitchen floor. He sat for a while trying to piece together what little memory he had of last night's events. He was still finding it impossible to fill in the blanks and grew frustrated. He thought about the events leading up to the phone call from Liam. Usually, E.R. and Liam worked the same schedule every week. They were not only partners on the job but best friends away from work. Earlier that night, they went to Bourbon Heat, a bar on Bourbon Street in New Orleans. That wasn't unusual because they often went to the bars after work to socialize and unwind before going home. E.R. remembered that Liam met a girl from Houma, Louisiana, and spent the night dancing with her. Because of the Covid-19 Pandemic, capacity in the bar was limited, so while Liam and the girl were in the outside courtyard, E.R. stayed inside by the bar with other friends. When he was ready to leave, he couldn't find Liam and assumed he had left with the girl. *Could she be involved in this? She was hot and Liam is always a sucker for the lookers.*

E.R. spent the next hour trying to remember every detail of the girl and the events from that night. He and Liam met the girl, Charley Ann, while they ordered drinks at the bar. She said her last name, but he couldn't recall what it was. She told them that she was a student at Nicholls State but taking a semester off. She was a good height with long lean legs. E.R. remembered the slight stir he felt in the bottom of his stomach when he first saw her. Her emerald-green eyes pierced his and his first thought was, *I could get lost in those eyes.* E.R. quickly realized that Liam was making a move, so he suppressed his desire and sipped his drink. He and Liam were always respectful of each other when it came to women and had managed to avoid any conflict.

E.R. remembered seeing Liam throughout the night but didn't really pay enough attention to know when he left. He made a mental note to contact some of the guys to see if they remembered seeing Liam leave and whether or not he was alone. He wished he could remember more about Charley Ann but once she became off limits, his attention was focused elsewhere. He vaguely remembered her talking about an ex-boyfriend, but the details were sketchy. Again, she was off limits for E.R. and even though *Bourbon Heat* wasn't as busy as normal, it was dark and loud like most bars.

E.R. stayed on the floor in his kitchen for hours going in and out of consciousness. Finally around 10 pm, he decided to call the one person he could always rely on. He dialed the number and waited for his grandfather to answer.

"Hey man. What's up?" Griff was surprised to hear from his grandson so late.

"Hey Paw. I think I need your help. Can you come over? I'll explain when you get here."

"You don't sound too good. I'll be there in a few." Griff hung up the phone and grabbed his keys. E.R.'s voice was weak, and he delivered each word slowly almost with a whisper. His grandson wouldn't have called that late if he weren't in trouble. Griff was grateful that E.R. lived about 5 minutes away because he felt a sense of urgency come over him. *That boy needs help now*. He thought about calling 911 but decided to wait to see what shape he was in first. E.R. was always a smart guy and if he thought he needed immediate attention he would have called 911 instead of Griff.

Out of nowhere, Griff thought about his own brother Christopher. When he and Griff were young, they were inseparable. They were a family of five living in a small two-bedroom, one bathroom house. His parents struggled financially but what they lacked in money they made up for with love and support. Christopher was much younger than Griff, but they were so much alike. Anytime Griff got into any kind of conflict, which was more often than not in his younger years, Christopher had his back. They were still very close and his grandson, E.R., reminded him of Christopher all the time. Griff had two daughters and his only grandson E.R. was like the son he never had.

When E.R. started school, he met Conner and the two became inseparable. They remained best friends all through school but unfortunately, after graduation they had a fallout. Conner went on to college in Alabama and ended up living there and even though he wouldn't admit it, E.R. was hurt by Conner and would probably never get over it. Griff tried for years to get the two to reconcile but to no avail. E.R. was a good, warm person that would do anything for anybody. He treated people with love and respect and expected the same. Griff knew deep down that E.R. would always love Conner, but he would never let him into his life again. In fact, he knew that E.R. found it difficult to let anyone new into his life.

As he approached E.R. 's house, Griff looked around cautiously. His grandson sounded like he was in trouble when they spoke but didn't indicate what that trouble was. The house was dark and quiet. The streetlights were on but the trees in front of E.R.'s house deflected what little light broke through and cast a shadowy darkness across the front. Griff parked across the street and sat for a moment. He was anxious to get to E.R. but didn't want to run into a dangerous situation. Since Griff had retired, he teamed up with his best friend Tab and started a detective agency. Tab shared his expertise with Griff and guided him over the past few years, but the most important lesson he learned was patience, because before that, he would've rushed into a situation like this without thinking.

Griff crossed the street and walked around the house. He wasn't sure what he expected to find but nothing seemed out of the ordinary. E.R.'s house was one of many old shotgun style houses on that street. The house had a front porch and several rooms that were in a straight line. It was an old neighborhood and most of the families had lived there for years. He made his way to the rear of the house and noticed the back door was open and broken glass was scattered on the ground. He drew his weapon and identified himself. From inside the house he heard E.R. mumble, so he rushed in. He found his grandson crouched against the wall in the kitchen, near the back door.

"E.R. are you alright?" Griff quickly looked around before holstering his weapon and reaching his grandson.

"I'm good. I hit my head last night and I think I have a concussion. Can you help me up?"

With his grandfather's assistance, E.R. made his way to the sofa and sat down. He still had a terrible headache, but the fog had gone away a while ago. He looked up at his Grandfather who was waiting for an explanation and E.R.'s whole body tensed, and his heart raced like he was running a sprint. Behind his grandfather, E.R. saw the same vision of the woman he'd seen by the gravesite. He squeezed his eyes tight as his chest began to rise and sink rapidly, and then he inhaled long and deep before he looked up again. It was gone. *I must be hallucinating.*

"Sorry to call you so late. I couldn't reach Liam and I panicked. Last night he called me and asked if we could meet at the Fleming Cemetery."

"In Lafitte? What was he doing there? The cemetery's not the smartest place to meet someone. It's so isolated not to mention spooky at night." Griff sat down on the sofa and waited for E.R. to continue.

"I know. I have no idea why he wanted to meet there and the sense of urgency in his voice distracted me from asking questions. I figured I would meet him and get answers but here I am no closer to finding out what's going on. I can't even remember how I got home. When I woke up this morning, I called Liam and he said he was on his way here. I fell back to sleep and the next time I woke I called him again and it went straight to voicemail. I'm really beginning to worry now. It's not like Liam to just disappear like that. I tried calling his phone over and over, but it goes straight to voicemail every time." E.R. tried to get up again, but Griff stopped him. E.R. continued to fill Griff in about Bourbon Heat and the mysterious girl. He decided to keep his dream, if that's what it was, to himself until he made sense of it.

"Whoa man. Take it easy. It's late now and you have a nasty bump on your head. Let's sit for a while and try to come up with a plan. We can't just go running around blindly looking for Liam. I'll call Mr. Tab and have him go by his place and check it out. You'll be no good to

Liam if you end up in the hospital. Maybe we should call Piper just in case. I know she would be happy to come check you out. I think it's been 24 hours since you hit your head so go take a shower and lay down. I'm gonna make some calls, and E.R., don't worry we'll find him." Griff helped E.R. to the bathroom and turned on the shower. He went back to the kitchen and dialed his niece Piper and then his friend.

Griff and Tab had been friends since college. Tab was his partner in their newly formed detective agency. He used to work for the D.A.'s office and had helped Griff when his family was recently in danger. He was someone that Griff always depended on and when he decided to open up a detective agency, Tab decided to join him. He had been contemplating retiring from the D.A.'s office but he didn't want to retire completely. When Griff suggested the partnership, Tab knew it was a sign and didn't hesitate to accept. Now it's been over a year and things were going great. They worked well together and surprisingly had more than enough cases to keep them busy.

After giving Tab the details, Griff remembered the broken glass on the back door. The glass was on the floor in the kitchen which meant that it was broken from the outside. E.R. told Griff that he thought he heard the glass break and then footsteps. Griff walked around and noticed some of the grass was bent over where someone recently walked. He hoped whoever it was would be long gone by now. *What were they after? E.R. doesn't know why Liam called him but maybe that has something to do with it.*

Griff walked around the house and checked the rest of the windows. He headed back in to check on E.R. and get him settled. Griff helped E.R. to his bed and brought him a bottle of water. He tried to get him to eat something, but he refused.

There was a knock on the door and in walked Piper. She and E.R. were born a month apart and the two had always been close. She lived around the corner and rushed over when Griff called her. Piper was a nurse and Griff felt better knowing that she could address E.R.'s injuries.

"What did you do now E.R.?" Piper was smiling at her cousin as she walked into his room.

"I'm good! I just hit my head last night when I fell into an open grave at Flemings cemetery in Lafitte." E.R. smiled to himself because he knew that would shock Piper.

Piper stood for a second with her jaw wide open. "Really? I'm not surprised. You always find some mess to get into. What were you doing there? Never mind." Piper lifted her hand and went on. "Can you lean up a little so I can see the back of your head?"

"Liam called me and asked me to meet him there. Have you seen Liam around? Wait. Weren't you at *Bourbon Heat* the other night when we were there? You came in with Harper around the time I was leaving. I forgot about that. Did you see Liam leave? I think he's in trouble and I can't reach him."

"I didn't see Liam when I was there. We only stayed a little while after we saw you because Harper had clients early the next morning and it was already late when we got there. Why did Liam want you to meet him in the cemetery? That's kind of creepy even for y'all." Piper motioned for E.R. to lean back.

"That's the problem. I don't know what he wanted but he sounded stressed out." E.R. leaned back on the pillow.

"You already know you have a nasty bump on the back of your head. The cut on your forehead could've used stiches but it's too late for that now. I would say go to the hospital, but I know you won't go. It's been almost 24 hours now so you're probably fine. If you have any dizziness or nausea, please go get it checked out." Piper got up to leave. "Unc, I think he'll be fine but check on him every once in a while. Call me if you need me. E.R., take it easy okay."

"I just need to lie down for a while. Thanks for coming Piper. I really appreciate it. Paw you can go home too, I'll be okay."

"Not a chance. I'll be on the sofa if you need me. Lucky for you, Honey is out of town this week on a girl's trip. Get some sleep and we'll tackle this in the morning. Love ya man." Griff watched over his grandson for a while and after he fell asleep, went to the sofa, and tried to relax.

E.R. was a smart kid and Griff knew that he was good at his job. When he told Griff that he wanted to be a game warden instead of an engineer, he knew that was the right choice for him. Griff was aware that the job was some-times dangerous, but he really didn't think about that side of it when he gave E.R. his blessing. Now, with his grandson laying in the other room, he wasn't sure that he made the right decision. Griff felt the tension throughout his body and tried to relax. *Liam better have a good excuse for not showing up here. Where could that boy be?* His conversation with his grandson hadn't offered any explanation to what was going on. He told Griff everything he could remember leading up to that moment, but they were both still in the dark. Apparently, Liam was in some kind of trouble and with the broken glass on E.R.'s floor it appeared that somebody was looking for something and thought that he was involved.

****

The darkness came as an unexpected comfort. Even though the space he was in wasn't tight, it was definitely confining but at the same time provided a sense of security. From the time he regained consciousness, pieces of recent events reminded him that he was in serious trouble. He knew that soon he would come face to face with true evil. When he was asked to help her escape a life of abuse, he didn't hesitate. He was familiar with what a life of abuse was like because he was told that as a boy, his father had abused him. The faded memories still haunted him but thankfully, his mother cared more for her child than the monster she married and got him to safety. His heart quickened as he thought of that time and his chest rose and fell with each breath. He felt his lungs struggle for air from the confinement and before he knew it, he became dizzy and then completely still again.

CHAPTER 3

Griff woke up early to make sure that E.R. was alright. His grandson was in pretty bad shape when he arrived last night, so Griff checked on him periodically throughout the night as Piper had instructed. He was still sleeping so Griff decided to go get donuts and let him rest a while longer. He was still worried about his health but was more worried about the trouble E.R. seemed to be in now. He decided to check in with Tab since he called Griff last night after passing by Liam's house to let him know that his house appeared empty. He offered to come by E.R.'s house but Griff told him that it wasn't necessary and that it could wait until the morning.

Arriving back to E.R.'s house with coffee and donuts, Griff found his grandson in the shower. He alerted him that he was back and waited in the kitchen. E.R.'s voice was strong, and he sounded much better which was a relief to Griff. All night he toyed with the idea of bringing him to the hospital. Under normal circumstances, he might have pushed the issue but with the hospitals full of Covid-19 patients he wasn't sure that was a good option.

He heard the shower stop running and waited for him to talk about a plan.

"Good morning E.R. How is Cinderella today?" Griff loved to tease his grandson. "Good to see you up and around. How do you feel?"

E.R. chuckled at the comment. "I'm good. I have a slight headache, but I'm not dizzy today. I have a nice bump on the back of my head. Did you tell Honey or mom?" E.R. looked concerned.

"Honey knows you fell and hit your head, but I told her you were alright. I also asked her not to worry your mom. I do think you should call her and let her know what's going on. You don't have to tell her everything, but you need to let her know. I spoke to Mr. Tab, and he said Liam's house was empty last night. I think we should take a ride to the cemetery and see if we can get some answers. I bought some donuts so please eat one before we leave."

"I tried Liam's phone again, but it went straight to voicemail. Something is definitely wrong, and I'm really worried," E.R. said as he left the room.

The drive to the cemetery was quiet because both E.R. and Griff were thinking about the situation. E.R. was worried about his friend and was anxious to find answers.

"Did Mr. Tab say if Liam's truck was at his house?"

Griff looked at his grandson. "He said that there was no sign of anyone around and that there were no vehicles in the driveway. I couldn't remember what Liam drove and I didn't want to wake you. I'm sure we'll get some answers at the cemetery."

When they arrived, Griff parked outside the gates. Even though it was daylight, the cemetery still seemed spooky and put them on edge, especially since there was a light fog that hovered just above the ground. Again, the cemetery was quiet and deserted. They got out of the truck and looked around.

"Liam's truck was parked right over there. When I arrived, I noticed the driver's side door was open, but the truck was empty."

Griff bent down looking for tire tracks. Rain had been falling the last few days, so it was pretty muddy. There were tire tracks leading up to where E.R. said Liam's truck was parked. He couldn't tell if the tracks were from when Liam arrived or left because it was only one set. He would've had to back up the same way he came in which was very possible since it was a narrow entrance through the gate.

"Well it looks like a vehicle did drive through this gate but it's not here now. Why don't you go wait in the truck and I'll check things out?" Griff waited for the response he knew he would get.

"Not a chance! I want to retrace my actions from the other night. I remember exactly where I saw something moving in the cemetery and I want to check it out." E.R. was already headed into the cemetery.

Close on his heels, Griff followed making a mental note of his surroundings. Even though there was a nasty wind blowing, there was a sense of tranquility in the air. Griff never did like cemeteries and would prefer to be anywhere else but abandoning E.R. was not an option. As far as Griff could see, the place was deserted. He watched E.R. as he moved with purpose through the gravesites towards the back of the cemetery. He stopped suddenly and leaned in as if he were listening for something. After a few moments, Griff spoke up.

"Did you hear something? E.R, did you hear something?"

E.R. waited a few seconds more before responding to Griff.

"Didn't you hear that? It sounded like a voice, maybe Liam's voice. The sound came from that direction, but I can't understand what he's saying." E.R. started to walk in the direction he pointed to. Again he came to an abrupt stop. He noticed an open grave and remembered that last night he saw someone dragging something in that direction. E.R. began to panic and with each breath he drew minimal air into his lungs. *What if Liam's in that grave? It couldn't be him because he brought me home the other night. I spoke to him on the phone yesterday morning, didn't I? Liam is alive, he has to be.*

Griff sensed that his grandson was beginning to panic and took the lead. When he reached the grave, it was empty. The ground was sloppy and the bottom of the freshly dug grave was covered with a milky mixture of rain and dirt. Griff picked up a nearby broken branch and poked around in the grave.

"Nothing in here. Just a lot of dirt and water. Are you sure this is where you saw movement?"

E.R. slowly approached the grave and nodded. He was grateful that Griff was with him for back-up and emotional support because he was about to lose it. Head still pounding he plopped down on a tree stump and tucked his head down to get control of his breathing. Looking over towards Griff, he noticed a trail in the mud. He quickly jumped up and pointed for Griff to see.

"That looks like something was being dragged across the ground. I knew I saw something." E.R. Jumped up and ran to Griff. Both men inspected the ground around the gravesite and determined that the trail began about ten feet from the grave and ended by its opening. After searching the area for more clues and coming up short, they decided to head back towards the grave that E.R. fell into. Oddly, there were no signs of another open grave. E.R. insisted that it was there and was baffled by its absence. Just when they had decided to give up and go home, they heard a noise closer to the bayou.

"What was that?" Griff motioned for E.R. to go to the left side of the place they heard the sound while he went to the right. Whatever it was started moving towards the bayou and appeared to be crawling on the ground because they couldn't see anything but the brush move. They were gaining ground from both sides and just when they reached the bayou an alligator slid into the water. Griff started to laugh first and then E.R. joined in. It's not uncommon to see alligators there especially lurking in the weeds on the edge on the bayou. They were just expecting to find a person creeping through the high grass trying to escape not a gator.

"I think it's time to get out of here. We're both on edge and I think we need a fresh mind to look at things. Let's head back to my office and meet with Tab. He might have some ideas. Things are not adding up, and from what I saw at the cemetery something apparently happened there. E.R., tell me again what you remember about that night. Are you sure you didn't fall into the open grave we found? It was dark and rainy, maybe you are confused."

E.R. was annoyed that Griff asked him that. "Yes, I'm sure! I didn't hit my head and become confused until after I fell into the grave."

"Chill out. I believe you. Like I said, things are just not adding up. That would mean that someone went to a lot of trouble to cover up what happened, but why? What could be the motive? You said Liam met a girl who lived out of town and had an ex, so maybe Liam was caught with the girl and things got out of hand. I'm not sure he would come back to the scene of the crime to fill in a grave. It seems to me that he would just leave town. Contact your buddies that were with you when Liam met the girl. Maybe they will remember something. A name would be great." Griff had hoped for some kind of lead to get things moving.

The ride to Griff's office was quiet. Griff finally broke the silence and suggested that they should file a missing person's report even though it wasn't quite 24 hours since Liam last called E.R. and failed to show up. He also suggested that E.R. check in with his job and anyone else he could think of to see if they heard from him. E.R. quickly reminded Griff that Liam didn't have any family and was currently single. E.R. was like family to him so if he were capable, he would've reached out already.

Tab was waiting for them when they arrived. He filed the missing person report and then joined them in the conference room to go over the events leading up to Liam's disappearance. He didn't say anything, but he felt like time was running out to find him alive. The first few days were always critical, and the clock was ticking. They discussed a plan to question all of E.R.'s friends and the bartenders that were tending bar that night.

When they had decided on a plan, Griff, and E.R. headed to Liam's house. E.R. knew where Liam hid his key and hoped to find something inside his house that would give them some answers. It was highly likely that Liam brought Charley Ann back to his place that night. When Liam called E.R. for help, it was 1:00 in the morning and he had just fallen asleep. He jumped up and headed out the door without thinking.

Griff cautioned E.R. to take it slow and stay alert. "Obviously, something is going on with Liam and we don't know what that is. You said he sounded anxious when he called you that night so we can assume he was in trouble."

E.R. retrieved the key from its hiding spot and approached the front door. He checked the handle to make sure it was locked. Griff motioned that he was going to go around to the rear door. E.R. inserted the key and slowly turned the handle. He stepped through Liam's front door, as he had done a million times before and called out his name. After a few minutes he cautiously entered.

Everything seemed to be in place. E.R. walked through the house towards the back door and let Griff in. There were dishes in the sink and two glasses and an empty bottle of wine on the table. E.R. knew Liam to be extremely neat, so the dirty dishes concerned him. The two men searched Liam's two-bedroom house, one room at a time. Aside from an unmade bed, another red flag, everything was in place.

"Let's get out of here. We can grab some lunch and then head over to Bourbon Heat to question the bartenders." Griff headed towards the kitchen. He stopped at the table and carefully bagged the two wine glasses. Hopefully, one of the glasses would have Charley Ann's fingerprints or DNA and would reveal information they needed.

E.R. looked down the hall as he turned to leave and jumped back. At the entrance to the bathroom he saw the woman from his dream, and she was pointing. Before he could react, the vision was gone. E.R. slowly walked towards the bathroom not sure what to expect. He hesitated but only for a moment then turned the corner into the bathroom. He didn't see anything out of the ordinary. As he was about to turn and leave, he noticed the shower cur-tain move. It was a slight wave but definitely movement. He looked up towards the ceiling and followed the posi-tion of the vent to the shower curtain. The vent was facing the other way so that couldn't be the source. He slowly backed up and softly stepped into the bathroom. Griff no-ticed E.R.'s behavior and came up behind him for back up. The bathroom was spacious, and it seemed to take forever to cross the room to the tub. E.R. looked back at Griff who had his weapon drawn and motioned that they would give a count of three. E.R. mouthed one, two, three and jerked the curtain back. Slouched down in Liam's bathtub, fully clothed and completely terrified, was a dark-haired girl with emerald, green eyes.

"Charley Ann?"

CHAPTER 4

E.R. had the same feeling in the pit of his stomach that he had the first time he laid eyes on her. Charley Ann was definitely a beauty even with bloodshot swollen eyes and that long dark hair in a ponytail sitting on the top of her head. Her trembling hands and terrified stare suggested that she was clearly upset and scared of something. At the site of Charley Ann, E.R. forgot about seeing the lady in the flowing dress again.

E.R. sat on the side of the tub and attempted to calm her down. Griff holstered his weapon and backed towards the door to give them some room. He was anxious for answers but figured they could get her to cooperate if they took a bit of a slower pace.

"Charley Ann, right? Do you remember me from *Bourbon Heat*? I was with Liam at the bar that night." E.R. spoke softly hoping to gain her confidence.

"I'm not going to hurt you. Let me help you up so we can go into the kitchen and talk." He held out his hand and waited for her to respond.

She didn't move. E.R. could see she was trying to reason things out in her mind but was still too afraid to move. She looked up at E.R. with pleading eyes that revealed just how panic-stricken she was feeling. Finally, she reached for his hand. Together they stood up and walked from the bathroom to the kitchen. For a moment, E.R. thought her trembling legs were going to fail her but she made it to the kitchen and sat down.

Griff grabbed a bottle of water from the fridge and handed it to her. He backed up again in fear of scaring her.

"My name is Evan, but my friends call me E.R., which is the name I used when I introduced myself to you the other night. This is my Grandfather Griff. We have some questions. We're here because Liam is missing. The last time I saw him was at the bar. I remembered your first name but couldn't recall your last. I also remembered that you talked about an ex-boyfriend or husband." E.R. watched her carefully and knew that she was trying to assess the situation and at the same time, was looking for a way out. He wasn't too concerned that she would try to run because she looked weak and disorientated.

Griff spoke up. "I'm a private investigator and trying to help E.R. find Liam. We need to know when you last saw him and what has happened since then." Charley Ann looked up at Griff and he was struck with sympathy and worried about how fragile she looked. He softened his approach and tried again.

"We are really worried about Liam. If you have any information that could help us locate him, please tell us."

"I don't know where he is." Charley Ann's trembling voice came out as a whisper.

"Okay. When was the last time you saw him?" E.R. anxiously waited for an answer.

"Yesterday morning. He said he was going over to your house to check on you and let you know what was going on. He was worried about you because you hit your head."

"And you've been here waiting for him since then? Did you hear from him any time after he left here? He called me yesterday morning to say he was coming over, but he never made it." E.R. was trying to be patient but he wanted more answers, and he wanted them fast.

Griff recognized his grandson's growing frustration and decided to step in. He wanted to call Tab and get him over there but didn't want to leave E.R. alone.

"Listen Charley Ann. Obviously, Liam is in trouble. Do you know why he called E.R. to meet him at the cemetery the other night? We need to know. I think Liam was trying to help you with something." Griff hoped she would open up soon.

"Liam was trying to help me hide from my ex-boyfriend. We lived together in Houma for the past six months and after the first few months he became physically abusive. I tried to leave him several times, but he would always find me. He threatened me and my family and I was afraid he was going to kill me. Earlier this week I packed a bag and left him. I didn't know where to go but decided to head to New Orleans. I ended up in *Bourbon Heat* that night and met Liam. I was honest with him from the moment we met, and he offered to help me." Her lip began to tremble, and she started to cry. "He was so nice to me. I am so sorry I got him mixed up in this. When we were leaving the bar, I thought I saw my ex, Brian, across the street. I freaked out and ran back in the bar. Liam followed and I told him but when we went back outside there was no one there. He suggested we go back to his place and call his best friend for help." She looked into E.R.'s eyes. "I guess that would be you."

"Why would he ask me to meet him at Fleming Cemetery if y'all were coming to his house?"

"We didn't make it to his house at that time. Liam thought that we were being followed so he kept driv-ing. We drove down a long road and across a bridge. He felt like we had lost whoever was following us, so he decided to turn down one particular road that led to the cemetery. That's when he called you. I pan-icked and jumped out the car. Liam ran after me and tried to stop me, but it was so dark and foggy that it was difficult to see. I tripped on an old gravesite and twisted my ankle. Liam heard the truck pull up and stop so he quickly pulled me behind another gravesite. We thought that it was Brian."

E.R. was confused. "Why did he leave his truck there? How did y'all get home? How did he get me home?"

"Again, we were both scared that it was Brian. By the time he realized it was you calling out for him, he went to look for you. He could hear you moaning but didn't know where you were. He feared that Brian had done something to you. Finally he found you and after getting you out of that grave, we got into your truck and brought you home. You were in and out of consciousness but seemed to be okay. Liam thought that it was best if he left his truck at the cemetery for a while. We took an uber back to his house."

"So, you thought you were being followed by Brian?" Griff was trying to piece it all together.

"I'm not sure. I'm not even sure if it was Brian that I saw outside Bourbon Heat. I was clearly on edge since I decided to leave Houma, and I was definitely paranoid." Charley Ann looked completely exhausted.

"Is there any way you can find out if Brian is still in Houma or if he in fact came to New Orleans after you? Maybe there's someone you can contact back home?" E.R. wanted to be sure that it could be Charley Ann's ex-boyfriend before they went in that direction.

"I wanted to call home, but I was afraid to use my cell phone. Liam told me to leave it at the bar, but I was scared and didn't want to be without a phone. When he didn't return yesterday, I smashed my phone and threw it in the trash. I was afraid that Brian would track it and find me at Liam's house alone."

"So Liam must've taken an uber to the cemetery to pick up his truck yesterday morning. E.R., that must be when he called you. So, something happened after he left here and called you. Liam's truck was gone, and we just assumed he picked it up. Was someone waiting for him at the cemetery? Did Liam pick up his truck or did something happen to him and someone else took his truck? At least we have a timeline to start with. Let's let Charley Ann go freshen up and settle down a bit. This has been overwhelming for everyone. I'm gonna call Tab and run all of this by him. Maybe he'll have some ideas."

E.R. agreed and encouraged Charley Ann to take a break. "Thanks for talking to us. I know things are crazy, but I really need to find Liam. We can talk some more later."

Charley Ann hesitated for a moment then got up and walked down the hall. She was already familiar with Liam's house. E.R. wondered just how close Liam and Charley Ann got last night. He was still intrigued by her but knew she was off limits. He tried to deny it, but that slight stir he felt in the bottom of his stomach the first time they met was getting stronger and that worried him.

"Hey."

Charley Ann turned and looked back at E.R. with a blank stare.

Her stare was captivating. "Is Charley Ann short for something?" He didn't know why but he needed to know more about her. E.R. convinced himself that it was necessary if they were going to find Liam, but deep down he knew that was not the only reason.

"No, just Charley Ann. Charley Ann Cheramie." She tried to smile as if everything were alright, but the pain she'd endured and the anguish she now felt showed through eyes that betrayed her.

Griff and E.R. discussed the best course of action to take. They both agreed that Charley Ann was telling the truth and that she needed protection. They also felt strongly that her ex-boyfriend was involved but wasn't completely sure how.

"E.R., I think you need to find someplace to stay other than your house, especially since someone entered your house yesterday. If they know where you live it's a good possibility that they followed Liam to your house and then to his." Griff was visibly troubled.

"I guess I could reach out to one of my buddies in Lafitte and stay at a camp, but I'm not going into hiding. I need to find Liam."

"I understand your frustration and concern but what about Charley Ann? It's evident that she needs help. We don't know if her ex is involved with Liam's disappearance, but we do know she is in danger as well. Until we get a handle on things, I think you need to step up and protect her. Once we locate this guy you can rest a little easier but until then, I don't think you have a choice buddy. Make some calls to friends and when Charley Ann is a bit calmer, we can swing by your house to pick up some necessities. Look, I know you don't like it but that's just how it is right now." Griff patted E.R. on the shoulder and walked outside. He needed some air and a moment to think. What was he going to tell Abby? His wife would kill him if he let anything happen to her golden boy.

When Charley Ann resurfaced again, they told her of their plans. She repeatedly apologized for getting them involved and thanked them for helping her. E.R. noticed that while she was still undoubtedly upset, the way she was holding herself suggested that she was relieved. E.R. felt sorry for her and was glad she decided to trust them. He wouldn't let her down.

CHAPTER 5

E.R. launched his boat and Griff drove his grandson's truck back to his house. Charley Ann didn't seem to mind that they would be staying at a fishing camp in Lafitte for a few days. Griff thought it was best for them to lay low for a while and E.R. didn't want to bring any danger to his parents or grandparents. He reached out to his friend Jason who owns a camp in Bayou Dogris that is only accessible by boat. That made it slightly harder for someone to sneak up on them. He didn't like to be isolated at a time when his best friend needed him the most, but there was Charley Ann's safety to consider.

"Is there anything you need before we get there? We could stop there." E.R. slowed down and pointed at Joe's Landing, a local marina.

"I'm fine. Everything I need is right here in my backpack. But thanks for asking. How much longer before we get there?" Charley Ann looked relaxed for the first time that day.

The ripples in the water were mesmerizing and the breeze was cool and brisk. At any moment things could change and the water could get choppy, or the skies could open up and they would be caught in an afternoon thunderstorm. E.R. wanted to get to the camp soon and make sure the generator started. Jason said that they were at the camp last weekend and that everything was good to go. E.R. was grateful that this camp had a separate bedroom. He wasn't sure that he could handle sleeping in the same room with Charley Ann. As it was, he was having trouble keeping his eyes off of her. The trivial things like the way her hair was blowing in the wind and the color of her eyes in the sunlight were driving him crazy. He tried to look away but then the wind would pick up the scent of her perfume and send it his way. *What is wrong with you? You know she's off limits. Get to the camp and stay away from her.*

"We should be there in a few minutes." The ride seemed like hours but he was in Bayou Dennis so it wouldn't be much longer. "Are you hungry? I know it's been a long morning and we are both exhausted, but we should eat. I brought some sandwich meat and chips. I'll start the generator and then make us some sandwiches."

When they arrived at the camp, E.R. jumped out of the boat and turned to help Charley Ann. She hopped out without any assistance which was better for him because the thought of their hands touching already had him on edge. The generator started right up. When E.R. walked back into the camp, Charley Ann had the sandwiches made and was waiting on him. He had a surprisingly warm feeling in his stomach that was all too familiar to him. He suddenly lost his appetite but knew he had to eat.

He didn't want to be rude, so he reminded himself that this woman was not Christina.

Before they left for the camp, Griff suggested Charley Ann call home and inquire about Brian. She borrowed E. R's phone and reached out to her sister Chelsea who said that she hadn't seen Brian but that she would ask around. Charley Ann explained what was going on and told her sister to report back to Griff and that she could be reached through him.

After some time, Charley Ann asked, "Did your grandfather hear from my sister yet? She was going to check around to see if Brian was still in Houma." Charley Ann's voice sounded hopeful.

"Not yet. I know it's none of my business but what's the deal with you and Brian?"

Charley Ann starred into her plate and remained quiet for a few minutes. "You never really know someone. Not completely. In the beginning, I thought he was amazing. He was generous, kind, gentle and patient, and after we moved in together, he was the complete opposite. He became controlling and possessive and tried to isolate me from my family and friends. My parents are gone but I still have my sister. The more he attempted to control me the more I pushed back. Eventually, things turned violent, and I knew I had to get away." She looked up from her plate and E.R. could see tears in her eyes. Her lower lip was trembling, and she shivered as she continued. "He was a likable guy and people had trouble believing that he could be anything but nice. I knew the only shot I had was to provoke him in public and hope that someone would be there to witness it and help me. The plan worked except most people don't want to get involved in other people's personal problems. They now knew the type of guy he was but didn't know how to help me. I finally left and got a restraining order against him, but he continued stalking me. That's when I knew I had to leave Houma. I had no idea where to go so I headed to New Orleans while I tried to figure it out. That's when I ran into you and Liam. Liam was very sweet and offered to help me." Again she hesitated and took a deep breath.

"Charley Ann, you don't have to go on if you don't want to." E.R. could hear the pain in every word she spoke. He realized that she was a strong independent woman struggling to keep her head above water.

"No. I want to help any way I can to find Liam. If talking about my relationship with Brian helps, I want to continue. I owe Liam that much."

"Speaking of Liam, was that the first time y'all met? Tell me what happened after y'all left the bar." E.R. wasn't sure he wanted to know but knew he had to.

"We walked out of the bar, and I thought I saw Brian, so I ran back in. When we walked out again, there was no one around. It was late and Liam said that there were re-strictions in place because of covid. We went to his truck and headed to his house. Once we were on the Crescent City Connection Bridge, Liam said that he thought some-one was following us. It was a dark colored truck, but it stayed far enough back that we couldn't get any more details. Brian does drive a black Toyota Tundra, but we couldn't confirm that it was him. It was foggy that night and visibility was low. Once we got off at the Barataria Blvd. exit, Liam thought he lost him. He said my paranoia was rubbing off on him and he was concerned about going straight to his house. We kept driving until we eventually arrived at the cemetery and that's when he called you. We didn't get to his house until early yesterday morning after we brought you to your house. We slept for a few hours and when we woke up, he went to go check on you. That's it. I didn't know what to do or who to call. I don't even know Liam's last name."

E.R. patiently listened to Charley Ann, giving her as much time as she needed. What else did they have to do but sit and wait. He wished that his grandfather would call with an update. As time passed, E.R. became more and more anxious. Even though he tried not to think about Liam being missing, it was eating away at him. He and Liam spent a lot of time at that very camp, sat at that very table and the memories were overwhelming. On the other hand, looking at Charley Ann and listening to her hoarse voice was soothing and that made him feel guilty. E.R. stood up and walked out the back door. He needed some air to clear his head.

He could hear noise from inside the camp and assumed it was Charley Ann cleaning up the mess in the kitchen. He felt bad that he got up and left her and was contemplating apologizing. He knew that none of this was her fault but couldn't help thinking that if she hadn't showed up at Bourbon Heat, Liam wouldn't be missing. As he reached for the door to the kitchen, his phone rang. Caller ID revealed that it was Griff. E.R. paused for a moment, took a deep breath, and answered the call.

"Hey Paw. Did you find out anything?"

"Hey man, how are you holding up? I know you hate being out there right now, but I promise you I am doing everything I can to help. We got a lead on Liam's truck and we're waiting for confirmation. It was found on River Road near the Harvey Locks. Tab's picking me up and we're going to head out there and hopefully get some direction on his whereabouts. Charley Ann's sister called and said that no one has seen Brian but that she was going to continue to ask around. My gut is telling me that he's probably involved somehow. Any word yet from Liam?"

E.R. was trying to process the information. *What was Liam's truck doing by the Harvey Locks? Did he drive it there or did someone else?* There were so many unanswered questions and the tension creeping up the back of his head caused him to rub his neck and shake his head.

"E.R. did you hear me? Have you heard from Liam?"

"Sorry. No. Nothing. I think I should come back and help look for him. I feel useless here and I know if I were missing, Liam would never give up searching for me."

"E.R., you are not giving up. You are trying to be smart and at the same time protect someone that needs help. Liam disappeared trying to help Charley Ann so don't you think he would want you to keep her safe? Just sit tight for the night at least. When we get more information about the truck, I'll call you. Until then, try to relax and focus on Charley Ann. Try to get as much information from her about Brian. Find out about their relationship, friends, hangouts, and anything else that might help us find him." Griff assured him that they would talk soon and hung up.

E.R. turned around to go inside and ran smack into Charley Ann. He didn't hear her come outside and was startled by her presence. She was even more beautiful in the sunlight and that made him nervous. He backed up and suggested they sit on the dock.

"That was my grandfather. He spoke to your sister, and she told him that no one has seen Brian. She was going to continue to ask around. Was there a particular place y'all hung out? What about certain friends that he would be with? Any family in the area?"

Charley Ann was feeling interrogated. E R. was so desperate for answers that he was almost shouting the questions at her. She sat at the end of the dock and let her legs dangle off the edge. The cool feel of the dark bayou water as she submerged her feet was comforting and energizing at the same time. *Who does he think he is? Why is he yelling at me? I'm trying to help him find Liam.* Charley Ann wanted to shout those thoughts at him but decided to give him a minute to calm down. If he decided to leave, where would she go? She wasn't happy with her current predicament, but she knew staying with E.R. was her best choice.

"Mahony's"

E.R. looked up to find Charley Ann starring into the bayou. His shoulders slouched and his demeanor changed as he looked at her. He was touched by her vulnerability and was unexpectantly embarrassed by his aggressive behavior. He needed answers but realized that he needed to do so in a more sympathetic way.

"What did you say?"

"Mahony's. That's where we usually hung out. It's a sports bar in Houma. Sometimes we went to Bubba's in Thibodaux. A lot of my friends go to Nicholls, and we would meet up with them. Deciding to take a semester off was a hard decision for me but I felt like I needed to get a handle on my life. Brian is originally from Lafayette, but had been living and working in Grand Isle, for the past few years. He doesn't have any family or friends in Houma, and he didn't talk about anyone in Grand Isle. He didn't talk much about his family but did suggest that they were estranged. We met at a football game and dated for nearly a month before he moved in with me. He was staying in a small apartment that he was renting month to month and suggested that he stay with me while he looked for a more permanent place. We were always together anyway so I agreed. I thought..." Charley Ann's voice trailed off. She pushed back the tears and wiped her eyes with her shoulder. "I thought I was in love. How did I not see the monster he was? How did I let him fool me?" She didn't wait for an answer. "My parents passed away when I was 14 and my sister was 17. We struggled but we were both determined to survive and make something of ourselves. We quickly learned that this world has a dark, ugly side but each experience taught us how to survive. I was always good at reading people from the start. We both could recognize a bad situation when we saw it and that helped us avoid a lot of misery."

E.R. noticed that Charley Ann was shaking. It wasn't cold but there was a chill in the air.

"If you're cold we can go inside."

Charley Ann shook her head. "I'm not cold." She looked down at her right hand and saw what E.R. had noticed. Her whole body was trembling, but she wasn't cold. She was scared, anxious, and uneasy, but not cold. She drew her legs up and pulled them close to her chest.

"When I met Brian, I did have my guard up. I ignored his advances, but he was persistent. He did little things like help an older lady down the stairs at the game. He was polite and kind to people around us. I began to see him in a different light and by the end of the game I agreed to go out with him. He continued to do things like open the door for me and treat me with respect." With her quivering voice failing her, Charley Ann took a deep breath and waited to start again.

E.R. could see the pain in Charley Ann's eyes as she described the betrayal that now has her on the run. She didn't seem to blame anyone but herself. He wondered if she was upset about her breakup with Brian or the fact that she didn't recognize the threat. He had a feeling that she was more upset about the latter and that caused the all too familiar sensation in his stomach to dance.

"What about Liam? Did you read him correctly? How did you know you could trust him?" E.R. felt bad about pointing that out to her, but he had to keep his guard up.

Charley Ann knew those questions were meant to remind her that she could have been vulnerable once again when she trusted Liam or E.R. for that matter. She could feel the animosity that he felt towards her. She didn't blame him because if someone she loved was missing, she would feel the same way towards the person responsible - her. She was responsible for Liam's disappearance and the constant bile in her throat reminded her of that.

"Do you mind if I take a nap. I'm exhausted and I just need time to refuel. We can continue to talk later." Charley Ann didn't wait for a response. She got up and walked away from E.R. leaving him to deal with his growing admiration for a girl he hardly knew.

CHAPTER 6

Griff and Tab went to the Harvey locks to confirm that it was Liam's truck that was found. He got out of Tab's truck and noticed the beauty of the area. From the top of the levee you could see across the Mississippi River to the beautiful city skyline. New Orleans was an old city but with the view of the Superdome surrounded by all the buildings it was a remarkable site to see. He tore himself from the mesmerizing view and focused in on the task he was there for. Liam's truck was parked along the levee but there were no signs of Liam and as far as they could tell the truck was not vandalized in any way. Unfortunately, there were no cameras in the area which would've confirmed who was actually driving the truck. The police dusted the truck for fingerprints and questioned people in the area. They questioned a couple walking their dog on the levee and they said they were there when the truck arrived yesterday morning. They gave a description of the man that got out of the vehicle but said they were too far away to be accurate. They reported that it was a tall white male that was on the thin side, but they didn't see when he left because they were just walking by. Today, when they noticed that the truck was still there, they called the police to report it.

"Let's go get some lunch. The officers have my number and if they get any information, they'll contact me. We need to get a picture of Liam and Brian. You said that Charley Ann destroyed her phone but I'm sure her sister must have a picture of Brian. Ask E.R. to send one of Liam and ask Charley Ann to give us more details about Brian. Maybe the couple could ID a photo or at least eliminate one or both of the men." Tab was trying to cover all the bases.

Griff made the phone calls as he walked to the car.

"E.R. sent a photo of Liam and said he would send info from Charley Ann soon. Charley Ann's sister didn't answer the phone, so I left a message for her to call me back. Where are we going?"

"Gattuso's Restaurant is right up the road. How's that sound?" Tab waited for Griff to answer.

"Sounds good to me. I love their appetizers."

The two men were seated right away, and the waitress took their orders. They were used to the demands of their work, but this case was personal and therefore taxing. Tab was reminded of a few years ago when Griff's wife was in danger.

"How's Abby doing? This can't be easy for her. I know how protective she is of E.R., and I'm surprised that she's not here with you."

Griff shifted in his seat. "She doesn't know. She knows that he hit his head, but I didn't tell her that Liam was missing, and that E.R. was protecting Charley Ann." Griff put up his hands. "I know. She's going to kill me, but I promised E.R. that I wouldn't say anything. And we don't know that E.R. is actually in any danger. He fell into that grave and bumped his head while he was looking for Liam. I will tell Abby if we don't get answers soon. I just don't want to worry her. After the ordeal she went through a while ago, it took her some time to get back to normal. I don't want to mess that up."

Tab just shook his head. "That's on you man. But I think you're right about one thing, she is going to kill you."

Griff dreaded the thought of telling Abby and was uncomfortable thinking about the results of that conversation. While he was deep in thought, some familiar faces walked up to the table. Gattuso's was frequented by the locals because of its good food so Griff wasn't surprised to see his good friends Greg and Pam there. He and Tab stood to greet them both and insisted that they join them. He looked forward to the distraction and always enjoyed their company. He was careful about the topic of conversation at the table because Pam and Griff's wife Abby were best friends, and he didn't want anything to get back before he had a chance to tell her.

****

E.R. decided to let Charley Ann have some time alone. She was dealing with some major issues, and he figured she needed to make some decisions. What would be her next move was what was on his mind. It took courage to leave everyone and everything you know and start a new life. A part of him even wondered if her relationship with Brian was over. He listened to his grandfather talk hypothetically about some of their cases and too often the abused went back to the abuser. E.R. felt the rage begin to boil deep inside at the thought of someone hurting Charley Ann. He could feel the heat that creeped up the back of his head and he subconsciously began to rub his neck. The stress was starting to get to him. *I can't just sit out here and wait.*

E.R. took out his phone and called his Uncle China. He knew that China was always booked up with fishing charters ever since he started China's Charters and thought that he might be in the area. When it was decided that he and Charley Ann would hide out at the camp, he packed the essentials and left. He didn't think about bringing fishing gear. There were a few poles at the camp but not too much bait.

"Hey Uncle China. What's up?"

"Just got back from a morning charter. What's up little cuz?"

"I'm out here by Jason's camp in Bayou Dogris and thought you might be close by. I need some bait." E.R. knew what was coming next.

"Dang brah, you went out there without bait?" China shook his head but wasn't surprised.

"Yeah, I was in a hurry. I'm helping out a friend and she needed a place to hide out for a while."

"She? Come on brah. How you gonna impress a girl when you forgot all your stuff? Let me see what I can do." China was grinning at the thought of E.R. at that camp with a girl. It's been a while since E.R. even talked about a girl. He was pretty torn up after the split with the last one.

China had just filled up his boat with gas and was taking it for a test run because earlier he heard an unfamiliar noise and wanted to check it out. The waters were getting a little choppy, probably from an afternoon storm brewing, but he had another early morning charter the next day and needed things to be running right. As he came around a bend. he noticed something floating between two logs next to the bank. At first, he thought it was a monster redfish chasing minnows but as he got closer, he ruled that out. He was still pretty far away to identify it but thought maybe it was a small bull shark or dolphin. Whatever it was it looked to be covered in seaweed and flanked between two logs.

"E.R. I'll holler back at you in a minute." China hung up before E.R. had time to answer. He didn't know why, but he had a bad feeling. Reluctantly, he trolled towards the bank to get a closer look and that's when he realized that it wasn't all seaweed but in fact a wig floating in the water. He chuckled to himself as he got on the front of the boat to fish it out of the water. He couldn't believe he was frightened by a wig floating in the water. He used a fishing pole to try and maneuver it closer to the boat. The wig was heavier than he thought and appeared to be stuck on the log. Suddenly, the wig broke free of the log and attached to it was a body.

"O my God!" China jumped to the back of the boat. It took a few minutes for his mind to register what he was looking at and he sat down when he realized it was a dead body. It wasn't just a wig, but someone's hair still attached to their head. China pulled out his phone and called 911. He gave them his location and a description of the body. They told him to remain there, and that they were on the way.

The body was face down, but he thought it looked like a man. He didn't want to get close again, but he was afraid it would float away. He pushed on the middle of the body to get it back closer to the shore where he had found it. When he pushed a second time, the body flipped over. Disgusted by the site, he gave the body one more push and it snagged on another log sticking out of the bank. This was the first time China had seen a dead body. It's funny that the site of a dead body freaked him out because he had no problem skinning a deer, cleaning fish, and doing other things most people found disgusting. He was having trouble keeping his lunch down and decided he needed a distraction. China called his nephew Chad and told him what was going on. He felt better talking to someone while he was waiting.

"Brah, they better hurry up!" China tried not to look at the body.

"Do you know who lives there?"

"I've been trying to figure out who, but I'm drawing a blank. I'm across the bayou from Boutte's restaurant." China looked towards Boutte's and noticed that they were open for business. He thought about going over there but was afraid to leave the area. The 911 dispatcher told him to stay there but he really didn't want to. He gave them his information and told them he was leaving, but as much as he wanted to go, he felt bad to leave the scene. The man didn't look familiar but there was seaweed partially covering his face so he couldn't be sure. He didn't want to get any closer to a dead body and decided it was best to wait for someone else to make the identification. After he hung up with Chad, he sat for a minute then made the decision to leave. That's when he heard the sirens in the distance. They were on the way.

****

Griff and Tab enjoyed their food and were waiting to pay the bill. There was a band setting up in the corner of the restaurant for that night. Griff recognized his buddy Billy and went over to talk to him. While he and Billy were catching up, Tab's phone rang.

"We gotta go." Tab tapped Griff on the shoulder and headed for the door.

Griff ended his conversation with Billy and followed Tab out of the restaurant. He knew by Tab's abrupt behavior that something was up. He must've received some news.

"What's up man?"

"I just got a call from a friend who heard that they found a body in the bayou in Lafitte. Looks like it's been in the water about 24 hours. Your nephew China found the body and reported it to the local police. I think we better get down there and quick." Tab was already out the door.

Griff didn't want to think about what finding a dead body in Lafitte could mean. He had spoken to E.R. a few minutes ago so at least he didn't have to worry about him. However, if the body turned out to be Liam, it would destroy E.R. to say the least.

"Did they say if China identified the body? He knows Liam and would recognize if it were him." Griff secretly said a prayer that it was not Liam.

"They didn't say. I told him we were on the way, and he could fill me in when we get there. I know you are rattled man but let's not give up hope that it's not Liam."

Griff's thoughts jumped all over the place. He decided to share what he was thinking with Tab. "If the body was in the water for only 24 hours and floating, that would indicate that death occurred before it hit the water and drowning was not the cause. The body sinks when the lungs fill up with water then it takes several days for the gases inside the body to make it float up again. That would mean that it could be Liam and that he was killed at the cemetery and dumped in the bayou. And that would also mean that it was not Liam who drove his truck to the locks and left it there. I hope that's not the case man."

Griff's phone beeped. It was a text message from Charley Ann's sister with a picture of Brian. It wasn't clear, but he looked to be tall and slim, just like Liam. He forwarded both pictures to Tab's phone and started to call E.R. with the news. *Maybe I'll wait until we get more information. I don't need him freaking out and getting in the way.* In a fit of terror, Griff realized that if that was Liam's body E.R. was in serious danger. He looked at Tab and saw that the same thought had just occurred to him.

CHAPTER 7

Griff and Tab approached the scene in Lafitte where the dead body was found in the bayou. The area was full of police cars and emergency vehicles. In the small town of Lafitte everyone knows everyone, and news traveled fast. Traffic had begun to back up on the two-lane highway but was still moving. As they approached the scene, Griff noticed that traffic was being directed by some local deputies. It seemed it was going to take forever to get there, and his anxiety level was reaching its limit.

Griff had met Liam a few years ago when he and E.R. became partners and he had considered him part of the family ever since. He was a genuinely good person and wasn't afraid of working hard for what he wanted. Griff had always felt relieved to know that Liam had E.R. 's back and knew that the two of them were good agents. That's why it was no surprise to Griff that Liam had attempted to help Charley Ann even when he didn't know anything about her or her situation. He also knew that his grandson would make the decision to help Charley Ann, even though he wanted to be out searching for Liam. *Chivalry.* That was the word that popped into Griff's mind. Both of those boys lived their lives in a chivalrous manner on and off the job.

"I think we should probably park around here and walk. It might take another 15 minutes to get there in this traffic." Griff wanted answers now.

"I think you're right." Tab pulled the truck off the road and parked.

They made their way through the cars and finally met up with the detective in charge. Griff looked around for China but didn't see him. They were told that the body was still in the water and hadn't been identified yet. The detective led them to the bayou and that's when Griff spotted China. He was still sitting in his boat that was tied up along the dock. Tab continued to confer with the detective and Griff headed towards China. He could see something in the bayou but was hesitant to look that way. The thought of it being Liam shook him to his core. He was so anxious the whole ride there and now he couldn't bring himself to make the confirmation.

"Hey man. How's it going?"

"Not so good Unc. I'd rather be fishing." China forced a smile.

"Did you recognize the body? They said you were the one who found it and called it in."

"Oh my God Unc, that was a trip. I'm never gonna get that image out of my mind. The face was covered with seaweed, so I couldn't really see it, but I could tell that it was a man. Did they identify him yet?"

"I don't think so. When we arrived, we spoke to the detective in charge, and he was leading us to the body. That's when I saw you and came over. I guess I need to go see what's going on. China, Liam's missing. He called E.R. and asked him to meet him the other morning at Fleming's cemetery. When E.R. arrived Liam was gone, but his truck was still there. We haven't been able to locate him yet. I pray that's not his body in the water." Griff stood up and adjusted his hat.

"No joke. I just spoke to E.R. a little while ago. In fact I was on the phone with him when I found the body. I could tell the body was a man, but I wasn't getting any closer. It did look like it wasn't in the water too long. Man, I don't think it was Liam, but I can't be positive."

"So E.R. knows about the body?" Griff's mind raced.

"No. I didn't know what it was at first and I told him I'd get back to him. I've been so freaked out that I forgot to call him back. He wanted me to bring him some bait to use for fishing. He said he was at Jason's camp with a girl. Should I call him back?"

Griff thought for a moment. "No. Not yet. The girl he is with at the camp is a girl Liam was trying to help get away from her abusive ex. Someone tried to break into E.R.'s house yesterday so he's hiding out to protect the girl. We believe that Liam's disappearance and the break in are connected to Charley Ann, the girl, and her ex-boyfriend Brian. If E.R. knew that you found a dead body in the bayou he would come here without hesitating. I need him to stay put and stay safe." Griff took a deep breath. "I guess I need to go see if I can find some answers."

"Let me know what you find out. This is crazy man. I'm ready to get out of here. They asked me to stay around so I am, but they need to hurry up." China couldn't seem to calm down.

"I will."

Griff headed towards the location of the body. It wasn't but about ten yards away, but the walk seemed to take forever. *What if it's Liam. How will I tell E.R. that his best friend is dead? I should've listened to E.R. the night he called and gone to search for Liam. E.R. was too weak, but I could've sent Tab. Now it's been more than 24 hours and things are starting to look grim.* Griff was feeling guilty and would never forgive himself if the body turned out to be Liam. He was finding it more difficult to stay positive the closer he got to the scene.

****

E.R. was sitting on the dock waiting for China to call him back. He hung up before E.R. could respond and that made him wonder what was so important. E.R. loved that time of the day on the water. The winds usually died down making the water glassy. Often you could see the sky so vividly in the water that it appeared as a painting. He sat there trying to go over the events from the last few days again. He had retraced every moment again and again but couldn't help feeling like he missed something. *Who moved Liam's truck? Where was the grave I fell into? Why would someone break into my house? Can I really trust Charley Ann?* As he contemplated that last thought, Charley Ann tapped him on the shoulder. E.R. sprung back with a sudden jolt and almost knocked her down. He was noticeably shaken by her unexpected presence but still attempted to steady her fall.

"I'm so sorry. You startled me. I didn't hear the door open. Are you okay?" E.R. felt embarrassed of his reaction and was worried that he hurt her at the same time.

"I'm fine." Charley Ann was subconsciously rubbing her arm.

E.R. reached for her arm, but she backed up. He was surprised by her reaction but let her have her space. He did almost knock her over so maybe she was startled herself.

"Were you able to get some rest? I hope I didn't wake you. I called my Uncle China to bring us some fishing bait. I'm waiting for him to call me back."

"Yes, I did sleep a few minutes. I guess events of the last few days have taken a toll on me. I just can't seem to put all the pieces together. Brian was abusive to me, but I don't think he had the guts to kidnap or kill someone. I believe that he would follow me to try and get me to go back home but I don't think he would confront Liam in the process. Something's just not adding up."

"I hope you're right. I am really starting to worry about Liam. If Brian is not involved, then what could've happened to him? He would never disappear without a word to me or work, so something is definitely wrong. I'm sure you realize just in the short time that you knew him that Liam is a stand-up guy. Everyone loves him and I can't think of one person that would want to hurt him. He's been like a brother to me since we met and if he had any enemies, I would know about them." E.R. paced back and forth from one side of the dock to the other.

"I'm sorry that Liam is missing. He was so nice to me and as you said I realized what type of guy he was right away. I was apprehensive at first because of my experience with Brian. I still can't believe that I was fooled by him and that I allowed myself to be in that situation. I always thought that I was a good judge of character." Charley Ann's eyes were glossy as she continued on. "When I met Liam, he knew that I was in trouble. He was genuinely concerned and listened to me explain what was going on. When he offered to help me, I was so relieved. I didn't know where I was going to go or what to do. He said that he knew people that would help me figure things out and that in the morning he would contact them. I don't know what made me trust Liam, but I did, and I agreed to go with him. If he hadn't come along, I don't know what I would have done. I think he was talking about his grandparents, but he didn't say their names."

"When I met Liam, he said he didn't have any family. He said that he lost his parents a long time ago and didn't have any siblings. We fast became best friends and he's become part of my family now, so he was probably talking about my grandparents because Liam is very close to them. He knew that they would do everything in their power to help you. And Honey works with women's shelters and would know what to do."

"Honey?"

"Yeah. That's what we call my grandmother. She started volunteering at a woman's shelter last year and like my grandfather and Liam, would help anyone in need. I wonder if he called her before he disappeared. My grandfather told Honey that I hit my head, but I asked him not to tell her what was going on. She loves Liam like a grandson, and I didn't want to worry her. Maybe he could find out if she heard from Liam. I'll ask him when he calls. I wonder what's keeping Uncle China. I hope he didn't forget." E.R. checked his phone to make sure he didn't miss his call. He knew his Uncle China wouldn't forget so he probably got busy. He remembered that he said his boat was giving him trouble so maybe that's what kept him.

It was getting late in the afternoon and E.R. was trying to keep calm. He could tell that Charley Ann was feeling the same way but was surprised that she hadn't complained. Going out to the camp was a good idea because they were isolated but at the same time the isolation was trying. It had only been a few hours but seemed like forever. E.R. was losing his mind. He was worried sick about Liam, but he was also dealing with his growing attraction to a girl he wasn't sure he could trust.

****

As Griff approached the crime scene, Tab was leaning over the bank looking at the body. He stopped and held his breath while he waited for his response. Tab knew Liam and if it were him, Griff figured he would know from his reaction. China said that the face was covered with seaweed, but it appeared that someone had already removed the seaweed from the body. The wind had died down a bit and allowed the murky bayou water to calm down. The bank was uneven, made up of rock and oyster shells that made it difficult to keep up. Tab stood up and started talking to the detective. Griff exhaled and held out hope that Tab did not recognize the body. He turned just as Griff approached.

"It's not Liam." Griff was staring at the body and didn't react to Tab. "Griff did you hear me? It's not Liam."

Griff heard Tab but was busy staring at the body. From where he was now standing, he could see the body clearly and he could tell that it was definitely not Liam. He didn't have time to be happy about that because from where he was standing, he could identify the body and the body that was floating dead in the bayou was Brian, Charley Ann's ex-boyfriend.

CHAPTER 8

A few hours had passed since E.R. called his Uncle China. He and Charley Ann stayed out on the dock both showing signs of complete distress. Not knowing what was going on was grueling and took tremendous patience and self-control not to give in to those feelings. A thousand times E.R. considered jumping into the boat and heading home, but each time, he reminded himself that he was doing it for Charley Ann and that would be what Liam would want him to do.

"We need to do something to keep busy. I saw a cast net over there that we could use to catch some small bait fish. It looks like Uncle China got tied up with something. Have you ever fished before?" E.R. hoped that she had.

Charley Ann shot him a look that suggested his question was an insult.

E.R. held up his hands as to surrender. "Hey. Sorry. I know plenty of girls that have never fished and have no interest in it what-so-ever. I just thought I would ask."

"I grew up in Houma. I know how to fish and hunt. It's been a while but I'm sure I can keep up."

Before E.R. could answer, Charley Ann was on her feet and headed to grab the cast net. He was impressed that she even knew what a cast net was. Most of the women he'd been around lately may know how to fish but it's not their choice of fun things to do. Christina joined him when she wanted something in return. He learned that trick early on, but it was easier to just let her think she was fooling him.

Early in their relationship, E.R. felt like he and Christina were so compatible. They both loved the same things, fishing being one of them. They enjoyed eating out and listening to music. After the second month, things changed, and E.R. found himself in a relationship that required more work than he wanted to do. He knew that the relationship was headed in the wrong direction, but he couldn't pull the trigger to end things. He liked having someone special in his life and wasn't ready to go back to being alone.

At the time, E.R.'s best friend Conner had recently broken up with his girlfriend. The two men were friends since childhood and E. R was concerned that Conner wasn't taking the break-up well. Christina started spending a great deal of time with Conner supposedly cheering him up. E.R. was blindsided and blamed himself for not seeing what was coming.

There was a splash in the water, and it jolted E.R. back to reality. He jumped to his feet just as Charley Ann pulled up the cast net full of small perch. He ran to grab a bucket and they gathered up as many fish as they could before they escaped back into the water. E.R. grabbed the fishing poles and baited one of them. Charley Ann grabbed the other one and baited her own pole before dropping it into the water.

"I guess I underestimated you. You weren't joking when you said you could fish. Let's see who catches the first one." E.R. dropped his line in the water and smiled. He found himself enjoying the day and hoped that feeling would last for a while.

The low putter of a motor filled the air. It grew louder as it approached Bayou Dogris. Without saying a word, both E.R. and Charley Ann reeled in their poles and looked at each other. E.R. motioned to move towards the camp door so that they could see who was coming without being seen. Once inside, E.R. grabbed his gun and told Charley Ann to stay out of sight. He was surprised to see that she listened and crouched down beside the sofa. The frightened look in her eyes tugged at his heart. She pretended to be tough and in control, but she was scared and that made him angry. He wondered just how abusive Brian was and to what length he would go to find her.

The boat had entered the Bayou and was headed towards the camp. E.R. walked right outside the door and squatted against the wall. He was alert and intended to find out who was in that boat before they docked. His boat was tied off in the back of the camp and if he didn't recognize the person, they were going to jump in the boat and take off. He felt like they would have a better chance on the water than in the camp. With a watchful eye, he waited.

"E.R. it's Paw. I'm with China." Griff thought it better to announce their arrival because he knew his grandson would be alarmed by an approaching boat." I tried to call your cell phone, but it went straight to voice mail."

E.R. frantically reached in his pocket to find his phone dead. *How could I be so stupid.* He acknowledged that he heard them then went inside to get Charley Ann. Relieved to know who was in the boat, she stood up and they both walked outside.

"Hey Uncle China. I was waiting for you to call me back. What happened? I thought maybe you were still having trouble with your boat, but I see that it's running fine." E.R. caught the rope and tied off the boat. He hugged his grandfather and then China as they climbed up on the dock.

"Sorry little cuz. I got caught up in some freaky stuff."

"Uncle China this is Charley Ann. That's my Uncle China that was supposed to bring us some bait. We found a cast net and Charley Ann caught some small perch to use as bait." E.R. noticed the look on his grandfather's face and knew that he probably had information to share.

"What's going on? Why are you with Uncle China? Do you have news about Liam?" E.R. wanted to know exactly what was coming about.

"We don't have any news about Liam. Still no word from him?" Griff hated to upset E.R. but it was inevitable.

"No. I thought maybe that's why you were here."

"We're here because China found a dead body in the bayou. It's not Liam. When China was on the phone with you, he spotted something in the water and when he realized what it was, he called 911. Mr. Tab got a call, and we headed down there thinking it could be Liam."

"Wow that's crazy. Man, Uncle China that must've freaked you out. Thank God it wasn't Liam. What did it look like? Was it in the water for a while?"

You could see the relief in both E.R.'s and Charley Ann's eyes. Her reaction looked genuine, and Griff hoped she would take the rest of the news well. After all, she was involved with the guy for a while. She must've had feelings for him at one time. Griff was hesitant to tell them that the body was Brian's.

E.R. sat down on the edge of the dock. His emotions were all over the place. He was glad that the body wasn't Liam's, but he was also tormented with the realization that they still don't know where he was or if he was even alive. The silence in the air was almost deafening with everyone thinking the same thoughts. E.R. looked up with a halfhearted smile and tried to read his grandfather's mind. He noticed his lip twitch and knew that his grandfather had more to say. The sullen look told E.R. that it wasn't good news. He felt his heart quiver and decided he was tired of that old sick feeling in the pit of his stomach.

E.R. glanced at Charley Ann and then back to his grandfather. *Does the news involve Charley Ann? What aren't you telling us?* It was clear that he was holding something back and E.R. knew his grandfather well enough to know that it was because the news would be disturbing.

"Hey Paw. Did you see the upgrade Jason did to the camp?" E.R. made eye contact with him that suggested they needed to talk alone.

"No. I haven't been here in a few years. I do need to use the restroom." Griff headed to the door with E.R. in tow.

Once inside E.R. patiently waited for Griff to use the bathroom. Looking around he noticed that Jason had done some renovations and the place looked great. He recognized some of the changes when they arrived but with everything on his mind it didn't register.

Griff tapped his shoulder and brought him back to reality.

"What aren't you telling me? I can see in your eyes that somethings up."

"Well I told you that the body in the bayou was not Liam, but I didn't tell you that I recognized the body."

E.R. ran his fingers through his hair and waited for the rest of the story.

"E.R., the dead body was Brian." Griff couldn't tell what emotion he saw in his grandson's eyes. He looked relieved and distressed at the same time.

After a moment, he jumped up and was headed for the door.

"Whoa man. Where are you going? Slow down and think for a minute. How are you going to handle Charley Ann? Are you going to tell her that Brian is dead? Do you know how she will feel about that news?"

E.R. stopped abruptly. The relieved look was again replaced by the distressed one and Griff could see the torment his grandson was feeling.

"If Brian is dead that means Charley Ann should be safe and I can get back to finding Liam. Paw, I don't want to waste any more time." E.R. looked at Griff and without saying a word, Griff knew that he was worried about the time that had already passed and the slim chance that Liam was still alive.

"I think we need to tell Charley Ann the truth, but can we try to break it to her gently. You can't just go drop something like this on her and then leave. E.R., you need a plan. She doesn't have anywhere to go. Are you prepared to continue to help her or are you abandoning that idea all together?"

His first reaction was to put finding Liam above everything else. But his grandfather was right, he couldn't just abandon Charley Ann. And even if he could, would he want to. As much as he hated to admit it, there was something between them and even if he couldn't be with her, he wanted to make sure she was safe. He would never wish harm on anyone, but Brian's death made it easier to help Charley Ann. And that cleared the way for Liam once they find him.

While Brian's death made some things easier, it also complicated them. *Did he have something to do with Liam's disappearance? If he didn't, who did? Apparently, it was Brian that Charley Ann saw on Bourbon Street, so he is the most obvious choice. He was angry at Charley*

Ann and followed them. E.R.'s thoughts were scattered, and it left things messy. The top of the list of his chaotic thoughts were: *Who killed Brian? Did Brian have something to do with Liam's disappearance and finally, where is Liam?*

Griff opened the door and went to join Charley Ann and China. He wanted to give E.R. time to digest everything and come up with a reasonable plan. He had some tough decisions to make, and it was imperative that he make the right ones. As the screen door slammed shut, he heard E.R.'s phone ring.

"Liam? Where are you? Liam can you hear me? Liam!"

CHAPTER 9

The light creeped through the cracks announcing the start of another day. *How long have I been here? Where am I? How did I get here?* The light illuminated the area just enough for him to see his hands and to reinforce the fact that he was not there of his own free will. His vision faded again, and he slipped into a subconscious state. He found comfort in a reoccurring dream about a young boy that made no sense to him but felt familiar.

It was a typical Saturday night at his house in Miami, Florida. He wasn't sleepy and insisted on staying up with the adults well into the night. His pleading eyes won the battle as it most often did. He loved listening to the music and watching his parent's dance. He was only four years old but already knew that he wanted to be just like his father. He watched his mother sway to the music and could feel the love she had for him with every look. It was almost 2:00 am and most of their guests were gone long ago. His father and several other men were in his office. He could hear his Uncle Dominick and his Uncle Thomas talking, but the conversation was muffled. They weren't really his uncles but like most of his father's friends, they were considered family.

He didn't know exactly what his father did for a living, but he knew that he was an important man because their house was always full of people day and night. He also knew that his father was busy, so he learned to embrace every opportunity he had to spend time with him. Tonight was a special night. It was his parent's 5th wedding anniversary. The celebration started earlier that day with all of his family members present and ended with only his parents' closest friends.

He idolized his father and mimicked everything he did. Sometimes he would hide under the desk or behind the sofa so that he could be close to his father. One time his father caught him and became terribly upset. He was shocked that his father would scold him like that just for trying to be close to him. That day his father made it clear that he wanted him to stay as far away from his business as possible and made him promise to never do that again. He was so startled by his father's reaction that he made a promise that he did not intend to keep.

Jolted back to reality, he looked around to assess his situation. He seemed to be in a tiny dark room the size of a very small prison cell. There were no chains or bars but without a doubt, it was meant to keep someone from leaving. He was lying on his back and closed his eyes to keep from getting sick. When he opened them again, he focused on one of the cracks in the wall. *What's happening? My body feels numb. Did I hurt myself? Was I in an acci-*

dent? I have to get out of here! He dialed E.R.'s number but when he went to talk, his words were slurred. He tried to get up, but the floor seemed to disappear, and the ceiling rippled like clouds in the sky right before the darkness came again.

CHAPTER 10

After considering all of the factors, E.R. agreed that it would be best if he and Charley Ann stayed at the camp for a little longer. Griff was going to try to trace Liam's phone, but he wasn't too optimistic about it because they already tried that and came up empty. E.R. agreed with his grandfather that he needed to tell Charley Ann about Brian but wanted to do it later when they were alone. He didn't know how she'd react and didn't want her to have an audience when she found out. Griff and China said their goodbyes and headed back to the dock. His grandfather promised him that he and Tab would work around the clock to find answers.

As soon as the boat left the camp Charley Ann stood in front of E.R. with her hands on her hips.

"Okay. Spill it. What were y'all keeping from me? I know something is up so quit tiptoeing around me."

E.R. was speechless. He didn't know what to say. He planned on telling her about Brian, but he didn't know how to start. Each time they spoke about Brian, he searched her eyes looking for some clue of her true feelings. She usually had a cold, hard look when she spoke of him, but he wasn't sure if that was how she felt in her heart.

"Come on E.R., I can handle whatever it is. I've spent my whole life dealing with disappointments and disasters so…"

"Brian's dead!" E.R. waited for a response. "Did you hear me? I said Brian's dead. The body they found in the bayou was Brian. He's dead Charley Ann."

"Wow. That's not what I expected you to say." Charley Ann sat down on the dock and gazed into the water. Her tensed shoulders slouched, and her body seemed to relax. It had been so long since she felt that way that she didn't trust it to last.

E.R. didn't know what to say. All he wanted to do was pull her in and hold her tight. He wanted to shield her from the world and anything that would steal the sparkle from those beautiful eyes. He wanted her to know that he would never let anyone hurt her ever again. But instead of telling her how he felt and acting on his feelings, he just sat down next to her and gave her time to process the information.

The sun was disappearing, but bits of light continued to shower the bayou. The cooler evening air started to return and even though she was numb all over, a slight shiver ran up Charley Ann's body. E.R. looked at Charley Ann and felt like he's known her his entire life. After about a half hour, E.R. stood to go inside. Charley Ann reached for his hand and turned towards him. When she looked up at E.R. there was sadness in her eyes.

"Thank You." Charley Ann let go of his hand and stood up. "I'm okay. Look I would never wish harm on anyone, not even Brian, but I can't say that I'm sorry he's gone. He was not a nice guy and when I left him, I had no intentions of ever going back. I learned quickly that he was trouble and now I wonder how many other people he abused before me. Do you think someone murdered him? Did your grandfather say how he died?"

E.R. was still reeling from Charley Ann's declaration that she was done with Brian the moment she left him. His heart soared silently in his chest. The slight glimmer of hope he felt was short lived when his thoughts turned to Liam.

"I'm not sure how he died. I don't think they know anything yet. My grandfather promised to let us know if there are any updates." E.R. shoved his hands in his pocket and looked away.

Charley Ann felt a connection when she touched E.R.'s hand. She thought that there was something there for a moment, but his reaction made it clear that he was not interested. He'd sent mixed signals from the first time they met, and she didn't know why. When they met at Bourbon Heat, she thought they had a connection. Then he just looked away uninterested. Liam asked her to dance, and she went with him. She had no idea that she would end up with E.R. and wondered just how he felt about the situation. She was grateful for his help and decided to leave it at that for now.

"Why do we need to stay out here if Brian is dead?"

"I'm not sure what to do. Brian is dead but we don't know what happened to him. And where is Liam? If the two are linked, then we have at least a third person involved who is probably dangerous. I've been going over everything that we do know and still can't connect any dots. What do you think we should do?" E.R. noticed a surprised look on Charley Ann's face.

"You're asking my opinion?"

"Yeah. This involves you too. We're out here to keep you safe. You're right if Brian is dead maybe the threat to you is gone. Do you know of anyone that would want Brian dead enough to kill him?"

"I can't say for sure. Like I said he was a different person in the beginning and when I started to see the real Brian, I was planning my exit. I think we should go to Grand Isle and ask around."

"That might not be a bad idea. Unfortunately, Hurricane Ida is headed this way and predicted to hit in the next couple of days. We can wait and see what the weather looks like in the morning and possibly make it there and back before it gets too rough. I definitely don't think we should go tonight. They just issued mandatory evacuations for Lower Jefferson parish which includes, the Lafitte, Barataria, and Crown Point area as well as Grand Isle, so we might not get too far. Let me run this idea by my grandfather first, okay?"

****

Tab was at the office when Griff arrived. It was getting late and both men were tired but knew that things couldn't wait. Every minute that passed was crucial to finding Liam alive.

"I don't have an official cause of death yet, but the unofficial cause is strangulation. The bruises on the neck would indicate that someone strangled him then threw him in the bayou. I'm waiting for confirmation from the coroner, but I feel confident that it was a homicide. How's E.R. holding up?" Tab could see the concern in Griff's face.

"He's anxious and ready for some answers. I told him about Brian, and we left before he told Charley Ann. I don't think she'll be sad that he's dead, but you never know. How often do we see an abuse victim go back into a bad situation? I think E.R. is growing fond of her because I can see the way he looks at her. Man, if Brian was murdered where does that leave Liam? Just because we didn't find his body yet doesn't mean he's still alive." Griff was pacing.

"We need to stay optimistic that Liam is still alive. I think we need to go back to the cemetery and look for clues. We don't know that Brian was even there. Maybe someone followed him from Bourbon Heat and killed him when Liam was not around. Let's not jump to conclusions. We can go there first thing in the morning unless you want to go now. It's getting dark soon and the thought of being there at night is not inviting to me."

Griff agreed with Tab that they should wait until morning. He just couldn't help worrying about time running out for Liam. They made plans for the morning and headed out the door. Griff's phone rang and it was E.R. calling.

"Hey Paw. I told Charley Ann about Brian, and she agrees that we're no longer in danger. She suggested that we go to Grand Isle to ask around about Brian to see if we can figure out who would have wanted him dead. I told her I was gonna pass that by you. I think it might be a good idea. We could take my boat at first light and be there early enough to check things out."

"Man, I don't know. Tab said that Brian was strangled and thrown into the bayou. E.R. he was murdered. We don't know the connection yet to Liam, but you could encounter a murderer. Are you ready for that?" Griff knew that his grandson had already made up his mind. "And what about the hurricane. That thing is coming right for us, and you don't want to get caught out there in heavy rain and wind bands. If you do go it would have to be at first light and only for a short time. E.R. be careful man."

"I think I have to do something. I agreed to stay here for Charley Ann, but it was her idea to go. I needed to see what you thought about it."

"I think it's a good idea to check out Grand Isle but I'm not sure it should be you and Charley Ann that does it. I trust whatever decision you make but please be careful and stay in contact. Tab and I are headed back to the cemetery in the morning to try and place Brian there. We don't even know if he was there or not. Washing up in the bayou would indicate that he was close by, so we'll see what we find. I'll keep you posted. Love ya. Be careful!"

Tab came barreling back into the parking lot of the office. He rolled down the window and motioned for Griff to get in.

I got a call from a buddy about a 911 complaint they received. They reported a suspicious car parked in the street and noise coming from a nearby house. Griff, the address was Liam's house."

Tab raced to Liam's house and hoped that the car was still there. Neither of the men thought that it was Liam but secretly hoped it would be. When they turned down the street, things looked quiet. Apparently, they beat the cops there. Tab decided to park near the end of the block and walk.

"What was the description of the car?"

"It was a black Nissan Maxima. Dark tinted windows, probably illegal." Tab pointed to a car that fit that description parked on the opposite side of the street from Liam's house. Griff went around to the passenger's side of the car while Tab approached the driver's side.

"It's empty." Tab looked up and in the reflection of the window, he saw Griff headed to Liam's house. "Griff, wait! We don't want to announce our presence. We were lucky to beat the cops here. Don't ruin everything by barging in there."

Griff knew that Tab was right, but he was anxious for answers. When he reached the other side of the street he stopped. He shook his head and relaxed his shoulders. He was reminded of his wife's techniques to calm down and put them into motion. He took a deep breath and held it before a long exhale. By the time Tab reached him, he was back in control. He was grateful that Tab was there to reel him back in because he could've ruined everything by barging into Liam's house.

"Did you hear that?" Tab motioned Griff to stay still and listen. "It sounded like a loud thump! I think we better get in there now."

Griff went to the front door while Tab headed to the back door. If someone were in the house, both exits would be covered. Tab drew his weapon as he approached the back door. He stood and listened for a moment, and it was quiet. Griff heard two noises, the humming coming from the air conditioner and his own heartbeat. *Deep breath man. You got this.* He leaned to the side of the porch and gestured to Tab that he was headed into the house.

The house was dark thanks to curtains that kept the light from coming in. The small foyer led Griff into the living room and kitchen area. He was familiar with Liam's house even though he'd only been in it a few times before. He saw light coming from the back and figured it was Tab. Just to be on the safe side, Griff tucked against the wall and waited for the door to open. Whoever it was didn't enter the house right away. Griff held his breath and waited. Tab finally entered the house and Griff exhaled.

There were still dirty dishes in the sink and the empty wine bottle was still in the same place. Things seemed to be just as they left them earlier that day. Griff headed down the hall just as Tab's phone beeped alerting him that he had a message. Griff quickened his step and without warning, stumbled over something on the floor. He reached for the wall to break his fall and brought down the pictures that hung there. Tab rushed in to find Griff on the floor on top of a duffle bag.

"Griff! Are you alright? What happened?"

"I tripped over this bag." Griff held up a duffle bag for Tab to see. "Where did it come from? I was just here this morning with E.R. and this bag was not. Let's check out the rest of the rooms. As the day goes on, things are getting stranger."

Griff went into one bedroom while Tab searched the other. They didn't find anything else that would indicate someone was in the house. But someone had been in the house and that worried Griff. They grabbed the duffle bag and headed out the back door. There was an old shed in the back yard that they wanted to check out. Griff's stomach dropped when he noticed the condition of the shed. It looked like it would fall down at any minute, especially if disturbed. Tab recognized that look on Griff's face and went ahead of him. He knew his friend to be afraid of two things: needles and heights. By the look on his face, he would now add getting trapped in by old fallen down sheds.

He whispered to Griff, "Cover me. I'm gonna open the door slowly. Stay back in case this thing goes down or if someone runs out. Either way I need you out here ready."

Griff nodded and stood ready for whatever happened.

Griff couldn't shake the idea that someone entered the house after he was there earlier. *Was it Liam? Why wouldn't he call E.R. first. He had to know we would be looking for him after disappearing for days.*

"Sirens! Tab, do you hear that? The cops are on the way. We better hurry up before they get here."

Tab reached for the door and at the same time the whole shed went down. He could hear moaning from inside and looked towards the direction it was coming from. Thankfully, some of the shed was held up from reaching the ground by wood that was stacked in there. He saw the body of a man in the middle of the shed under some boards and broken sheetrock. He was barely moving but Tab could hear his groans. He was afraid that the rest of the shed was going to go at any minute. He grabbed onto the man's legs and pulled him towards the door. Griff joined in and they were able to get him out of the shed just as it collapsed completely.

They turned the man over and gasped. His face was swollen, and he had two black eyes that suggested that someone had beaten him.

"Liam! Oh my God! Tab it's Liam." Griff stood shocked.

CHAPTER 11

Things happened so quickly that Griff was still coming to terms with finding Liam in his own backyard. "Liam, are you alright? Liam, can you hear me?" Griff was careful not to move him too much. They just pulled him out of a collapsed shed and wasn't sure about the extent of his injuries.

"Liam can you open your eyes?" Tab checked his pulse and looked at Griff. "His pulse is strong, but we better call 911." He grabbed his phone and placed the call.

Griff stayed at Liam's side. He appeared to be unconscious and would let out a moan every so often. He didn't have any visible injuries, but something was wrong. *If the building fell on his head, he could have a concussion which would explain the problem.* Griff said a quick prayer, held Liam's hand, and waited for the ambulance to arrive.

While he waited, Griff started to worry about E.R. and Charley Ann. Finding Liam at his own house, apparently of his own accord, brought up all sorts of questions. *Did he have something to do with Brian's death? Why hadn't he called anyone to say he was alright? Was he hiding out from Brian or the killer?* There were still so many unanswered questions. Griff took out his phone and dialed E.R. to give him the news. It went straight to voicemail.

Tab decided to search the house and the grounds again while they waited. He couldn't understand what was taking the cops so long to get there. When they arrived, they heard the sirens but apparently that was for a different call. As he headed towards the house, he heard a loud low growl and noticed the dark clouds rolling in. He looked back and saw that Griff heard it too. He doubled back to see what he wanted to do.

"Hey man, do you think we should try to move Liam inside. I think the skies are about to open up. I hate to move him, but we can't just leave him in the rain." Just as Tab said the word rain, the first cold drop hit Griff in the face. The slow drizzle quickly picked up momentum and before they realized, a hard steady rain had begun to fall.

Griff acted quickly and started to examine Liam for noticeable injuries. He slowly touched his neck and waited for Liam to respond. He looked at Tab and motioned for him to grab the other side of Liam. Griff had decided they were going to move him inside.

"Wait. I think I hear a siren and this time it's close." Tab looked up and saw the flashing lights that illuminated into the back yard. They had finally arrived, so he ran to the front of the house and directed them to Liam's location. They assessed Liam and proceeded to load him onto the gurney. Both Griff and Tab walked with the technicians back to the ambulance answering questions they were asked. Aside from his identity and fact that he was in the shed when it collapsed, they didn't have much information to share. When they were loading him into the ambulance, he opened his eyes. Griff rushed to his side and said his name. The terror in Liam's expression when Griff said his name, suggested that he was not only scared and confused but that he was looking at a total stranger.

Although it was still drizzling, a crowd had begun to gather in the street and around Liam's house. Everyone wanted to know what was going on. Tab and Griff split up and started to question the neighbors and hoped that someone would have information that would be helpful. After the ambulance drove off, the rain picked up and ran everyone inside. Griff and Tab hurried back to Liam's house to lock up so that they could get to the hospital and check on Liam.

Griff remembered that he had left the duffle bag he tripped over earlier in the backyard. He told Tab that he'd meet him at the car after he retrieved the bag. He stood at the back door looking out. It was dark and with the heavy rain falling, it was almost impossible to see the fallen shed that collapsed on Liam moments ago. He descended the steps carefully taking one at a time. The old wooden steps that led to the back yard needed repair, and like the shed, could give way at any time. As Griff looked around, he was surprised at the condition of the back yard. At a closer look, the wood fence that surrounded the yard was dilapidated and had sections that were completely missing. Griff figured that Liam was probably too busy to get to the repairs out there.

Griff reached the last step and moved towards the area he had left the duffle bag. He was always amazed at how sounds stood out more in darkness. He heard the hoot of an old owl that was claiming his territory. There was a howling that came from a neighborhood dog that was probably still startled from the earlier ambulance sirens. In the distance, he could see the swarm of termites around a neighbor's back porch light. Griff shivered at the thought of termites and subconsciously scratched his neck and arm.

He reached the bag and picked it up. He thought about seeing what was inside but decided to wait until he got back into the car. He turned to leave but something caught his attention on the side of the shed. He stopped and stared, waiting for some sign that it was something to be concerned with. He didn't see anything move but he heard the sound of someone rustling through the grass. *Someone's out here.* Without thinking, Griff ran towards the sound which was around the back of the shed. There were more fence boards missing back there and by the way one of the boards was swinging back and forth it was an indication that someone had ran through there recently. Griff made his way to the fence but didn't see anyone around. He waited there for some time, but the area remained quiet and empty. His heart raced and he no longer heard the sounds of the night just the loud beating of his heart. He slowly headed back to the house to lock the back door.

He marched up the steps and into the house. A darkness covered the room like a blanket and that created more anxiety for Griff. He couldn't wait to get out of there and wished that Tab would have stayed with him. He set the lock from inside and attempted to walk out when he was grabbed and thrown to the ground. Before he could react, the duffle bag he had slung over his shoulder was pulled off and the assailant ran. Griff tried to get up and chase the person, but pain shot up his leg and prevented him from moving. He yelled for Tab while he reached for his phone.

By the time he reached Tab, whoever attacked him was long gone. Tab checked on Griff and then ran in the direction that Griff indicated but found no one. When he returned, he found Griff standing and unsuccessfully trying to walk.

"Hey buddy, take it easy." Tab ran to Griff's side and gave him a shoulder to lean on. "What happened man?"

"I went in to lock the door and when I attempted to leave someone grabbed me and shoved me to the ground. They grabbed the duffle bag and ran. Man, it all happened so fast. When I came back here to get the bag, I thought I saw someone behind the shed but when I checked, it appeared that someone was there but had run off. I was locking up to come and tell you what was going on when he must've come back to get the bag." Griff kept moving and attempted to walk on his leg. "I don't think it's broken but it sure hurts. I think I twisted it when I landed. Let's get out of here before something else happens. There's already been too much going on tonight.

Tab helped Griff back to the car and the two of them headed to the hospital. Tab wanted Griff to get his leg checked but he refused. Griff dialed E.R.'s number and reached his voicemail again. *Where are you E.R.?*

They checked in at the nurse's station and inquired about Liam. They were informed that he was still unconscious and were instructed to wait in the waiting room. After a while, Tab talked Griff into going home to get rest and return in the morning. They made sure the nurse had their information and left for the night.

CHAPTER 12

E. R. woke up before the morning sun and was surprised how well he slept. Both he and Charley Ann were mentally and physically exhausted and decided to turn in early. The plan was to head to Grand Isle at first light where they hoped to get clues about Brian's death. There was bad weather last night that interfered with his phone service. The service in Bayou Dogris was sketchy to begin with, so it didn't take much to knock it out. E.R. checked his phone and found that there was still no service. Thankfully, the storm didn't last long, and they woke to calm waters. The ride to Grand Isle by boat was about 25 minutes if the conditions were right. E.R. checked radar and saw that they were expected to get more rain later that afternoon so they should be safe if they hurried.

"Are you ready? It shouldn't take long to get there, and we will hopefully get phone service back again so I can call my grandfather. I know a place where we can dock my boat while we're there. I would like to head back here no later than one this afternoon if we can." E.R. walked back and forth from the camp to the boat loading everything they needed. They were not planning on staying long but decided to pack a backpack just in case.

"I'm ready to roll." Charley Ann noticed a surprise look on E.R.'s face. "What?"

"Nothing. That's just what my grandfather always says. Let's roll or I'm ready to roll."

Charley Ann smiled and got into the boat. E.R. handed her the rest of the stuff and jumped in next to her. She wondered about his life. He didn't talk about anyone special, except Liam and his family. She didn't think that he had anyone special in his life but there was a sadness in his eyes that said he did at one time. He was always guarded when they spoke and steered away from anything that was personal. Just like last night, she felt that there was a connection building between them but then like before, he became closed off. Charley Ann got the impression that E.R. was a very loyal, dedicated person when it came to someone he loved. The way he spoke about his grandfather and the effort he was putting into finding Liam told her that he was an 'all in' kind of guy and someone you could count on. Too bad that he wasn't interested in her, she was really beginning to like him.

It was a beautiful, crisp morning. The water was slick as ice, and thanks to the storm last night, the air smelled sultry yet felt clean. As the day progressed, the humidity would rise but for now Charley Ann was enjoying the air as it touched her face, almost like a cleansing, washing away the bad. She thought about Brian and for a moment felt bad that he was dead. She never wanted things to end that way, but she couldn't help feeling relieved that he couldn't hurt her anymore. She just hoped that they would find Liam soon. Her gut told her that Brian could never kill anyone, so she believed that he was alive. She was glad E.R. agreed to go to Grand Isle because she hated sitting around doing nothing. She hoped that his grandfather would find some answers back at home while she and E.R. looked for some in Grand Isle.

They could see the Island draw near and slowed down to a wake as they approached the dock at Bridge Side Marina.

"That name sounds familiar. I think Brian might have worked here for a while. I know he worked at a fuel dock among other odd and end jobs. Maybe someone will remember him." Charley Ann jumped off the boat and grabbed the rope to tie it off to the dock. E.R. looked at Charley Ann with amazement and yearned to know more about her. Before he could say anything, she was off headed towards the door. He ran to catch up and reminded her to take it slow.

"We don't want to come on like gangbusters. Let's just go pay for docking the boat and check the place out."

Charley Ann held the door open for E.R. and they both went to the counter. Charley Ann noticed the restroom sign and headed in that direction while E.R. paid.

"I love your jeans. Where did you find them?"

Charley Ann looked up from washing her hands and saw a waitress standing behind her.

"Thanks. They're old. I just can't seem to get rid of them." Charley Ann looked down at the ragged-out bottoms of her old jeans. She noticed the girl's name tag – Sam.

"Definitely do not get rid of them. I wish I could find me a pair. They look so good on you."

"Thanks, Sam, is it? I'm Charley Ann." Charley Ann pointed to the name tag. "How long have you been working here?"

"I just started. I've been out of work due to covid and decided to come down here and stay with my cousin for a while. Usually I come for a short visit but now I have nothing but time. I'm working the morning shift here and then on to Artie's Sports Bar for the late shift. I really need to work, and I love to stay busy. Are you here for a visit or do you live here?" Sam asked while she washed her hands to head back to work.

"I'm just passing through. I'm here with a friend to spend the day. We took his boat here from Lafitte. I was hoping to hook up with an old friend that lived here. Do you know Brian Moreau?" Charley Ann stared into Sam's face waiting to read her response.

"Name don't sound familiar. Is he a local? Like I said, I just got here and I'm not good with remembering names. Do you have a picture?" Sam waited for Charley Ann to respond. Her break was almost over, and she didn't want to be late.

"No I don't. I lost my phone and hadn't had time to get another one. Thanks anyway." Charley Ann walked towards the door.

"Hey, are y'all staying on the Island tonight?" Charley Ann shook her head no. "Well before y'all leave come see me at Artie's. I'll ask around and let you know what I find. I gotta get back to work." Sam ran out the door.

E.R. was seated at a table waiting for Charley Ann to come from the restroom. "Are you hungry?"

Sam approached their table and before looking up asked what they were drinking.

"I'll have a coffee and a glass of water. What about you Charley Ann?"

The waitress looked up from her pad and smiled. "Hey Charley Ann. I guess y'all decided to stay for breakfast. What can I get ya to drink?"

E.R. looked confused. Charley Ann didn't mention that she knew anyone on the Island.

"You two know each other?"

Charley Ann smiled. "We just met in the lady's room. Sam this is E.R. and E.R. this is Sam. She works the morning shift here and she's going to Artie's after."

"I know that place. I've been there a time or two." E.R. never understood women. *How do you meet people in the bathroom?*

"I'd like a breakfast platter. Eggs over medium, bacon crispy and grits. And coffee is good for me too."

"I guess you are hungry. I'll have the same except I don't like my bacon crispy." E.R. noticed Charley Ann's nose crinkle up when he ordered his bacon. "You have a problem with the way I like my bacon?"

"No problem at all. E.R., can you show Sam that picture of Brian? She didn't recognize his name but thought that maybe she would know him from a picture."

E.R. flipped through his phone for the photo Charley Ann's sister sent him. He stared at it for a minute noticing how happy Charley Ann looked standing next to Brian. She had a beautiful smile that was contagious even through a photo. E.R. smiled back before he realized that they were looking at him.

"It's not too clear but I think you would know if you saw him before. Charley Ann said he worked around here for a while." E.R. shifted in his seat and was glad that the attention was focused on the picture instead of him.

"No, I don't know him. I can ask my cousin and see if she knows him. He doesn't work here now but maybe he has in the past. I'll send over the manager and maybe she can help you. She's been here for years." Sam headed to the kitchen to find the manager.

The rumbling sound of thunder followed by a lightning strike caused Charley Ann and E.R. to jump. E.R. wasn't aware that the weather was supposed to get bad already. He excused himself and headed towards the back door. The sky was dark, and the wind rushed across the dock. Lightning lit up the sky in the distance. The smell of rain in the air surrounded E.R. and compromised his original plans. He hoped that the approaching storm would pass quickly but he couldn't be sure. He grabbed his phone to check the radar. He put in his password and saw that he had two missed calls and two messages. He hadn't had phone service since last night. He checked when they docked, but it was still out. Both missed calls were from his grandfather. He pressed recent on his phone and waited for his grandfather to answer.

"E.R. man where are you? I tried to call you a few times. I was starting to worry when I didn't hear from you this morning. I have some news for you. Liam…"

"Hello. Pawpaw are you there? Hello. Can you hear me?" E.R. looked down at his phone and noticed that they were disconnected. He tried to dial back but it wouldn't go through. There was a loud cracking sound followed by another loud boom and the parking lot lit up. E.R. dashed for the door and ran inside. Charley Ann looked up as he made his entrance and could tell he was frightened by the sound they all heard.

"E.R. are you alright? What happened?"

"I'm good. Lightning must have struck something in the parking lot. The weather is getting really bad out there." Before he could finish talking, the lights went out.

The manager informed them that there was a generator that would kick on in a few moments. She went to the back door and opened it up to let the light in while they waited. There were windows all around, but the shades were still down.

"Let's go outside and see if I can get service on my phone. My grandfather called but we got disconnected. He said he had news about Liam but didn't have time to tell me what it was. I really need to talk to him." E.R. grabbed Charley Ann's hand and headed towards the door. As he approached the bar he asked if they had a phone he could use. The person behind the bar checked the house phone and it was dead.

The sky darkened as the storm approached. The angry waves smacked the dock and rocked E.R.'s boat as they rolled in. The gloomy weather matched E.R.'s mood. The possibility of getting back to Lafitte by boat grew dimmer with each second that passed. He looked at Charley Ann and noticed that she didn't seem to be worried at all. In fact she looked calm and peaceful.

"I take it you're not afraid of bad weather."

Charley Ann smiled at E.R. and shook her head. "I'm not a fan of it but as long as I can get out of it, I'm okay. I guess this means we have to stay here longer than planned."

E.R. just smiled back at her. The thought of spending more time with Charley Ann pleased him but he was still worried about Liam. *What was the news he had for me? We gotta get someplace that has phone service soon. Did he not tell me right away because Liam's dead? God, please let him be alive.*

CHAPTER 13

E. R. and Charley Ann stayed in the Bayside Marina until the rain let up. They finished their breakfast and talked with the other waitress and the manager. The manager remembered Brian but said that he only worked there for about a week.

"After his first check he quit, and I hadn't seen him since."

"Is there anyone else here that might remember him?" E.R. hoped that there was but doubted it.

"No. I'm the only one that has been here for more than six months. We have a high turn around with waitresses and staff. Hey y'all do know that we are under a mandato-ry evacuation, right? Right after breakfast we are closing up and headed inland. I suggest y'all do the same." She smiled then declared that she had to go check on things in the kitchen.

The light flickered a few times but remained on. There were only a few customers in the place but by the sound of the clapping and hollering going on, it would appear to be full. Charley Ann smiled at E.R. and waited to hear what their next move would be.

"It's still raining so I don't think it would be safe to go home yet. How about we just sit under the patio and wait it out? It's too early to go to Artie's and too wet to sit on the beach."

Charley Ann chuckled. She hadn't noticed the color of E.R.'s eyes before. They are brown but not a boring brown. They're more like a milky rich color that was almost heavenly. She realized that it was the way he looked at her with compassion that drew her in. She had decided when she first met E.R. that he was trustworthy but didn't know why she felt that way. Now she understood exactly why and it's because of his strong compassionate eyes. *Get a grip Charley Ann! What are you doing? He is clearly not into you!*

Charley Ann stood up and headed for the door and without looking back said, "Ya coming?"

E.R. followed her out onto the back patio and found a few chairs they could sit in while they waited for the rain to stop. They were quiet for a while and E.R. wondered what changed. Charley Ann seemed on edge and avoided eye contact with him. Inside the restaurant she was laughing and looked relaxed. He was about to ask her what was wrong when his phone vibrated in his pants pocket.

"We must have service." He retrieved his phone and answered, "Hello."

"E.R. I've been trying to call you back. Where are you?"

"We're in Grand Isle. The weather has turned bad, so we are waiting it out at Bridge Side Marina. You have news about Liam?" E.R. didn't want to lose service again before he had answers.

"We found Liam. He's alive but unconscious."

"Thank God!" E.R. looked relieved. "I'm putting you on speakerphone so Charley Ann can listen."

Griff went on to say, "There was a 911 call from someone in his neighborhood last night, so we went to check it out. We found him in that old shed in his back yard, but it collapsed before we could enter. He's in the hospital and they expect that he'll be alright. Like I said, he's still unconscious this morning, so I don't have any details of where he's been or if he was involved in Brian's death. Tab requested security to be placed outside his door just to be safe. I'm not leaving until he wakes up."

"As soon as this storm lets up, I'm heading there."

"E.R., why don't you calm down and sit for a while. I'll stay with Liam, I promise. Do what you went there to do and find some answers. We don't know when he's gonna wake up and as far as we know someone dangerous is still out there. I checked the radar, and it looks like things are going to clear out of there soon. Take that time to find out what you can and call me when you head back to Lafitte. I'll let you know if anything changes here. Be careful, okay?" Griff didn't tell his grandson about being knocked down and Liam's duffle bag being stolen. He decided that he would tell him once he was back home safe.

"You're right. The rain is at a drizzle now so as soon as it stops, we're headed to Artie's. I'll call you when I leave here. Love ya. Bye." E.R. felt like his grandfather was holding something back, but he pushed that thought aside to be dealt with later.

When Griff hung up, E.R. sat motionless. He was so happy to hear that Liam was alive but still worried that he was unconscious. He was concerned that Liam could've been the one to kill Brian. He knew Liam and if that was the case it had to have been in self-defense.

Charley Ann reached for his hand. "He's gonna be okay. Look it stopped raining. Let's go find out what we can so we can get home."

E.R. didn't respond but rather got up and followed her. He didn't know what to say because he knew in his gut that there was more bad news waiting for them at home.

Artie's was just a few miles up the road from where they were. Sam offered to borrow her cousin's car and give E.R. and Charley Ann a ride down there since she was on her lunch break. They gladly accepted because the sky was still dark and was threatening to burst open at any moment. E.R. stayed quiet for the ride while Charley Ann and Sam discussed fashion and girl things. The two women were best friends by the time they arrived at Artie's.

Sam said, "I'll see y'all in a little while. My shift is over at 12.30 and I'll head here then. Call me if y'all need anything." She smiled then drove off.

"You two seem to hit it off pretty quickly."

Charley Ann just shrugged her shoulders. "She's nice and easy to talk to. We could definitely be friends."

Artie's had just opened at 10:30 and it was already busy. It was a different atmosphere than that of the Marina. E.R. noticed a stack of plywood by the door and assumed that they were also preparing for the hurricane. The sun attempted to show its face, peeking out from behind the clouds every now and then. E.R. hoped it was finished raining because the gloomy weather was adding to his bad mood. The last few days had been like a roller coaster, and he was feeling the effects.

Charley Ann grabbed a table inside. It felt like they just ate but that was around 8 that morning. E.R. wasn't too hungry, so he just ordered an appetizer. Charley Ann ordered a burger and fries. Most of the tables were taken and the bar was full. Their waiter was a short stocky guy named Freddie. He wasn't very friendly and seemed to be in a hurry. He took their orders and left without smiling once.

"Makes you miss Sam, huh?" Charley Ann smirked in the direction Freddie went.

"He must be having a bad day," E.R. remarked before he excused himself and headed to the restroom.

While E.R. was away from the table, Freddie brought their drink orders.

"Have you worked here long?"

Freddie looked up from his platter and seemed to be confused. He wondered why she would ask that question. "It's been a while." He placed the drinks on the table and turned to leave.

"Wait. I'm looking for a friend. I think he used to work here. His name is Brian Moreau."

The blood drained from Freddie's face, but he quickly recovered and smiled at Charley Ann. "Never heard of him, sorry." He walked back to the bar and then out the back door.

What was that? Charley Ann decided to wait a few seconds then follow him outside.

Outside, Charley Ann looked around for Freddie but didn't see him. There were only a few people scattered out there because of the rain. She noticed someone standing against a large container that sat on the far-left side of the dock He was having what appeared to be a heated conversation on his cell phone. He had the same build as Freddie, but the dark cloudy sky hindered her vision so she couldn't make a positive identification. She thought about calling his name but decided to try to get close enough to hear what he was saying. Charley Ann could tell by his reaction when he heard Brian's name, that even if he was telling the truth and didn't know him, he knew of Brian and that made him anxious.

The beach that was shadowed with dark clouds a moment ago now glistened like a thousand tiny diamonds. The gritty, powdery feel of the sand was replaced with a sticky clumpy texture that stuck to Charley Ann's shoes every step she took. She was reminded by the burning in her calves just how difficult it was to walk through the sand, especially wet sand. As she approached the container, she realized that the only way to sneak up on him would be to go around the back side. Charley Ann glanced back towards the door, towards safety. She wondered if E.R. made it back to the table. How long would it take him to come looking for her if she didn't return soon. She hesitated but only for a minute then she inhaled deeply and made the turn. As she reached the back of the container, she found the doors open and the area deserted. Or so she thought.

****

Griff was at Liam's bedside waiting for him to regain consciousness. The doctors were optimistic that he would wake up soon. As he watched him lay there, he thought of E.R. and reminded himself that what ever happened to Liam was probably not over. He prayed that Liam was not responsible for Brian's death but the odds of that being true were stacked against him. They know from the information Charley Ann gave them that Brian had followed them the night he was killed. If it comes back that Brian died at the cemetery, that puts both Liam and Charley Ann at the scene of the crime. Griff shifted in his chair suddenly becoming uncomfortable with the fact that E.R. was with Charley Ann. When they found her, she gave the impression that she was afraid and didn't know what was going on. Griff was all too familiar with the lengths in which people go in order to hide something. *What if it was all an act? E.R. could be in danger.* He pushed those thoughts away and tried to focus on what they knew so far.

Griff was deep in thought when the slightest movement from the bed Liam was lying in caught his attention. Glad to be pulled from his disturbing thoughts, Griff went to Liam's bed side and searched his face for signs of life. Liam's eyes were still closed but they had begun to flutter as if he were trying to open them. Griff watched him closely and hoped that it was a sign that he would wake up soon. They only had Charley Ann's side of the story and Griff was ready for some answers.

"Liam can you hear me? It's Griff man. Can you open your eyes?" Griff stood by waiting for a response. He repeated those questions a few more times.

Liam's eyes continued to flicker, and his body became restless. Griff wondered if he should call a nurse. Before he decided, Liam's eyes burst open, and he sat up in the bed. He immediately flopped back down and moaned. Griff pushed the button for the nurse but didn't wait to question him.

"Hey buddy. Take it easy. Do you know where you are?" Griff grabbed his hand and squeezed it tight hoping to reassure Liam that he was safe.

Liam became completely still. Griff thought that it was because he was in a strange place and disoriented.

"Liam, you are in the hospital. You had a nasty accident and have been unconscious since yesterday." Griff thought that informing him of his whereabouts would bring him comfort but he still seemed uncomfortable.

"Liam, does anything hurt you? Do you..."

"Who are you? Why are you calling me Liam?" The man lying in the bed just blindsided Griff with his questions.

Dumbfounded, Griff sat back into the chair that he had spent hours in waiting for Liam to wake up. *This can't be good.*

The door to the hospital room opened and two nurses rushed in. They immediately checked Liam's vitals and started to explain to him what was going on. A tall man entered the room wearing a white lab coat and holding a chart. Griff was so disturbed by Liam's reaction that he was at a loss for words. He got up, shuffled past Liam's care team, and headed for the door. He desperately needed some air. On his way outside, he called Tab and updated him. He wanted to call E.R. but didn't want to upset him with the news until he had a chance to talk to Liam again. He was probably confused, after all, he had been unconscious for a while. He waited for Tab to arrive and the two of them headed back towards Liam's room.

****

Concern started to bubble up about five minutes after E.R. returned to the table. When he got back Charley Ann was gone. He assumed she was in the restroom, but he couldn't be sure. Something didn't seem right but with all the crazy events of the past few days he wasn't sure he should trust his gut. He waited a little longer then decided to go check the restroom. He stood outside the door at first waiting to see if anyone came out. Finally, he opened the door and called her name. There was no answer and without thinking, E.R. barged into the women's bathroom. He checked each stall, but it was completely empty. He rushed back to the table searching every corner of the room on the way. She was not there. Charley Ann was not in the restaurant.

E.R. tossed cash on the table for lunch and headed to the back door. There were a few people enjoying the nice feel of the air that happens right after a thunderstorm passed. Once the sun returned it would be back to the unbearable heat that burdened the south well into the fall. E.R. forced himself to stay calm and look for Charley Ann. She probably just went outside for some fresh air. He made his way towards the beach and noticed a man who was trying to start a boat. He yelled to get his attention but instead of responding, the man jumped out of the boat and took off running. E.R. kicked into gear and followed the guy. *Why would he run?* He continued to keep his anxiety at bay while he chased down the guy. E.R. noticed that he was wearing a hoodie which in this heat was a little suspicious. However, with the pandemic going on, people were covering up in different ways. He was so close that he could feel the wind coming from his body as he ran. He reached out to grab his hoodie which was flying up behind him and didn't see the curb. E.R. stumbled to the ground and the guy ran away.

E.R. was momentarily baffled until he remembered Charley Ann was missing. He got to his feet and started to run back. *Why did I chase him? What about Charley Ann? She might need my help*. The urgency to find Charley Ann overpowered his exhaustion and pushed him forward. He stood in the back of Artie's again and still no sign of Charley Ann. *What made him run?* Once again, E.R. felt panic stricken at the thought of Charley Ann and her absence. *He must have had something to hide.* He zeroed in on the boat where he found the guy and dashed in that direction. There were several boats there, but he knew exactly which one the guy was in.

"Charley Ann! Charley Ann! Where are you?" When he reached the boat, it was empty. E.R. stopped to catch his breath. Hands on his knees and slow deep breaths helped him to regain his composure. *My God Charley Ann, where are you?* Again he canvassed the area with his eyes. There were a few people hanging out on the back deck now. Maybe they saw Charley Ann and knew where she was. He started towards the deck and noticed that there was a large container off to the side, but the doors were closed and looked to be locked. E.R. kept walking towards the restaurant checking out everything along the way. He stopped and looked towards the containers again before ruling it out. He turned to go back inside the restaurant hoping that she was back at the table when suddenly, the woman from his visons appeared. She was so close to his face he imagined that he could feel her breath. E.R. froze and was completely intimidated by her ghostly presence. She was angry and wanted him to know it before she motioned for him to turn around. He blinked then she was gone. He thought he heard a thumping sound and turned towards the noise as he tried to isolate its location.

Thump. Thump. Thump. E.R. froze again and waited. The sound was coming from the area that the container was in. He cautiously moved towards the sound looking around for the woman. E.R. was led to the back door of the container that he knew was shut and locked.

"Charley Ann! Charley Ann, are you in there?" He struggled with the doors as he tried to gain access to the container.

At first, he thought it was just the wind he was hearing because even though the storm passed it was still very windy. He stopped breathing and strained to listen.

"E.R. is that you? Get me out of here. Hurry! Please!" Charley Ann's voice cracked and indicated that she was frightened.

E.R. put his ear against the door and spoke.

"Charley Ann! Charley Ann! Yes, it's me. Are you okay?" E.R. was so relieved to hear her voice even if it was from inside a locked container.

"If you mean being locked in a dark hot container okay then yep. I'm good!" Then she yelled, "Please get me out of here. It's so hot it's hard to breathe."

"There's a chain lock on the door. I have to find the key or get something to cut it off."

"E.R. don't leave me, I'm scared."

His heart sank in response to the distressing sound of her voice, but he reassured her that he would be right back. He ran back to the restaurant to retrieve the manager

Jude, and the key. Together they rushed to the container that imprisoned Charley Ann and fumbled with the locks. There were about twenty keys on the key ring and unfortunately had to use the process of elimination to find the right one. Finally there was a click, and the lock was released. E.R. ripped the chains free and tugged at the doors. All at once, the doors burst open, Charley Ann bolted forward and landed right into E.R.'s arms. She was shaking uncontrollably and continued to hold on to E.R. for dear life.

CHAPTER 14

The doctors were still in Liam's room when Griff returned with Tab. They sat outside waiting for an update. Griff was worried that the doctors wouldn't consult with them because they were not family and Liam didn't recognize him. Tab assured him that he would get answers. Again, Griff's thoughts strayed to E.R. and Charley Ann, and he hoped that everything was alright. He told Tab of his concerns and discovered that he shared the same concerns.

"I think I'm gonna check in with E.R." Griff walked back towards the entrance to the hospital. Before he dialed the phone, the doctor walked out of Liam's room. Griff hurried back to the waiting room and arrived just as Tab stopped the doctor. He told him that they were personal friends of Liam and that they were also detectives investigating his disappearance the last few days. The doctor studied both men before saying anything. He appeared to be struggling with something and proceeded to reveal what was bothering him.

"Liam? Did you say his name was Liam?" The doctor looked at them with a skeptical look.

Griff jumped in the conversation. "Yes. His name is Liam Barrios. He works for Louisiana Wildlife and Fisheries with my grandson E.R. and has been missing for a few days. I was in the room when he regained consciousness, but he seemed confused when I spoke to him. Is he alright? Can we see him?"

"Are you related to the patient?"

"No. I just told you he was my grandson's coworker. And Liam doesn't have any family. He has been a part of my family for the past few years. Aside from working together, he and my grandson are best friends." Griff was quickly losing patience.

"Maybe we should sit down." The doctor gestured towards some chairs in the waiting room.

Griff was reluctant to cooperate but did it anyway. *Something is not right here.* The doctor was holding back information, and Griff wanted to know what it was. He also knew that he needed to be careful not to alienate the doctor before he had answers.

"Look, you can call the Department of Wildlife and Fisheries and confirm that what we are saying is the truth." Griff reached for his phone. "Here are pictures of Liam with my grandson and my family. Can you please tell us if he is alright?"

The doctor hesitated but began to talk. "The patient is stable. He has a concussion and a few scrapes and bruises. He has a couple of cracked ribs and a sprained ankle. Other than that, I don't see anything else that is life threatening. There is however another problem. Like you said earlier, he seems confused which is probably due to the head injuries."

Tab stepped into the conversation. "We found him in his backyard shed. We responded to a disturbance call that came from his neighborhood and when we got to his house, we heard a noise that lured us to the shed. We moved closer to investigate but before we reached the shed, it collapsed. We pulled a man out of the shed and realized that it was Liam. He was unconscious and stayed in that state until recently when Griff was with him. Do you think he will make a full recovery?"

The doctor stood and wrote something in the chart he was holding. Griff and Tab joined him. He looked at both men and asked for their names. He added that information to the chart then filled them in to the rest of the problem with Liam. "Gentlemen, I don't doubt that what you say is what you believe to be the truth. However, the problem comes in when the information he gave me contradicts what you are claiming. I'm afraid you may have the wrong man. The patient in that room claims that his name is Lucas Ricci and that he doesn't know who you are."

Griff's voice elevated as he proceeded to protest that information. Tab squeezed his shoulder in an attempt to help calm him down. As his mind shuffled the information around trying to make sense of it, Griff became frustrated. *We found him in Liam's shed, in Liam's backyard. He looks like Liam. How could it not be Liam?* He realized that he had spoken all of those thoughts out loud.

Griff snapped back to reality and contemplated what to say next.

Tab made some suggestions. "Why don't we take a break and try to figure out what's going on. Doctor, can we see Liam? As you've noticed, we have a lot of questions for him."

"That is entirely up to the patient. I have a few more patients I have to see then I'll go back in and talk to him. I'll let you know if he agrees, but if he refuses, I won't be able to allow you access to his room. I hope you understand." Without another word the doctor walked off leaving the two men behind more baffled than before.

"Tab, I know that's Liam in that room. I don't understand why he would claim to be someone else. Even if he lost his memory as a result of his injuries, it wouldn't be normal to think he was someone else, would it?" Griff ran his fingers through his hair and shook his head. The tightness in his forehead and his furrowed brow indicated that stress was taking over. "And who else was at Liam's house?"

"We really need to get into that room!"

Tab was concerned about Griff and hoped that he could maintain control of his emotions. He knew that although Griff was worried about Liam, E.R. was his main concern. Things seemed to get more difficult with each new turn of events. Now, Liam may not be Liam which means Liam was still missing. And whoever was in that hospital bed had been attacked by the anonymous person that snatched Liam's backpack from Griff. Tab decided that it would be best to head back to the office and try to piece together everything they knew so far. Convincing Griff to leave the hospital wasn't going to be so easy.

"Hey man. Let's go back to the office and regroup. Maybe if we can write it all down and look at the whole picture, we'll get some answers. We'll leave my number for the doctor to call after he talks to Liam again. This case is getting crazier by the minute, so we need some clarity." Tab grabbed Griff's arm in an attempt to stop him. "Griff, call E.R. and see how he's doing. Then let's go to the office."

Griff stopped pacing and started to protest. He needed to talk to Liam. He knew that Tab was right, but he was afraid to leave the hospital before talking to Liam. What if he disappears. He knew that was a long shot, but the way things had gone so far made him apprehensive. Finally, he shook his head in agreement. He dialed E.R.'s number while Tab headed to the nurse's station to leave his cell number for the doctor.

Tab waited for someone to come to the nurse's station so that he could leave his number. After a few minutes and no one showed up, he debated going into Liam's room. His room was directly across from the nurse's station and there wasn't anyone around. Tab crossed the hall and stood outside Liam's door. He leaned against the door and listened. He thought maybe he would hear the television or a nurse's voice, but it was quiet. Slowly, he pushed open the door and walked in. Liam was laying on his side facing the window. Tab walked over to the other side of the bed and found Liam asleep.

The fresh scent of Clorox tickled Tab's nose but didn't surprise him. The room was spotless and well equipped. Under normal circumstances rooms were sanitized but with covid the cleaning schedule had increased. Even though the room was small, it was pleasant. There were chairs for visitors situated beside the bed and large windows to make it feel more open. The drapes were closed and sadly there were no visitors.

Tab contemplated his next move. He carefully examined the room and found that Liam's clothes were in a bag that sat in the corner of the room. When he lifted the bag, it created a soft crackling sound. He glanced over to Liam who was still sound asleep. Even though his clothes were filthy, they were folded neatly and placed in that bag. Tab pulled out his shirt first and then his jeans. He heard activity pick up outside the room, so he quickened his search. He checked the pockets of the jeans and found a pocketknife and a few dollars. *Where's his wallet?* Tab started to put the clothes back in the bag and remembered that he didn't check the small watch pocket. He fumbled with the jeans and stuck his finger into the pocket. There was a small napkin folded inside. He pulled out the napkin and opened it up. Tab wanted to examine the napkin but a knock on the door startled him. He shoved it in his pocket and waited to be discovered. The door started to open, and Tab held his breath. He heard voices from the hall.

"Jen, can you come help me in Mr. Martin's room please?"

The door shut, and Tab exhaled. He made his way to the door and cautiously exited Liam's room. He quickened his pace and reached Griff just as he had entered the nurse's station. Without saying a word, Tab motioned for Griff to head out the door. Once they were safely outside the hospital, Tab put his hands on his thighs and inhaled deeply.

"Man! Can things get any more bizarre with this case?" Tab's pulse was slowly getting back to normal.

"Tab did something happen. What took you so long?"

"Griff, I went into Liam's room. When I got to the nurse's station it was empty. Without thinking, I decided to slip into his room and talk to him. I know I was taking a chance, but the hall was completely empty, and I thought maybe Liam would recognize me."

Griff was surprised by Tab's actions. Tab was usually the one that always followed the rules and thought things through before reacting. He could see that he was physically shaken and wondered what happened.

"Did you get caught? What did you find out?"

"It was close, but no I didn't get caught. Liam was sleeping when I got in there, so I didn't wake him. I searched the room and found his clothes in a bag on a chair." Tab reached in his pocket and retrieved the napkin. "I found this in his pocket. He had it stashed in the little watch pocket of his jeans. Someone started to enter the room, so I shoved it in my pocket."

"I thought you said you didn't get caught."

"I didn't. By some miracle, the nurse that was coming into Liam's room was asked to help with another patient before she entered."

Griff looked at the napkin in Tab's hand. Tab unfolded it and found two clues. The napkin was from Bourbon Heat and there was a phone number written on the back.

"This proves that the patient is Liam because he was at Bourbon Heat with E.R. when he met Charley Ann. It has to be him man. I don't recognize the phone number. Call it and see who answers."

Tab took out his phone and dialed the number. It went straight to a generic voicemail message. "Well that didn't help. Let's get to the office and I'll call a friend to trace this number. This is the first real clue we have. I would have to agree with you that the odds that someone that looks identical to Liam would be at the exact same place recently are slim. How much do you know about Liam? I know you said he didn't have any family but what happened to them? Did he have any siblings? Maybe he has a twin brother but if that were the case and the man in the hospital bed was his twin, he would've recognized Liam's name. Where was he born? Where did he grow up? I think that's a good place to start digging. We need to find out everything we can about Liam. Did you get in touch with E.R. yet? Maybe he knows some of these answers. They seemed to be very close."

"Yes, but the call dropped and now it goes to voicemail. I'll try again when we get to the office. They were supposed to go to Artie's and ask around about Brian and it's really loud in there. He probably didn't hear the ring. I'm sure he'll call me back when he sees that I called. All I know about Liam is that he doesn't have any family and he moved here two years ago from Florida. I think you're right that we need to investigate Liam, but I think it would be a good idea to check out Charley Ann also. I know you didn't get to meet her yet, but my gut tells me that we can trust her. I hope that's true because I think E.R. is beginning to take an interest in her. I don't want to see him betrayed again because that would kill him." Griff started to reflect on the past while they drove to the office.

One thing from the past that stood out the most to Griff was that everyone loved E.R.'s girlfriend Christina from the start. She was nice and outgoing. She really seemed to like E.R. and treated him good. Griff often wondered if she regretted what she did but E.R. broke things off immediately and they all lost contact with her. She didn't stay with Conner but instead broke all ties that involved E.R. and his family. Griff figured that she knew she messed up but also knew that E.R. would forgive her but never forget.

E.R. had been cautious since his break-up with Christina and hadn't had a serious relationship since. Griff saw the way his grandson looked at Charley Ann and prayed that she was truthful with him. He didn't want to see his grandson hurt again and hoped the next relationship he was in would bring him peace and happiness. Griff planned on doing a little research on her to see if she had any skeletons in her closet, but for now, he just prayed.

CHAPTER 15

Relief came over E.R. like a wave when he saw Charley Ann. "Are you alright? Are you hurt?" E.R. wanted to comfort her but at the same time was worried that she was hurt and in need of medical attention. "How did you get in there?"

"I don't know exactly. I followed Freddie out here and was trying to get close enough to listen to his conversation. I went around the side of the container and when I reached the back it was open, and Freddie was gone. Before I knew what was happening, someone pulled something over my head and shoved me into the container. I didn't see who it was. With the cloudy sky looming over it was pretty dark and I was facing the container. Have you seen Freddie? Is he still here?" Charley Ann looked around.

"I don't know. When you weren't at the table when I got back from the bathroom I started to worry. He wasn't around then and after that I was searching for you. When I came looking for you there was a man in a boat getting ready to take off. When I approached, he ran, and I chased him. I tripped and he got away, but I don't think it was Freddie. If I remember correctly Freddie was short and a little overweight. The guy I was chasing was tall and definitely in shape. Let's go inside and see if he's still here. Maybe he has some answers for us." E.R. waited for Charley Ann to start walking and followed her inside.

They went to the bar and asked for Freddie. The bartender said he was gone for the day. They made their way back to the table they had occupied before, and it was completely cleared. They decided to sit down again and question their new waitress. They were both shaken and weren't in the mood to eat anything.

"I just want a coke. I don't think I can stomach food right now. Do you think we should call the cops?" Charley Ann searched E.R.'s face for answers.

"Yes. I think we should report what happened. Someone attacked you and wanted to get rid of you. Thank God you were able to call out for help. I still don't know who would do that. Why would they pick you to assault? Do you know anyone here?"

"No. Just you and my new friend Sam." Charley Ann tried to crack a smile, but the slight lift of her lip wasn't enough to have that affect.

"Why were you following Freddie?"

"I asked him about Brian, and he turned pale white. From his reaction, I think he knew him, but lied and said no. He left the table so fast and headed out the door with his cell phone. I just thought that I could follow him and listen to who he was calling. I know in my gut it had to do with my question about Brian. E.R., do you think it could've been Freddie that locked me in the container?

What if you didn't hear me? I could've been locked in there all night." Charley Ann's body involuntarily shook.

E.R. moved closer to Charley Ann and covered her hands with his.

"That must've been scary for you. I know it was dark in there. Are you sure you're alright? I'm gonna call 911 and report this."

"I still don't see the connection to the guy in the boat. Why did he run from you? Do you think that maybe Freddie called him when he went outside? That would be…"

"Hey guys. What's up?" Sam came to the table with the biggest smile that involved her mouth, cheeks, and eyes.

"Sam. What are you doing here?" E.R. found her presence disturbing.

"I told y'all I was coming to work here after I left the marina. Y'all didn't eat yet. What can I get ya?"

"Sam, do you know Freddie that works here?" Charley Ann watched Sam's face closely for a reaction. She didn't know who she could trust anymore.

"Can't say that I do. I've seen him before when I came with my cousin but he's not a real friendly guy, kinda rude sometimes. Was he rude to y'all? You need to let the manager know because I'm sure it's not the first com-plaint against him. You know in our business you have to be nice to the customers." Sam turned and looked for the manager.

"No. Sam. He wasn't rude. Well, he was rude but that's not the problem. I asked him if he knew Brian and while he said "no" his facial expression told a different story. I followed him outside and then someone locked me in a container." Charley Ann tried to continue her story, but Sam interrupted.

"Oh my goodness, you poor thing." Sam seemed genuinely concerned. "Did Freddie do that? I'm gonna kill him!"

"I don't know who did it. The sky was clouded, and the light wasn't good back there. Do you think Freddie is capable of doing something like that? I know he's rude but is he capable of assault?"

"I don't really know. Like I said, he's not a friendly guy. I can ask around. Maybe some of the other wait staff know him better." Sam looked around again.

E.R. called 911, asked for the manager and decided to look around again. He wanted to check out that boat but didn't feel comfortable leaving Charley Ann's side. Maybe Griff could find out who owns the boat and run a background check on Freddie.

"Hey Sam. What's Freddie's last name?" E.R. waited for her response.

"I think...ya know, I don't know. Like I said, I don't know him personally but here comes the manager. I'm sure he knows his name." Sam turned and left the table before the manager arrived. Charley Ann noticed that Sam was suddenly ready to move on and wondered if there was something to that, or had she read more into it because she was on edge. Either way, Charley Ann was going to keep an eye on Sam.

The manager Jude recognized them from the container incident. "Hi. Did you need something else?"

E.R. spoke up first. They didn't shake hands because of covid. He nodded and introduced himself.

"Yes Jude. We're looking for Freddie. He was our waiter earlier but didn't come back to the table. Is he still here?"

"No. He left a while ago. He got a phone call and said he had to leave. Is everything alright?" Jude loved his job but hated dealing with complaints.

"Can you tell us Freddie's last name and where we can find him?"

Jude shifted his weight and became alarmed. "Did he do something wrong?"

"We don't know yet. What's his last name?" E.R. voice demanded answers.

"Freddie Jackson. His name is Freddie Jackson. I don't know much about him because he just started about a month ago and only works part time. I really can't give out his personal information, but I can call him and give him your number."

E.R. asked Jude to sit down and reminded him what had just happened to Charley Ann.

"Man. I'm sorry. I don't know what to say."

E.R. realized that Jude was trying to cooperate and decided to switch his tone to befriend him rather than scare him.

"We called 911 and are waiting for them now. Thank you for your help. I understand your position I wouldn't want to get you into trouble. We were just trying to get some information. Don't call Freddie. We don't even know if he was involved. We'll wait and see what the cops have to say." E.R. wanted to get Jude away from the table and back to work.

Jude apologized again and left the table. E.R. waited a second and then followed him to the back. E.R. listened from right outside the kitchen door. Jude shouted out some orders to other employees and then came back out to the bar. The bar was packed, and E.R. blended in making himself discreet. As far as he could tell, Jude went on with business as usual. E.R. just wanted to make sure he didn't call Freddie and warn him. He returned to the table and listened as Charley Ann and Sam were deep into conversation again. He noticed that while Sam rambled on about everything, Charley Ann asked some very pointed questions. He smiled to himself. *She's smart.*

E.R.'s phone rang, and it was Griff.

"What's up Paw?" E.R. walked towards the back door to hear better but kept Charley Ann in his sight.

Griff updated E.R. with what seemed like a long explanation. Last time they talked, Griff reassured E.R. that Liam was safe and would be fine. E.R., who was understandably upset, listened to all the bizarre turn of events that had happened at home while he was in Grand Isle chasing clues. He felt useless and was overwhelmed with the need to be at Liam's side.

Back at the table, Charley Ann watched Sam as she spoke. She felt bad about being suspicious, but her life was at stake, so everyone was a suspect. She noticed that Sam didn't have on an apron, just her regular clothes. Charley Ann looked around and realized that all of the employees had on street clothes. She relaxed a little and tried to focus on what Sam was saying.

"I know this place is crowded but believe me, if we didn't have to evacuate it would be more crowded than this. It'd be difficult to see the other side of the bar. Eve-ryone loves Artie's. Hey, how long are y'all staying on the Island? I don't really want to evacuate but I think we have to. Give me your number and I'll call you once the hurri-cane has passed and we are back to work." Sam kept rambling on.

Charley Ann didn't know why but that last question raised a red flag. "Give me your number. I lost my phone and didn't have time to get another one yet." She handed Sam a napkin to write on. "We're heading back home soon but I'll call you when I can."

Charley Ann noticed that Sam hesitated for a second then reached for the napkin. *She's hiding something from me. Or maybe she just has something to hide from every-one. Either way, she cannot be trusted.* Charley Ann watched as Sam scribbled her number on the napkin. She handed it to Charley Ann and said, "Call me soon."

She didn't know why, but Charley Ann yelled as Sam walked away. "Hey Sam. Have you ever been to Lafitte?"

Sam put her hands behind both ears and motioned that she couldn't hear her. She shouted, "See ya later, okay."

Charley Ann looked around for E.R. and worried that he went outside to investigate by himself. She spotted him by the back door talking to two officers. He looked in her direction and then with the two officers in tow, headed towards the table.

Charley Ann stood up and greeted the officers. "Hi. I'm Charley Ann Cheramie." Both officers were young and well fit. One of the officers was taller than the other but only by a few inches. Charley Ann watched E.R.'s reaction as she met them and was surprised to see discomfort. *Is he jealous?* She quickly turned her attention back to the officers and gave her account of the events leading up to her abduction. *Abduction? Is that the right word?* Charlie Ann stopped for a moment and thought about what she was saying. Exactly what happened finally started to register with Charley Ann and there were visible signs that she was shaken. E.R. stepped in and diverted the officer's attention to himself. He knew that Charley Ann needed some time to gather her thoughts. She wasn't the sensitive type, but she was just assaulted, and that sense of vulnerability could be overwhelming.

"Look, clearly someone pushed her into that container."

Charley Ann jumped back in. "I didn't see who it did, but I think Freddie should be our number one suspect. I think he lied to me about knowing Brian. Maybe something else was going on but he was clearly upset when he ran out of here."

E.R. suggested that they go outside and check out the container and the boat. Before they went out, one of the officers stopped and asked about the video cameras. They were informed that they didn't work but were being replaced the next week. He also asked about the container, but no one could explain why it was there and what it was used for. All they knew was that the key was on the main ring with all the other keys for Artie's and only the managers and the owner had a set.

"It's never been locked before. I don't know who locked it. When that guy ran in here yelling for the key, I ran outside with my set. I wasn't even sure which key it was. Luckily, we found the right one. Sure glad that girl was alright. Let me know if I can help with anything else. My name is Jude if you need me."

"Thanks Jude" The taller officer spoke up. "Can you give me the names of all your employees that worked here today? And give Artie a call. Tell him we will need to speak to him soon. Thanks."

When they were outside, E.R. ran to the boat dock yelling. "The boats gone. How did I let that happen? I should've stayed out here and waited until the officers arrived. The boat is gone." E.R. was trembling in disbelief. He wanted to kick himself for letting that slip by him. Normally, he would've had someone watch the boat if he wasn't able to do it himself. He was upset about the missing boat but more upset that he felt out of control and vulnerable.

"Hey. It's not your fault. Things are moving so fast there was nothing you could've done. We needed to find Freddie and talk to the police. He must've slipped back here and taken off. It's too bad that we missed him, but it's not your fault."

E.R. continued to beat himself up. He wanted to know why that guy ran. He felt desperate to get some answers.

The officers looked around and questioned people at the restaurant. "Apparently, no one noticed the guy take off in the boat. He was gone and there is no way to find him."

"Wait. E.R. didn't you take pictures of the bar and the dock when we got here. Look at your photos. Maybe you captured his boat in the picture." Charley Ann stood next to E.R. as he searched his photos.

"There it is. It's that white Carolina Skiff right there." E.R. showed the officers. "I think I can zoom in and get the numbers off the side."

One of the officers had E.R. send the photo to his phone. "We'll call this in and see where it leads. Now is there anything else you can think of that could help find who assaulted you Ms. Cheramie?"

The officers asked both Charley Ann and E.R. for their contact information. They reminded them that they had to leave the island because of the mandatory evacuation and looked around for anything that could possibly provide any clues before they left. They promised to keep in touch and reach out as soon as they got any information on the boat.

"I think I'm ready to get out of here. The storm has passed, and I want to get back before the next squall comes in and I need to check on Liam. Are you ready?"

E.R.'s voice was low, his shoulders slouched. He looked deflated and was visibly troubled. Charley Ann nodded and the two of them headed back to the Marina to get E.R.'s boat. They were both shaken from the day's events and felt like it was time to get back to Lafitte and try to put things into perspective.

CHAPTER 16

The drive back to the office took about 10 minutes. Both Griff and Tab were preoccupied with the newest developments on the case. Tab agreed that finding the napkin should be proof that the man in the hospital was Liam, but he wasn't convinced. He couldn't figure out why Liam hadn't contacted E.R. to let him know he was alright. He had to know they were looking for him and would be worried. Tab knew that Griff wasn't thinking straight because normally he would have been the skeptical one. He was very observant and diligent when he investigated which was why he was so good at his job. Griff also had extremely high standards and too often expected others to behave the same way. No, Tab knew that if Griff were thinking straight, then he would've admitted that there was a good possibility that the man in the hospital was not Liam.

As soon as Griff and Tab arrived at their office, Tab's phone rang. The nurse from the hospital was on the other end and informed him that Liam had agreed to see them. The nurse barked out instructions and then hung up.

Tab looked over at Griff and repeated what the nurse said. "That was the hospital. Liam agreed to see us."

Griff was about to exit Tab's car. "Yes! Let's get over there." He sat back down and hooked his seat belt. He realized that Tab was staring at him, and he knew that he was about to get a lecture. He started to defend his actions but decided to let Tab say his peace, after all, he had been by Griff's side since all of this started.

"Hey buddy. Don't you think we should go inside and reassess what we know so far? We can make a list of the questions we want to ask Liam. Remember the doctor said he denied being Liam so at any time he could ask us to leave. I know you think he'll respond to you, but what if he doesn't? We might only get one shot at him. Can we please slow down and make that visit count?"

Griff knew Tab was right. Normally, he would have behaved in the same way as Tab and would take things slowly, but this case was personal for him and had him on edge. He had been agitated and fidgety and Tab was right to call him out on it before he messed things up.

"You're right. I'm a mess but we need to solve this. Here we are three days later, and we still don't have answers. Who killed Brian? If that's not Liam lying in that hospital bed, where's Liam and who is the patient? And who attacked me and stole the duffle bag?"

"Those are all good questions but what do we do if he doesn't want to cooperate? Chances are he's still claiming to be someone else. We need to be prepared for that scenario and accept his answers. The main objective is to find out who is in that bed and if it's not Liam then we need to know now." Tab waited for Griff's response.

Griff reluctantly reached for the door handle and opened the car door. "You're right. Let's go inside and come up with a plan. I know that man is Liam, but I understand what you're saying. If by some miracle it's not, then we need to be searching for Liam before it's too late. He looked pretty sedated, so I don't think he'll be going anywhere anytime soon." Griff entered the office with Tab right behind him.

Tab jumped on the phone immediately requesting a background check on Liam and a trace on the phone number he found on the napkin in Liam's pants. He called his friend Trey whom he always relied on for help when he and Griff were too busy and needed someone that was good, and Trey was the best. Trey was young and when it came to modern technology, he could navigate through it all, especially social media. For a moment, Tab reflected on how things were when he was young. He and Griff got away with a lot of things back then because there wasn't anything like social media to catch you. He frowned at the thought of the effect social media had on young people today. They are too young to know better or even care, but in reality, their actions will follow them the rest of their lives.

"Trey's gonna run a check on Liam. I think we need to know everything there is to know about his life. I also asked him to run a check on Charley Ann. I know you're worried about E.R., and I thought maybe checking her out would ease your mind."

Griff shifted in place. He felt guilty about invading Charley Ann's privacy but under the circumstances he needed to know he could trust her. Griff really liked her, but he had some questions. The one thing that bothered him the most was her relationship with someone like Brian. He knew that people like Brian were good at hiding their true nature and were usually quite charming, likable characters, at least in the beginning. Griff just felt like Charley Ann was an intelligent, strong, independent woman and he had a hard time thinking that she could be fooled like that. Of course, he hadn't known her for long so he could be mistaken, and maybe she was the one hiding her true nature and was dangerous after all. Considering all the factors, Griff decided that it was necessary to have Charley Ann checked out and hoped that she wouldn't be offended by it and would forgive him.

"Thanks. I planned on checking her out, but I haven't had the time yet. These last few days have been crazy and it's not over yet. I think I should be the one to question Liam. He's been really close to my family for several years now and I think I'll know if he's telling the truth. If he doesn't respond to me then you can step in. Here's a list of questions I want to ask him." Griff handed the list to Tab. "Do you have anything to add?"

Tab looked over the list and added a few questions of his own.

"Let's head to the hospital and see what Liam or whoever it is has to say."

Tab was focused on that last statement. He wasn't sure that Griff was ready to accept what was about to happen at the hospital. The more Tab tried to make sense of the recent events the more he leaned towards the notion that the man at the hospital was telling the truth and that he was not Liam Barrios.

****

E.R. and Charley Ann were both exhausted. The events of the past few days were taking its toll on them, and E.R. shuddered to think what could have happened had he not found her in that container. He wondered why that container was even there. His mind raced as he imagined all the reasons for a container to be used. Before they left Grand Isle, E.R. examined the container and the area around it. The grass was knee high, and the container was rusted and in disrepair. It didn't look like it had been moved in years. The inside was in better condition and seemed to be empty less a few old cartons stacked in the back. The chain holding the lock was also rusted and old and didn't appear to have been opened lately. The manager denied knowing anything about the container except that it had been there as long as he could remember. He suggested talking to the owner to find out its purpose. When the officers arrived, they instructed the manager to have the owner call them.

The boat ride back to Lafitte was pleasant and supplied much needed down time for both of them. The winds had calmed down enough, and the sun rays glistened on top of the water. E.R. loved being on the water that time of the day, especially right after a thunderstorm. The intense heat was back but as they raced across the water, the wind was cool and refreshing. E.R. knew that it was time to go back home, back to reality, but he wished he had more time with Charley Ann. He glanced her way and felt the ever-building stir in his stomach to be disturbing. He was stunned by just how beautiful she was. Her long silky hair danced from the breeze, and she had a peaceful smile on her face. He wanted to know what caused those beautiful lips to curl up in such a way and hoped that maybe it had something to do with him.

They reached the camp and immediately started to straighten up and pack to go home. An important lesson E.R. learned from his grandfather long ago was "Leave it like you found it." There wasn't a lot to do because they weren't there long enough to make much of a mess. The camp had ceramic floors that were easy to keep clean and the rooms were nicely furnished but not too cluttered. Jason made sure that his camp was easily maintainable because that allowed for more time to enjoy other things like fishing. E.R. noticed that the smile had left Charley Ann's face and had been replaced with a brooding frown.

"Are you alright?"

Charley Ann nodded and continued to pack up her things. She grabbed the broom and started sweeping the floors. She shoved the broom back and forth with concentrated effort. She was definitely doing more than sweeping the floor. Charley Ann was upset, and she was taking it out on the floor. E.R. didn't know what to say so he opted to just leave her alone. He wasn't sure how things were going to play out, but he felt a sudden urge to grab her and never let her go. Instead, he kept his feelings to himself and held off his desire to run to her side and comfort her. He kept his distance and waited for her response.

Charley Ann stopped sweeping and started speaking in a low trembling voice. E.R. could barely hear her, so he moved in closer, still keeping a safe distance.

"I'm really, really sorry I got y'all mixed up in this mess. I wanted you to know that before we leave. I didn't know that Brian would follow me and involve y'all in our problems. He was never the man I thought he was, and I thank God that I realized it before it went on too long. I feel like such a fool, and I have to live with that, but I re-ally am sorry that I involved you and Liam. You've been so wonderful to me, and I don't know how I can ever re-pay you. I hope you can forgive me for everything." Charley Ann picked up her backpack and headed for the door.

She was sorry that she brought a monster like Brian into E.R.'s life. She said what she had to say and now it was time to move on. She was sure E.R. was ready to get rid of her when they got back to his house. She was apprehensive about leaving the camp for two reasons and both were equally terrifying to her. First, she wasn't sure what was going to happen when they went back home. Where would she go? The other thought that haunted her was getting back home and she and E.R. going their separate ways.

E.R. made a quick pass around the camp making sure everything was in order and then headed out the door behind Charley Ann. She was already in the seat of the boat, and he wondered just how eager she was to get back to reality. Again, that stir in the pit of his stomach came about but this time it was caused by fear, regret, and disappointment. He had hoped that there would be some kind of future with Charley Ann, but it was clear that all she felt was sorrow that she had involved them in her mess and nothing more. E.R. realized that he misjudged her actions since they met and that instead of starting to have feelings for him, she just felt bad that Liam was missing, and E.R. was now involved.

E.R. got into the boat and shifted the gear. He was anxious to get home and help Tab and his grandfather solve this mystery. E.R. had been so worried about Liam and was ready to get home and find out what happened to him. Earlier, his grandfather had told him that Liam was still unconscious, but he was expected to wake up soon. As much as he had enjoyed being with Charley Ann, he was eager to return to his old quiet life and feel normal again but first needed to get to the bottom of all that had happened.

CHAPTER 17

Getting out of the hospital was simple. People were so easy to manipulate, and he was the master of manipulation. He learned at an early age how to survive, and it had served him well. The bump on his head was throbbing and he was struggling to move. He wished he could see their faces when they realized that he was gone. He chuckled at the thought then winced from the pain it caused. He needed to get to a phone so he could tell them that he was alive. He was safe for now, but he wasn't sure for how long. Those detectives were smart and would be searching for him as soon as they found out he's missing.

He should've known better than to get himself caught. He knew that the place was unstable yet went inside anyway. He needed to stay out of sight and that unfortunately led to his bad decision. His partner had alerted him that the detectives had arrived, so he had to act quickly. That was just a little hiccup in their grand plan. He would bounce back quickly just like he always had. When he was young, everyone used to count him out because of his size but they would always regret that assumption. Fortunately, he grew up to be average size but still found people underestimated him. *Will they ever learn?*

He opened the back door to the building and walked right into a kitchen. The kitchen staff was busy, so he walked through unnoticed. He canvassed the area and noticed a small break area to the right of the kitchen. He made his way across the crowded kitchen and slid into the room undetected. There were lockers that stretched across the back wall with snack machines on the side. The tables were empty but showed evidence of being occupied recently. He looked down at his arm and cursed when he remembered that his watch was gone. That was his favorite watch, a souvenir from finally standing up and making sure that it was the last time his father would abuse anyone. He made a mental note to get that back.

As he was about to leave the room, he noticed a black sweater hanging from one of the chairs. He glanced back at the kitchen to make sure no one was coming. He didn't want to make another mistake and mess things up. He slowly walked along the wall to the other side of the room where the sweater hung. He reached into the left pocket and pulled out a pack of Marlboro's and a lighter. Instead of returning the items he slipped them into his own pocket for later. He reached into the other side and there it was, an I Phone enclosed in a pink glittery case with the initials KEG on it. *Please don't be password protected.* Before he could check he heard the break bell ring and decided it was time to move on. He shoved the phone in his pocket next to the cigarettes and lighter and walked back to the break room entrance. He was met with a crowd of people rushing in to take full advantage of their break time.

He ducked his head as he walked against the crowd. A few people mumbled, "Watch where ya going", and "Excuse me" but he ignored them and headed out the back door. He didn't make eye contact and was positive that if it came down to it, they wouldn't be able to identify him. He needed to make that call and he couldn't let anything stop him. His plans had been temporarily put on hold but not for long. He was back and they were going to find that out soon enough.

CHAPTER 18

Tab usually drove a black SUV for work and an old 1998 Chevy truck when he was off. The truck was emerald-green metallic, had 150,000 miles on it and was in great condition. Tab loved his truck and hoped to keep it for another 150,000 miles. Most people commented that it was time for an upgrade, but he ignored the suggestions and enjoyed his truck. Griff understood because his own truck was almost as old as Tab's.

Sometimes, when he worked locally, Tab would use his truck instead of the SUV. They were in his truck headed back to the hospital to question Liam. As they drove along, Tab looked in his rearview mirror then the side mirror. He repeated that action a few times before Griff caught on that something was happening. He looked back and noticed what Tab was looking at, a black sedan that seemed to be following them. Tab switched lanes and decided to take a side street. They drove for a few miles and was relieved that they didn't see the sedan again.

"Did you notice that black sedan? I thought it was following us, but I guess I'm just being paranoid. Be on the lookout for that car just to be on the safe side." Tab felt uneasy.

"I didn't notice it until I saw you looking back but when I did see it, I thought they were following a little too close. But who would be following us?"

"I don't know man. These last few days have me on edge and nothing would surprise me." Tab pulled over to make sure no one was following them. Griff got out of the car and called E.R. for an update. Service had been so spotty with the weather that he hadn't had a chance to update him about Liam.

"I just spoke to E.R., and they are heading back in from the camp. If you think things are crazy here wait until you hear what happened there. Someone locked Charley Ann in an old empty container in the back of Artie's and when E.R. was searching for her, he approached a man getting into a boat and the man fled as E.R. got closer. E.R. ran after the guy but lost him. Apparently, E.R. found Charley Ann and filed a police report. He also mentioned that he was suspicious of a waiter named Freddie because of his reaction when asked about Brian. I'm glad they are on their way home. I'll feel better with him nearby."

"Do we need to meet them at the dock now or do we have time to see Liam first?"

"They just left the camp, and we are only about five minutes from the hospital depending on traffic. Let's go see Liam and then you can drop me off at E.R.'s house so I can pick up his truck. They can wait a few minutes if they get there before we do." Griff needed to see Liam.

The men arrived at the hospital and parked on the 3rd floor of the garage. Tab thought he noticed a black sedan driving up to their level, but as it approached it turned out to be dark blue. *He can't wait until this is all over.* The idea that this case was personal was unnerving. Tab couldn't remember the last time he was this nervous about a case. *Abby.* This case reminded him of when Griff's wife Abby got caught up in something that still to this day he didn't understand.

Griff and Tab took the elevator to Liam's floor and approached the nurse's desk. The same nurse that contacted Tab sat behind the desk looking down at her computer screen. She was unaware that they were standing there until Tab cleared his throat.

"Can I help you?" She asked without looking up.

"We're here to see Liam Barrios. You called to say that he agreed to see us."

"Right. He's in room 214 across the hall on the left." The nurse pointed in the direction of the room then went back to working on her computer.

Griff was anxious and walked at a fast pace towards the room. He was afraid that Liam wouldn't know him and was still claiming to be someone else. They hadn't heard back from Trey on the background checks, but Griff had no doubt that the man in that bed was Liam. He looked exactly like him, same height, same color hair, same color eyes. He even sounded like Liam. If it wasn't Liam, he had to be related to him. *Could that be it?* Griff was startled by that scenario but pushed his thought aside because he had arrived at Liam's door.

Griff looked back at Tab and motioned that they were ready. Tab nodded and the two men entered the room. A familiar smell hit Tab in the face as he entered. He had learned recently that he did not like the smell of hospitals. When he was in Liam's room yesterday, the smell stayed with him the rest of the night. He followed Griff through the hall and around to the bedside. Both men stood in silence. The bed was empty, and the room was vacant.

"Where is he?" Griff rushed to the bathroom to see if Liam was in there. When they entered the room, they passed the bathroom, and the door was open. He knew that he wasn't in there but had to be sure.

Tab rushed to the nurse's station to find out if they took him for a test. This time, he didn't wait for the nurse to look up.

"Where is he?" Tab watched as the nurse looked up confused.

"Where is he? Liam. Where is Liam? Did they take him for test?"

The nurse responded to Tab's questions without haste. "Is he not in his room?"

Tab took a deep breath before he answered. "No. He is not in his room. Can you check to see if they took him for a test, please?"

Tab headed back to the room and found Griff holding an empty plastic bag that had contained Liam's clothes the day before.

"He's Gone! His clothes are gone! Where could he be? How did he get out of here? Did they release him?" Disappointment dripped from Griff's voice.

"The nurse is checking into it. I don't think they released him because the nurse had no idea what I was talking about. She jumped into gear and started to make phone calls when I left to come back here. Maybe he is having some test done."

Griff held up the empty bag. "Liam is gone. We need to look at the video surveillance to see when he left, if he left on his own or did someone take him." Griff marched towards the door determined to find out what happened.

There were several nurses at the front desk when he arrived. They confirmed that Liam was not scheduled for any test and that he should be in his room. Griff informed them that the room was vacant, and that Liam's clothes were gone. He asked to see the supervisor and patiently waited for answers

Tab joined Griff and they sat in the waiting room until the supervisor arrived. Griff spoke first.

"If that were Liam, why would he leave. I took the bag that had his clothes in it hoping that we can get some fingerprints from it. Can you call Trey to put a rush on the background check? I swear, that man looked identical to Liam." Griff shook his head in disbelief.

"I'm on it." Tab walked to the quiet side of the room to make the call.

Griff watched as the chaos grew behind the nurses' desk. They lost a patient, and everyone was scrambling to locate him. A tall, slim woman in her mid-thirties walked up, and everyone waited for their orders. Apparently, she was the supervisor. Griff stood up and walked towards the desk. Before he reached his destination, she came from behind the desk and introduced herself.

"My name is Laci Perrin. I'm the floor supervisor. I understand you found room 214 to be empty and reported the patient missing. I assure you that we have everyone looking for him. If you follow me, we can go down to security and review the surveillance video." She turned and headed towards the elevators.

Griff motioned to Tab, and they followed the nurse to security.

"Did you reach Trey?"

"No but I left him a message filling him in and requested that he speed things up. Griff, I hate to say it man, but I think Liam has a double. His behavior is too bizarre. Even if he has some kind of amnesia, why would he leave the hospital before being discharged? We need to talk to the doctor again to find out if he said anything else."

"I'm inclined to agree with you now." Griff stopped for a moment and looked at Tab. "Tab, where in the world is Liam? Are we too late?"

Tab grabbed Griff's arm and started to follow the nurse again.

"I don't know man but let's look at these tapes before we move on to that. Maybe they contain some clues for us."

The head of security for the hospital was waiting for them when they arrived. He introduced himself, offered them a seat, and then pressed play on the surveillance tape. The nurse had recorded that she had been in his room an hour before Griff and Tab arrived, so they started the tape ten minutes before that time. They all watched as the nurse entered the room and fifteen minutes later exited. Twenty minutes after the nurse left the room, the door opened, and a man walked out of the room with his head tucked down. He turned away from the camera and went into the stairwell. They switched cameras from the hallway to the stair well. Again the man had his head down and limped down the stairs.

They switched from camera to camera and followed the man to the first floor of the hospital. He went out a back door and then later entered into the cafeteria kitchen. He found a phone in a sweater pocket and left the same way he came in. They were able to track him as he walked up the street eventually out of sight.

"So he left on his own." Tab turned to the supervisor and asked if they could see the latest doctor's report. She agreed and led the two men back up to the 2nd floor. Griff and Tab had so many questions but remained silent.

The report was written at 6:30 am. The doctor's report stated that his patient was awake and seemed stable. It stated what they already knew that he had some cracked ribs and a sprained ankle. The doctor recommended that he stay another night in the hospital and be reevaluated the next day. He added a little side note that, "The patient again claimed to be Lucas Ricci not Liam Barrios which was suggested by the two detectives yesterday."

Tab and Griff thanked the supervisor and asked her to let them know if they get any information relevant to Liam. They wanted to get to Trey but first stopped by the cafeteria to check it out. They decided to follow Liam's steps to see if there were any clues along the way. They looked all around the stairwell and then the cafeteria. Tab noticed something shiny under the chair where Liam stole the phone. There, almost tucked completely under the front leg, was a small silver key. Tab took a napkin from the table and picked it up. He showed Griff and they decided to go back to the security office to see if they could tell if it belonged to Liam.

They watched the video again, but this time focused in on the moment Liam placed the cigarettes and lighter into his pocket. When he pulled his hand back out, something shiny dropped to the floor. It was difficult to see because of the angle of Liam's body to the camera but without a doubt it belonged to him. Again they thanked the security guard and left the building.

"How did we miss that?" Griff opened the passenger side door of the truck.

"The position of the camera blocked most of it making it difficult to notice, and it all happened so quickly. If we hadn't found that key, there was no way we would have noticed it in the video. I wonder who or what it belongs to?"

Earlier, when Tab checked Liam's pockets, he was interrupted by a nurse and hurried out of the room. He must have missed the key in haste. He recalled that there were only a few things in his pockets, so the key had to be important to him. They now added the key to the list of things to check out.

CHAPTER 19

E. R. received a text that Griff would be late picking them up from the dock. The boat ride back from Jason's camp passed quickly. Instead of waiting at the dock for his grandfather, E.R. suggested that they get something to eat at Boutte's Restaurant. Charley Ann agreed so they headed to the restaurant.

"Can we get a table for two, please?" Charley Ann waited for the hostess to respond.

E.R. secured the boat to the dock and joined her inside. After a moment, the hostess showed them to a table upstairs and reminded them that there was a mandatory evacuation order, and they would be closing soon. Charley Ann and E.R. were both on edge and took note of the room and the people in it. After the episode at Artie's earlier, E.R. was afraid to let Charley Ann out of his sight. He reminded himself that in just a few more hours she would no longer be his problem. Deep down he knew that time wouldn't make a difference at all. He had developed feelings for her, and no amount of time would stop him from worrying. He wouldn't relax until they got to the truth and that was going to take time.

Even though it was well past lunch time, the restaurant was full of locals looking for one last meal before they had to hunker down for the hurricane. The décor was fitting for the location of the restaurant. The walls were decorated with rope to display a nautical look and there was a wall full of beautiful lanterns. Boutte's was known for its delicious seafood and was not only frequented by locals but by tourists from all over. E.R. started to relax as he admired the décor but suddenly remembered that Fleming Cemetery was just up the road. His smile flattened and his bad mood returned. He shrugged off the impulse to check his phone again to see if his grandfather called.

Charley Ann watched as E.R.'s demeanor shifted back and forth and wondered what he was thinking.

"E.R., are you alright?"

E.R. was caught off guard and looked at Charley Ann puzzled. He wondered if she knew what he was thinking. It surprised him that she recognized his change in mood.

"I'm good. Let's order because the wind is picking up out there and I'm afraid that we'll start to see heavier squalls coming in soon. It's forecast to hit sometime on Sunday." E.R. hesitated then said, "There's no way I'm leaving town without finding Liam."

Charley Ann started to reply but the waitress came for their order. She understood how he felt and wished she could comfort him. She felt a twinge of guilt because if he hadn't been trying to protect her, he could've focused more on finding Liam. With Hurricane Ida headed that way, things were going to get more complicated. They didn't talk about what was going to happen when they got back but E.R. had suggested that she may still be in danger. She wasn't sure that she agreed with him but decided to pacify him and go along with whatever he wanted to do. She owed him that much.

"I feel like I'm failing Liam. I'm due to go back to work tomorrow and with the hurricane coming I have to go. We are already shorthanded and with Liam missing they need me. I'm grateful that they let me take the last few days off. I don't think Liam has missed one day of work in 2 years. He was very dedicated to his job and often talked about how much he loved what he did. We were good together. I don't know what I'll do if we don't find him soon. They say that the first few days are crucial. And I know that if he were able, he would contact me. Something is wrong and I'm afraid that it's not good."

The waitress brought their food and they both ate in silence. They needed time to go over all of the recent events and decide what direction to take.

****

Griff called E.R. and told him that they were on their way to pick them up. Tab had dropped Griff off at E.R.'s house to get his truck and they were both heading down. They wanted to go back to the cemetery before the weather got too bad. Ahead of Hurricane Ida, the flood waters would start to rise, and the roads would be impassable. Griff knew they were racing against the clock and that every second counted.

They were still waiting on Trey to call with an update. He did call to say that he came up empty on the phone number they found because it was for a burner phone. Griff shook his head at that thought and wasn't surprised that it was another dead end. He had started to feel like there was a force working against them and hoped that Trey would at least come up with something on Brian that would help them find answers.

Griff called Tab's phone. "Hey Tab. Did you remember to ask Trey to check up on the name Lucas Ricci? I know it's a long shot, but you never know. And I have that plastic bag from Liam's hospital room. I want to drop it off when we get back from meeting with E.R. and Charley Ann. I know with the storm coming they probably won't get to it right away, but I want it there just in case."

A gust of wind forced Griff to grab the steering wheel with two hands. He looked out towards the bayou and noticed that the water was extremely high, and the wind had started to send it over the banks. The tree branches were bent almost to the ground then sprung up to the sky as if to announce the coming of something big. Griff could see the boat launch ahead and hoped that E.R. and Charley Ann were there and ready to go. When he pulled into the parking lot there was another truck backed up in the launch. Griff pulled to the side and waited for them to finish. He searched the water for E.R. and noticed that he was off to the side waiting for Griff. Griff, relieved to see his grandson safe honked the horn to get his attention.

E.R. waved and directed his boat to get into position after the launch was clear.

"Man, it's good to see you!" Griff hugged E.R. and smiled. "Hi Charley Ann. How are you doing? I hope E.R. wasn't too much of a pain to put up with." He looked towards E.R. and waited for him to respond.

"I'm good. Thanks for asking. I'm just really tired as I'm sure y'all are. Did y'all find out anything else about Brian's death or Liam's whereabouts?" She anxiously waited for good news.

"I'm afraid not. We'll talk more about all of that when we get out of here. The water is going to start rising and I don't want to get stuck. E.R., we're going to stop at the cemetery to see if maybe we overlooked something. You and Charley Ann should get to your house and unload the boat. I still think y'all should stay somewhere else, but you need to secure your house for the hurricane first. I'll head there when we are finished." Griff jumped into Tab's truck and left.

E.R. was tempted to pull into the cemetery as they passed it but decided that maybe he should listen to his grandfather. He had Charley Ann with him, and he did need to secure his house. Even though he lived in Marrero, away from the projected landfall in Port Fourchon, Louisiana, his house was going to have devastating winds to contend with because it was expected to be a category 4 with 150 mph winds. E.R. reflected and even chuckled at the irony that Hurricane Ida was to make landfall 16 years to the day that Hurricane Katrina devastated that same area. He pulled into his driveway and was grateful to be home.

****

Tab parked his truck outside the gates to the cemetery. With all the rain they had the area was muddy. The cemetery was flanked by swampland on both sides and the water was rising.

"This place is going to be under water soon enough. Do you remember where E.R. said he thought he saw Liam or whoever he saw?" Tab motioned for Griff to lead.

"I do. There's an open grave over there to the left and that's where he saw something. We checked it out but didn't see anything unusual. We were both on edge so I can't say that we didn't miss something."

The two men walked to the left side of the cemetery. Tab noticed the dead flowers that fell onto some of the neglected graves. There was a mixture of floral and rot smell that circulated in the air. Aside from Griff, himself, and some pretty loud wildlife, the place was abandoned. He figured everyone was packing to leave or preparing to ride out the storm. There were a few gravesites that had fresh roses that stood erect amongst the dead. Tab walked around the area, careful not to fall into the slippery grave, and searched for clues. He noticed something shiny caught on a branch right inside of the freshly dug grave.

"Do you see that?" Tab bent down to get a closer look.

"What is it? Be careful because those sides look like they are going to collapse any minute. It looks like a bracelet."

Tab grabbed a stick from the ground and used it to reach closer to the branch. He was careful not to knock it off because the bottom of the grave was full of water, and they wouldn't have enough time to fish it out. He caught the edge of the object with the end of the stick and slowly tilted it so that it would slide towards his hand.

"That looks like a man's watch." Griff hoped it was a clue and belonged to the killer. He knew for sure that it wasn't E.R.'s and he was pretty sure it wasn't Liam's either.

Tab slowly lifted the watch to safety and handed it to Griff. It was full of mud but was still ticking. Griff reached for the red rag he had in his back pocket and tried to wipe it clean. "There's an inscription inside the watch with the initials, 'L.P.R' and the words 'Forever Love' inscribed underneath." Griff examined the watch and concluded that it was a high-end Rolex. He handed the watch to Tab. "Look at those diamonds."

"Did you hear that?" Tab ducked and pulled Griff down to join him.

While the two men were wrapped up in inspecting the watch a car drove up and stopped outside the gate. They were too far away to see who it was but heard the door open and shut. Somebody was entering the cemetery. Tab put his hand on his weapon and waited.

Griff looked at Tab and thought that maybe he was overreacting. "It's a cemetery so maybe it's someone coming to visit their loved ones that have passed on."

"I guess we'll see soon enough."

The sound of vehicles passing on the main road radiated through the cemetery. It suddenly occurred to Griff how ironic it was that just a few yards away, life was vibrant and busy and where he was it was final and constant. He shuddered and shook away the thoughts. In between the noise of the passing vehicles, there was a deadly silence. As the person that entered the cemetery walked, the dead grass that was still untouched by the rising water, crunched and rustled to reveal their position. They were walking away from the area where Griff and Tab were.

"Hello?"

Tab and Griff stayed silent.

"Hello. This is the Police Chief from the Lafitte Police Department. Lafitte is under a mandatory evacuation as of this morning. We need everyone to heed this warning and get out of harm's way. Hello?"

Griff stood up and waved. "Hey man. It's Griff. I didn't know that was you."

"Hey Griff. Sorry man but y'all gotta get out of here."

"We were just about to leave. You remember Tab?" Without waiting for a response Griff continued. "Did y'all get any information on the body they found in the bayou yesterday? We're still looking for Liam and trying to fig-ure out if the two incidents are related. We thought maybe we missed something here and wanted one last look before the storm came through and washed everything away."

"To tell ya the truth we have been so busy with hurricane preparations that we haven't had time. Go ahead and finish your search but try to hurry. We would like to get everyone out of harm's way as soon as possible. Good to see ya man. Stay safe."

Griff shook his hand and nodded.

When they were alone again, they searched the area for any other clues then decided it was time to leave. The traffic was going to start picking up and they didn't want to get caught down there. He was anxious to get to his grandson and find out what he had planned. Griff knew that nothing was going to get in the way of E.R.'s search for Liam, not even a hurricane.

The house was boarded up and the yard was picked clean of everything that wasn't secured down. E.R. was so used to the drill, taught by his father and grandfather, that it only took him an hour to completely secure his house. Charley Ann helped, and it showed that growing up in Houma where hurricanes were also a threat, prepared her as well. After everything was done, they sat on the porch swing and talked about their next step.

"I think you should stay here at least until the Hurricane passes. It's gonna come in at Port Fourchon so I think you'd be safer here instead of in Houma. I know Brian is dead, but we still don't know who killed him." E.R. looked right into those emerald eyes for a sign that she agreed.

"I don't want to be in your way. You've done so much already. I am..."

E.R. interrupted her. "Wait. What I should've said was that I want you to stay. I would like you to stay here with me until we get this solved."

Charley Ann, who was taken back by his frankness, smiled, and nodded.

E.R.'s phone rang, and it was Griff. He said he had some news and that they should meet at Griff's office in 30 minutes. The office was only about 5 minutes from E.R.'s house but evacuation traffic had been building all afternoon. Before they left, E.R. checked in with his office to see how things were going and to see if anyone heard from Liam. Regrettably, they hadn't. They did offer him more time off if he needed it, but E.R. thanked them and declined. He knew that they needed everyone to report to work so that they had enough manpower to handle the calls they were sure to get once the storm arrived. He locked up the house and they got into the truck to leave. Even after the distractions, E.R. was still caught up in the moment and wished he could have stayed on the porch swing with Charley Ann for the rest of the day. He put the truck in reverse, backed out of the driveway and drove away.

The black sedan that was parked down the deserted street edged its way towards E.R.'s house and parked in front of it. The two men got out of the car, one with a limp and clearly in charge, and walked towards the back yard with familiarity.

"It looks like Liam's girlfriend didn't waist anytime replacing him. I'm not surprised because they are all alike. Too bad he's not here to witness this betrayal because it would be nice to watch the pain it would cause him. It's about time for him to wake up and remember that we both came from the same place and that place was not a nice one. He escaped once but not this time. I'll just have to wait for them to return then bring the pain to him."

****

While they waited for E.R. and Charley Ann to arrive, Griff started a timeline with all the events from the past few days and tried to find connections. At first, they assumed that Brian was a target since someone killed him but if the person in the hospital wasn't Liam, then maybe Liam was the target. The man who claimed to be Lucas looked just like Liam. As Griff thought about it, it was dark, and he did have black eyes and a swollen face when he first saw him. And he was only conscious for a few seconds when Griff was at the hospital, so maybe he wasn't Liam but rather a close relative instead. But why would he leave the hospital and where is Liam. Did he get the bruises defending Liam from Brian? There are so many unanswered questions that it was difficult to piece it all together.

Griff walked away from the board to get some coffee and gather his thoughts. Tab hung up from a phone call with Trey and walked over to Griff.

"That was Trey. He made a fingerprint match from the plastic clothing bag you took from the hospital room, and it confirmed that the man in the hospital is Lucas Ricci as he said. I'm sorry man. Trey is trying to run a background check on him as we speak. We need to find out more about Liam and his past. I know he told y'all he didn't have family, but everyone had family at one time. Did they die? Did he grow up in foster care? We need more details of his life. We need a fingerprint from him so try to catch E.R. before he gets here and have him go to Liam's house to get something with his prints on it. I know it's a longshot and it could take a few hours to match a print from the database, but it's worth a try." Tab was frustrated that things were getting more complicated by the minute.

"That's a good idea. I'll call him now." Griff flipped open his phone and as he dialed the number, E.R. and Charley Ann walked into the office.

"I was just trying to call you." Griff walked to his grandson, hugged him, and said hello to Charley Ann.

Tab acknowledged the two and sat down at the conference table. "Sit down and we'll go over everything we know so far.

"Right now what we know for sure is that Liam is missing from Fleming Cemetery, presumably alive since E.R. has received a few calls from his phone. Someone tried to break into E.R.'s house the next evening. Charley Ann's ex-boyfriend Brian is found dead in Lafitte after we believe he followed Charley Ann and Liam from Bourbon Heat in New Orleans. We found his car at the Harvey Locks. We found someone that looks exactly like Liam at Liam's house, who claims to be someone named Lucas Ricci and has now disappeared. I found a napkin in his pocket that was from Bourbon Heat, and it had a phone number on the back of it that we now know was for a burner phone. We found a key in the cafeteria of the hospital that this Lucas character dropped out of his pocket when he stole a phone and snuck out. Griff took the bag that housed Lucas's clothes to Trey and the fingerprints confirmed that he is Lucas Ricci not Liam. Someone locked Charley Ann in an empty container in Grand Isle." Tab paused for a moment. He pointed to the board where all of this was laid out and continued. "Does anyone have anything to add to the board at this time?"

"Don't forget the watch." Griff walked to the board to decide where to add that information.

"What watch?" Charley Ann asked just as E.R. was about to.

Griff sat back down. "When we went back to the cemetery today, we found a watch hanging on a limb right inside the open grave which we believe you fell into the other night. And that's not all. Tab, remember we thought we were being followed the other day by a black sedan. It might be coincidence, but I think we need to add that to the board."

"When did that happen? Did y'all get a license plate number?" E.R. pushed the hair away from his face and stood up. "This is crazy. Every day things are getting more complicated, and we are no closer to finding Liam!"

"Look E.R., I know this is upsetting but we are not giving up. We are going to find Liam. We need you to go to Liam's house and get some DNA."

"DNA? Hey Paw, didn't you take those two glasses from Liam's house the night we found Charley Ann there? What did you do with them?"

"I forgot about that." Griff jumped up and ran out to his truck. He couldn't believe he had forgotten about the glasses. He had intended to use it to find out who was there with Liam that night but once they found Charley Ann, he forgot that he took them. They had Trey run a check on her and confirmed her identity.

When Griff walked back into his office, Tab was on the phone and E.R. and Charley Ann were standing in front of the board discussing its contents.

Griff walked up to them and touched E.R.'s shoulder. "Can you tell us anything about Liam's past? I know you said he doesn't have family, but everyone had family at one point, and we really need to find a connection between Liam and the guy in the hospital. Man, E.R., I'm telling you, he looks just like Liam. He had black eyes, had been beaten up, and still looked like Liam. Do you know where he was from before he moved here?"

E.R. shook his head. Ever since Liam went missing, he'd tried to remember their conversations and hoped something would stand out and give him a clue. He remembered the day he met Liam like it was yesterday. E.R. had just started at a new job the week before and was still learning the ropes. His boss called him and told him that he was going to be paired up with a partner. From the moment they met, E.R. and Liam were good friends. They both shared a brief account of their lives and then moved onto other subjects.

"All I remember is that Liam said he moved around a lot and was in and out of foster care since he was little. I know he lived in Florida and Alabama at one time or another, but he was very uncomfortable when we talked about his past, so we didn't."

Tab, who had just returned to the conversation chimed in. "Maybe we should start with the foster care system. You said he mentioned Florida and Alabama, but do you think he was ever in foster care in Louisiana?"

"I would guess not because I do remember him saying that he had never been to Louisiana before and had just moved here a few weeks before he got the job."

"I'm gonna make some calls and see what I can find out. Let's not forget that there's a Hurricane on its way here. We need to move fast if we are going to find Liam." Tab reached for his phone again and left the room.

Griff stood and grabbed the bag holding the two wine glasses. "I'm gonna run these in to see if we can get a fingerprint match for Liam. Who knows, maybe Liam is Lucas and is in some witness protection program. That would not surprise me."

As Griff walked out of the office, he heard the low howling of the wind that announced the arrival of more rain bands. Hurricane Ida was well on her way and the bending of the towering trees was an unmistakable sign that displayed her strength. She wasn't forecast to hit until midday on Sunday, but Griff knew from experience that things were gonna get worse way before that.

CHAPTER 21

E. R. was on edge and hated that his life felt out of control. He liked to be organized and kept things simple, but the last few days had proven to be quite the opposite and he wasn't sure when this would end. His grandmother had struggled with anxiety and he'd secretly worried that he might inherit the disorder. As far as he could tell, it skipped his mother completely unless she kept it hidden, but he doubted that. When he and Christina were involved, he felt anxious often and blamed it on the relationship. It was apparently clear to everyone else that they were wrong for each other, but it took a while for E.R. not only to realize it but to accept it. Since then, he'd been unable to trust anyone and was struggling with the feelings he had developed for Charley Ann in a short period of time.

E.R. chuckled as he thought about the recent events. He was not one to believe in ghosts but the reoccurring visions of the woman in white had him questioning that and, he hated to admit it but also had him spooked. He wondered if someone was playing a joke on him but knew that wasn't the case. When he saw her the first time, he thought he was dreaming or hallucinating because he had hit his head and was in and out of consciousness. After that, he was wide awake when she appeared to him. E.R. thought back to each time that he saw her and the only thing that stood out was that she appeared when he needed help. *Was she some kind of angel?*

"What?" Charley Ann was staring at E.R. "What did you say? Was who an angel?"

E.R. jolted up and realized that he had said that aloud. She would think he was crazy if he told her about the woman, especially if he claimed that she was a ghost or an angel. He had to think fast. He mumbled as he headed towards the kitchen.

He yelled back, "Would you like something to drink?"

"I'm okay but thank you."

E.R. heard footsteps and quickly headed towards the back door. He didn't want to explain what he said, and he didn't want to lie to her. He believed in complete honesty in a relationship and if they were to ever get together, he didn't want to have a lie between them. And he really hoped that they would be together because he was crazy about her.

"I'm going outside to check the yard again. I don't want to have anything flying around especially now that the winds are picking up." E.R. shut the back door just as she entered the kitchen. He needed time to think. How could he be so stupid and say that out loud. He was just so relaxed for the first time in days and got caught up in his thoughts.

Nightfall was approaching and the wind was blowing. Even though E.R. knew that this hurricane was going to be a bad one he couldn't help but admire the strength of her winds and the way it pushed against his body. He walked around the house a few times making sure that everything was secure. He and Charley Ann had spent time earlier in the day doing just that, so he was sure that all was good. He knew he would have to go back inside soon but still needed time to think. *I'll just tell her the truth about seeing the vision when I was knocked unconscious and leave out the rest. I did wonder if the woman was real or a dream. I'll just tell her about that and...*

"E.R.! Help!" Charley Ann screamed from inside the house. "Help! E.R.! Help! Get away! No!"

The screams startled E.R., and he jumped into action. He left Charley Ann in the kitchen, but the scream came from the front of the house. He bolted towards the house and stopped abruptly. There inside the back door was the woman in white. He froze and rubbed his eyes trying to get a better view. When he opened them, the vision was right in his face screaming without sound and then vanished. E.R. fell to the ground. He didn't hear her voice, but he felt it throughout his whole body. Charley Ann screamed again and without hesitation he ran into the kitchen and towards the screams. *Why did I leave her alone? I knew that she could be in danger, and I left her alone.* He continued to beat himself up as he ran through the house.

"Charley Ann! Where are you?"

Charley Ann continued to scream as E.R. made it to the living room. She was standing on top of the coffee table pointing to the ground. "E.R. watch out!"

He didn't understand what was happening but did recognize that something was wrong. He glanced at the door and around the room, but it was empty other than the two of them. As he started to move forward something black on the floor in front of him caught his eye and he froze. He found himself within inches from a large fat black snake that definitely saw E R. as a threat. He looked up at Charley Ann who was pointing to the other side of the table.

"There's another one over here." Charley Ann pointed to the other side of the coffee table. "What do I do?"

With one look E.R. knew exactly what kind of snakes they were. He couldn't see the other one but by the terrified look on her face he knew it was the same. He looked at Charley Ann and they both said, "Cottonmouths."

"Listen. Don't move, okay? I'm going to slowly back away towards the kitchen and get something to scare them with. They're not aggressive snakes unless they feel threatened. Just don't move. I'll be right back." E.R. smiled slightly for encouragement.

Charley Ann just nodded and stayed put. She kept her eyes on both snakes. She was familiar with the snakes because she also lived by the water. Normally she wouldn't be afraid but there were two of them and both were close enough to bite her if they wanted to. She shifted her weight and one of the snakes inched closer to her.

Instead of screaming which is what she started to do, she took a deep breath and tried to stay completely still. She glanced towards the kitchen and back towards the snakes. She trusted that E.R. was coming to help her, but she wished he would hurry up. When she was a teenager, a group of her friends were camping out in the woods and one of the guys encountered a cottonmouth. Unfortunately, he was too close before he noticed it and was bitten by the snake. Luckily, they acted fast, and he was able to get to the hospital for treatment, but still endured a lot of pain. Charley Ann shivered at the thought.

E.R. came back to the living room with his phone to his ear and a broom in his hand. He was whispering to the person on the other end and then hung up. He noticed that the front door was open, and he was certain that they had shut it when they came in.

"Did you open the door?"

Charley Ann followed E.R.'s eyes and noticed that the front door was open. She shook her head no.

"Okay. Listen I'm going to try and run this snake towards the door. The screen door is shut so they won't be able to get out, but it should contain them for a while. I called a friend to come and capture them. He lives around the corner and should be here quickly.

Charley Ann listened to E.R. and shook her head no. She held up her hand and softly said, "Wait. I need a minute." She wasn't sure that his plan would work and was worried that it would instead provoke the snakes to attack.

She stared into E.R.'s eyes and pleaded for him to understand.

"Charley Ann, we need to do something. I don't know how long these snakes are going to stay still. If they get loose in the house, we'll have a bigger problem."

She hesitated but then nodded that she understood and was ready. Just in case things went wrong and the snakes came her way, she looked around the room and contemplated her next move. The sofa was close enough that she could jump over the side and get away. She waited for E.R. to approach the snake because she didn't want to startle it and make it slither the wrong way or worse attack him.

How did two snakes end up in my house at the same time? The water hadn't even started to rise here yet. And why was the front door open. E.R. was trying to reason with himself when he noticed his friend Patrick at the door. He sighed with relief. He knew Patrick since they were in grade school. He, just like E.R., grew up in Lafitte and was always good at handling snakes. When they'd go hunting, Patrick would always spot the snakes and instead of killing them, he'd find a way to run them off or relocate them. He should've been a game warden but instead he went into law. E.R. never saw that coming, but Patrick was good at his job as an attorney and thankfully, just as good with handling snakes.

Patrick acknowledged E.R. without saying a word. Both men knew that the snakes could be easily spooked, and they didn't want to chase them down. Patrick held up

3 fingers and nodded at both Charley Ann, who was still on top of the coffee table and E.R. that they were ready. He counted down with his fingers and after the last one folded, E.R. swung the broom at the snake and Charley Ann jumped onto the sofa and attempted to hop over the edge but her foot caught the arm and she fell back onto the sofa. She leaped up and made another attempt and this time landed safely at E.R. 's side. The snake closest to them slithered under the coffee table and towards the door. Patrick had a large sack positioned right outside the screen door and when he opened it both snakes bolted for what they thought was freedom.

"E.R. are y'all alright?" Patrick was securing the sack that contained both snakes. "Man, those were cotton-mouths and pretty big ones. How did they get into your house?"

E.R. and Charley Ann were still standing in the same place trying to digest what just happened.

"I don't know man. I was outside in the backyard when I heard Charley Ann scream."

"I didn't scream! I yelled your name." Charley Ann looked annoyed. She looked towards the door and into a pair of lovely green eyes. E.R.'s friend was tall some-where about 5'11" and had an infectious smile. "I thought I heard the door, so I came into the living room to see if it was E.R. and almost stepped on the snake. I jumped over it and onto the coffee table. That's when I saw the second snake on the other side. She looked at E.R. with accusing eyes. "I had no idea that you had a snake problem here."

E.R. shot Charley Ann a look. "I don't. I have no idea how they got in here. And why was the door open?" He walked over to the door and looked around the porch.

Patrick walked into the house and the three of them went into the kitchen.

"Patrick, can I get you something to drink?"

"I'm alright. Man, I've never encountered two cotton-mouths together. They're usually solitary and aggressive towards other male snakes. I don't know what kind of booby trap you got yourself into, but I don't think that this was a coincidence." Patrick hated to sound alarming.

E.R. glanced at Charley Ann and could tell that she was thinking the same thing he was. This was no accident, but he just wasn't ready to explain the situation to Patrick especially when he wasn't sure what was going on. One thing he was sure of, he didn't want anything to happen to Charley Ann. She'd become very important to him lately and he was prepared to protect her at all costs.

E.R. extended his hand. "Patrick, thank you man. You were the first person that came to mind when I saw the snakes. I don't know how they got in here, but I doubt that it was by accident. I need to call my grandfather and let him know what's going on."

"How's he doing? I haven't seen him lately, but I often think about him. Do you remember all the fishing trips he used to take us on? Man, we had some good times, and I learned a lot from him. He taught me a lot about snakes actually. He used to call me the 'snake whisperer' among other things." Patrick shared his fond thoughts about

Griff. "He always encouraged me to follow my dreams and he's part of the reason why I became an attorney." Patrick laughed. "He used to say that one day all of the mischievous things I did would catch up with me and that I better know a good lawyer. That stuck with me because you know we did some crazy things, but thankfully we didn't get into too much trouble. Your grandfather made sure we were held accountable for the things we did that he found out about. Remember when he made us eat a whole pack of cigarettes when he caught us smoking?"

"I will never forget that! And it definitely worked on me because I never picked up another cigarette after that day." While E.R. enjoyed reminiscing with Patrick, his mind was on other things and without being rude wanted to focus on them. He walked over to Patrick and extended his hand. "Patrick it was really good to see you. Thank you for responding so quickly and coming to the rescue. You were right that this was no coincidence and unfortunately, I have to figure out what to do about it. There's a lot going on and I don't have time to get into it now. The storm is on the way and time is running out for us to find answers. Let's get together soon and have lunch. I promise I'll fill you in then."

Patrick agreed to lunch and assured E.R. that he was there if he needed him for anything. "Stay safe man. I hope you find your answers soon." He nodded towards Charley Ann and headed out the door.

"Thanks again Patrick."

E.R. and Charley Ann stood silent for a moment. E.R. was trying to wrap his head around everything, and Charley Ann was trying to keep hers together. She considered herself a strong, independent woman but at that moment she was grateful that E.R. was by her side. Her mind knew how strong she was, but the slight tremble of her body suggested that it hadn't caught on yet. She looked at E.R. and without saying a word, told him that she needed him.

E.R. looked into Charley Ann's eyes and saw the turmoil going on inside her. He gently touched her arm and then pulled her into an embrace.

Don't you dare cry! Charley Ann demanded that her body obey and used all her energy to control her tears. *How did things get so crazy? When will this nightmare end?* After what seemed like forever, Charley Ann whispered 'Thank you' in his ear. She wanted to say more but E.R. cancelled her words out with a gentle kiss on her forehead. She wanted the moment to last forever and didn't want to ruin it by saying anything. She had so many questions and wanted him to know that she was not only grateful, but she had feelings for him. She wanted him to know that she wanted to stay here with him because she had never felt like that before. She felt cared for and empowered at the same time. She was ready to declare her feelings for him and hoped that he felt the same.

"E.R." Charley Ann took a step back and gazed into his eyes that were dark with lust. Before she could continue his phone rang.

The moment was gone. E.R. looked away and reached for his phone. "It's my grandfather. I need to take this."

"Hey Paw, I was just getting ready to call you. E.R. looked back at Charley Ann and saw the disappointment. He couldn't think about that at the moment. He turned away and walked out onto the porch. The wind was blowing with incredible force now driving the rain to fall sideways as it pounded the ground like a train hitting a wall. E.R. wasn't sure how long the phone service would continue to work and needed to let his grandfather know about the snakes.

"Hey man, things are getting pretty rough outside right now. Where are you?" Griff was worried about his grandson.

"We're at my house. Paw, someone released two cottonmouths in my living room. I know that sounds crazy, but we were both in the living room just a few minutes before and the front door was shut and there were no snakes. I walked to the kitchen and Charley Ann followed me. I went out the back door and then moments later I heard Charley Ann scream."

"I didn't scream! Stop saying that!" Charley Ann shouted as he continued to tell Griff the story.

E.R. ignored Charley Ann and went on. "When I heard Charley Ann scre… I mean yell, I ran into the house and into the living room. I almost ran on top of one of the snakes, but Charley Ann warned me just in time. She was on top of the coffee table and pointed to the other one that was still by the door. Paw, I know the front door was closed which tells me that someone opened the door and put the snakes in here."

"Are y'all okay? Did anyone get bitten? I'm coming over that way now, stay put." Griff didn't wait for E.R. to answer. He called Tab to let him know what happened.

"I need to get to E.R.'s because someone released two cottonmouths inside his house. I'll fill you in later."

"Wait. What? This is a joke, right? Griff meet me back here at the shop and I'll go with you. I have a few errands to run but I can drop you off first." Tab laughed and added. "Don't you find it amusing that we've been in business for a while now and the only two difficult cases that we've had, that were beyond belief and incredibly intense, both involved your family?"

Griff couldn't help but laugh too. "Don't remind me. I hope we get to the bottom of all of this soon. Thanks man. Really, thanks for always being there."

CHAPTER 22

LORNA RICCI   SEPTEMBER 2004

When she met Lorenzo, he was the sweetest man she had ever been with. He was considerate and patient and treated her like a queen. She had heard the rumors but the man she spent so much time with was the complete opposite and she decided to believe that they were just that – rumors. They married just two short months after they met, and she was happier than she had ever been. Nine months after they were married their perfect little family grew. They welcomed two beautiful babies and shared so much love. She imagined that things couldn't get any better for them and Lorna thanked God every day for her blessed life.

After the boys were born, she began to notice small changes in her husband's behavior. The considerate patient man she had come to know was becoming inattentive to not only her but to the boys as well. He was spending less time at home and more time at the office. Lorenzo dealt in investments and as such provided them with a very lavish lifestyle. He never used to bring his work home but had started to spend most of his evenings in his home office with his colleagues coming in and out all hours of the night. One night Lorna decided to talk to her husband about her disappointment in the way things were going in their marriage. That was the first of many times she realized that she was wrong about him, and the rumors were true. That was also the moment she knew that she along with her children were in danger and she began to devise a plan for their escape.

It wouldn't be easy but for four years now Lorna had planned and prepared to escape the nightmare life she and her boys were subjected to at the hands of her brutal husband, and it was finally time to make a run. Lorna had always been a very spiritual woman and she tried to treat people with kindness and forgive often, but her current circumstances had taken its toll on her, and she prayed that she would be forgiven for wishing that her husband were dead. She cupped her hand around the small cross she wore on her neck and began to pray. She was terrified that he would find out about her plans and stop them or worse, but she couldn't think about that right then because she was more afraid that if she didn't make a move soon someone was going to die. Lorna was prepared to sacrifice everything to protect her boys and that included her life.

CHAPTER 23

Griff was glad that Abby was out of town and grateful that she agreed to stay there until the hurricane passed. His youngest daughter Harper was with Abby and his other daughter, E.R.'s mom, was with her husband and daughter in Atlanta. They left earlier that week for a gymnastic competition and decided to spend the weekend away from the storm. They were all worried about Griff and E.R., but he assured them that he would look after E.R., and that they would stay safe.

Griff and Tab headed to E.R.'s house to look into yet another bizarre episode. When E.R. told Griff that two cottonmouths were inside his house, Griff wasn't sure he heard him correctly and asked him to repeat it. Griff felt a quiver as he thought about the snakes. He wouldn't say he had a fear of snakes, but he also wouldn't want them in his house. He opened his phone, keyed in his password, and started searching "Cottonmouth Snakes." His research included pictures of the snake, information on their habitat and their general habits.

"Tab, E.R. said that there were two snakes in his house. This article says that they are solitary reptiles and wouldn't be together naturally in nature. That was my thought exactly but wanted to confirm it before we got to his house. I hate to admit it, but I think somebody put snakes there on purpose." Griff was sickened by some of the photos that popped up of the damage the venom could do to a person that was bitten by a cottonmouth.

Tab didn't answer right away because his mind was still on that black sedan that followed them earlier. He was positive that they were being followed but he couldn't figure out who would want to follow them. He thought about the vehicle that was parked outside Liam's house when they thought they found Liam. There were no plates on the car and with all the commotion he forgot to follow up. Griff was anxious to get to E.R., but Tab wanted to swing by Liam's house first to see if by some miracle the car was still there. They spoke to the neighbors last night and unfortunately found out that there were no cameras in the area.

"Hey man, I think we need to swing by Liam's house and see if that car is still there. With all the chaos we forgot to go back. It might give us some clue as to who is behind all of this."

Griff was focused on his phone and didn't answer.

"Griff. Did you hear what I said? We need to stop by Liam's house first."

"Yeah, I'm sorry. Believe it or not, there are some amazing facts about snakes on these sites. Why do we need to stop by Liam's house?"

"The black Nissan Maxima parked outside Liam's house last night..."

Griff's head popped up from the slouched position and he looked at Tab with an impatient expression on his face. It just registered what Tab was saying and he hoped that they hadn't missed out on that lead.

"I can't believe we forgot about the car! What if it's gone? They might've left fingerprints that would've given us a lead. Thank God you remembered. I just hope we're not too late." Griff was finding it difficult to sit still.

They turned into Liam's neighborhood and headed to his street. Usually the streets were filled with vehicles parked on the curbs, but because of the hurricane, it was mostly empty. They were surprised to discover that the one car left on the whole street was the black Nissan Maxima. Tab parked in front of the car and he and Griff got out. They were both skeptical as they approached and even considered that maybe it had nothing to do with their investigation. They assumed when they got the call, that it belonged to the person in Liam's house but maybe it was just dropped off there. It didn't have plates, so it was probably stolen.

"We need to get this car towed and checked for fingerprints soon. Let's go talk to any neighbors who have decided to ride out the storm and see if they know how long the car has been here. I'll call for a tow truck and then take this side of the street."

Griff was already headed to the neighbor on the right of Liam's house. A man was outside cleaning out a drain in front of his house. Everyone around that area knew that the water rises fast when it rains and making sure that the drains are clear helps keep the streets from flooding.

"Hi. I'm Griff, a friend of Liam's." Normally Griff would've extended his hand but with covid decided to just leave them in his pockets. "Can you tell me when that car was parked there?"

The man followed the direction Griff pointed to. "I'm not really sure. I just noticed it this morning. Hey, how is Liam? I saw the ambulance pick him up last night. Is he alright?"

Griff had no idea what to say. "When was the last time you saw Liam?"

"I saw him yesterday morning before I left for work. I just waved because I was in a hurry."

"Was he alone?" Griff was hopeful for something to go on.

"No he was with another man. They were headed towards the back of his house and now that I think of it, it looked like they were arguing. They weren't yelling or anything like that, but Liam looked annoyed." The man continued to clean out the drain." I don't mean to be rude, but I need to get this stuff done before we leave. My wife doesn't want to stay since Hurricane Ida has intensified."

"No problem. I completely understand. Thanks for your help." Griff talked to a few other neighbors, and nobody seemed to notice the car that was parked on their street and abandoned because everyone was busy with storm preparations and several people already evacuated.

Tab motioned for Griff that he was ready to go so they met at the truck and headed to E.R.'s house.

They arrived at E.R.'s house and Griff went inside. Tab followed to make sure that they were okay. His phone rang and it was his home alarm company. After he hung up, he informed Griff that he had to run to his house and check out why the alarm was triggered.

"No problem. E.R. can run me back to my truck. Thanks man."

When he left E.R.'s house, Tab decided to drive back to Liam's house and do a quick assessment. He went around the back to look at the fallen shed again. It was dark and raining last night and difficult to see. He didn't notice anything out of the ordinary, so he continued to walk around to the rear of the shed. From the side view, you got a good picture of just how lucky Liam, or whoever it was didn't get killed. The entire shed caved in and was supported by only a few boards. He had no idea that Liam's yard would be in that condition. Around the back of the shed Tab noticed that the fence was in the same shape and shook his head.

Tab wandered around the yard assessing the place and noticed that one of the fence boards was swinging. He just passed back behind the shed and was certain that they were still. The wind was gusting at times but had been quiet since he'd been back there. He wanted to call Griff but didn't want to bring attention to himself. Instead he continued to walk around and out of caution had his hand on his weapon.

By the time he saw the guy laying on the ground it was too late. Tab felt a blow to the side of his leg. He went down and the person that hit him jumped up and ran through the fence. Tab popped up but fell forward when he tried to chase him. His leg was hurt but it wasn't broken. He got to his feet and ran in the direction of the man. By the time he made his way to the street, he saw someone jump into a black sedan and speed away.

Tab ran back from the street behind Liam's house and through the fence to get to his truck. He raced to the end of the street and caught site of the sedan. He gunned it and started to chase the car as it bolted through the neighborhood and ran towards the old highway heading towards Lafitte. *Doesn't he know that this way brings him through the Jean Lafitte park and that there are no through streets to get away?* Tab thought that he must not be from the area or didn't really want to get away. *Is that it? Does he want to get caught? Is this some sort of trap?* Tab stayed close enough to keep him in site but was waiting for the big curve by Bayou Coquille to try and catch him. They would have to slow down there and that would give Tab a chance to catch up or at least see who was driving the car. *Is this guy alone or is someone else with him like Lucas?*

Tab subconsciously rubbed his leg. He knew he was being followed by a black sedan earlier, and that was the same car. He wondered why they were following him and determined that Liam was the connection. He thought that they could be headed to the Lafitte Cemetery but why would they want to lure him there? The big curve was only a couple of miles from where they were so Tab dialed Griff to let him know what was happening. A Verizon message came on and informed him that his call could not be completed as dialed. He tossed it on the seat and pressed the gas. He stayed his distance up until then but wanted to make sure he was close enough when the curve came.

Aside from the bright head lights of the vehicles, darkness ruled the area and casted an eerie stillness to the swamp. Even though there was a hurricane approaching, the winds were subdued by the thick forest that lined both sides of the highway. At times, the winds would gust and penetrate the trees that protected the area. Tab concentrated on the vehicle ahead and was only a few yards back when he caught a glimpse of something to his left. All at once, it smashed into the front of his truck, onto his windshield and Tab was forced to jerk the wheel to the right as he'd tried to avoid it. His truck went off the road and because of his speed, shot through the trees, and hit one before it bogged down in the swamp and came to a halt. The front of the truck was submerged about two feet in the swamp. Tab's body thrust forward with mighty force and then rested on the steering wheel before everything went still.

CHAPTER 24

Charley Ann wanted to stay at E.R.'s while he ran his grandfather back to his office, but E.R. wasn't comfortable leaving her alone. Whoever gifted them the snakes was probably still around, and her life was in danger. He was smart enough to know that he could be in danger as well, but she was important to him, and he didn't want anything to happen to her. She put up an argument but finally agreed to go with him. He suggested that they run by the Verizon store to get her a cell phone. E.R., like most people, didn't have a landline and relied completely on his cell phone. That was one of the reasons he used to convince her she shouldn't stay there alone.

They dropped off Griff and were at the Verizon store buying Charley Ann a phone when E.R.'s phone rang. He stepped outside to answer a number he didn't recognize. It was one of the officers from Grand Isle. E.R. was surprised to hear from him so soon because Hurricane Ida was barreling towards the island and almost guaranteed catastrophic flooding and destruction.

"I have some information about the owner of that boat you were looking for. The boat is registered to a Douglas

Breaux and his last known address was in Marrero, Louisiana. Isn't that close to where you're from? I remembered you said that y'all came from Lafitte."

"Yes, it is." E.R. was startled by those details. "I live in Marrero myself. Can you text me the address and any other information you have on him?"

The officer was very cooperative and before he hung up asked about Charley Ann and then wished E.R. good luck. Instead of going back into the store where Charley Ann was nervously watching him through the window, he dialed Griff.

"The officer from Grand Isle just called with a name of the owner of that Carolina Skiff. It belongs to Douglas Breaux. I'm going to forward you the address so you can run a background check on him. I'm still at the Verizon store with Charley Ann but we should be finished soon. Let me know what you find out."

E.R. hung up and went back into the store. Charley Ann was waiting for the guy to finish putting her protective screen on the glass. She looked at E.R. with questioning eyes. He met her gaze and nodded that he would explain as soon as they were finished.

The sky had been dark and gloomy all day but as nightfall approached it brought with it a feeling of hopelessness and discouragement. E.R. felt like he was racing against a time bomb and that time was running out for Liam. He told Charley Ann what the officer said, and that Griff was checking it out. She could tell that he was upset just from the lack of energy in his voice as he spoke. He had been so upbeat and positive that they would find Liam but as the days passed, he was forced to face reality and that was taking its toll on him. E.R. found a chair in the corner and waited for Charley Ann. He was so tired and worried that they wouldn't find Liam in time. He laid his head back against the window and closed his eyes.

E.R. opened his eyes and was startled to find that he was back in the Fleming Cemetery. He looked around and saw the dirt walls that were washing away with the rain. How did I get here? The water was rising so he jumped onto his feet and attempted to climb the wall. His anxiety started to take over as he scratched endlessly at the mud. He stopped, stretched out his arms and felt the rain on his skin. How is this possible? I must be dreaming. He closed his eyes again and willed himself to wake up. When they opened again, he was still in the grave but realized that he was not alone. Hovering just above the water just a few feet away was the woman in white.

E.R. remained completely still. Each time she had appeared to him it was brief, and he reacted frantically. He hoped that if he didn't move, she wouldn't disappear so quickly. As he looked at her, he noticed that her dress was once beautiful and white, with details that looked to be very old fashioned. She had long hair, a face that was ashen and unlike before, she had an exhausted appearance. E.R. felt an overwhelming feeling of sympathy take over and found himself intrigued rather than frightened. He wondered who she was and what she wanted with him. She was clearly a ghost, a fact that he was still troubled about, and wanted his attention. The sadness in her eyes told him that she needed his help. But why him? The first time she appeared to him was when he fell into the grave while searching for Liam. She must have a connection to Liam and maybe she could help find him.

E.R. didn't know how to communicate with her. Every other time she emerged, she made strange noises without speaking. She had a way of conveying her thoughts to E.R. without speech. How does that work? E.R. tried to concentrate and tap into her mind but found only silence. She began to float upwards towards the top of the grave and E.R. panicked and yelled, "Wait! Please wait." He adjusted the tone and volume of his voice and asked again. "Wait please. I need your help. I'm looking for my friend Liam. Do you know him?"

She didn't speak but instead appeared to be crying softly as she shook her head yes and pointed.

"What are you trying to tell me?"

She grew impatient with him, reached down, and grabbed his hand. Before she could continue, there was a loud voice from above that called his name.

"E.R.! E.R.!" He felt his body shake. "E.R.!"

E.R. watched as the vision of the lady vanished and he was thrust back into reality. His eyes flew open as he yelled "Wait! Don't go!"

He looked around and noticed that Charley Ann was standing over him with her arms on his shoulder.

"Hey. Are you okay? You must've fallen asleep. I'm finished and ready to go."

E.R. took a moment to respond and instead of answering Charley Ann, he got up and headed to the car. He didn't know what the lady in white wanted from him, but he was certain that she had the answers he needed to find Liam. He knew he had to talk to her soon but had no idea how to reach her. He wished he would've paid more attention to those horror flicks his grandmother loved because then maybe he would know how to communicate with a ghost. *Is that what she is – a ghost? And just how do you conjure a ghost?* E.R. glanced at Charley Ann and toyed with the idea of telling her about his visions but wasn't sure what her reaction would be. He knew that if it were reversed and she told him that she was having the visions, he would've had a hard time believing her.

At first, he thought he was going crazy or at the very least was affected by the hit on his head. Now he wondered if maybe that hit to his head caused something to happen that allowed him to see the dead. He'd heard of people that were struck by lightning gaining certain abilities. And Hollywood was full of stories that involved trauma and superpowers. He grinned as he thought about that and concluded that he would wait to tell Charley Ann about his visions – his new superpower.

E.R. watched as Charley Ann played with her new phone and smiled. For him she'd become a light in all the darkness. He didn't know much about her but her attitude towards everything that had happened the last few days told him that she was strong and a survivor. She hadn't complained once about anything and seemed very content. Again he smiled and hoped that soon they would find Liam and he and Charley Ann would get the chance to get to know one another better.

"Do you think that it's safe for me to call my sister. I really want to talk to her and let her know that I'm alright."

"Let me call my grandfather and see what he thinks. I know Brian is dead but I'm still a little concerned about someone locking you in that container. I believe that it had to do with us asking about Brian, but we can't be sure." E.R. felt bad for Charley Ann but wanted to keep her safe.

Griff picked up quickly. "I was just getting ready to call you. I have some information on Douglas Breaux. He has a long rap sheet that includes assault, theft, several DUI's, and possession of illegal drugs. He was arrested just last week on a drug charge and posted bail. E.R., he was bailed out by Lucas Ricci. I'm in route to Douglas' house to question him now. I tried to call Mr. Tab but he didn't answer. I'm sure he'll call me back soon. Are y'all back at your house?"

"Turning on my street now. Charley Ann wanted to call her sister, and I thought we should run it by you first. What do you think?"

"I don't want to tell her what to do but if she could just wait a day or two, I would feel better about it. I can call her sister and check in if she would like. Talk to her and let me know what she wants to do. I'll call you when I find out something. Love ya. Be careful and stay alert." Griff hung up.

E.R. shared what he learned about Douglas Breaux with Charley Ann. The chilling facts didn't sit well with either of them. E.R. immediately realized that Douglas Breaux was probably the person that locked Charley Ann inside the container in Grand Isle. Before he relayed his thought with her, she blurted out, "He locked me in that container! Why would he do that? What would he want with me? I don't even know the man."

"I'm not sure it has anything to do with knowing you. I'm beginning to believe that everything revolves around Liam. My grandfather said that the man, Lucas, looks just like Liam. In fact, he's not ruling out that Lucas and Liam are one in the same. I refuse to believe that Liam would be involved in anything illegal, and he would never shut me out. Maybe it's an alienated relative I don't know. My grandfather asked that you wait a few days more before you contact your sister. He offered to check in with her for you. Of course he said that ultimately it was your decision, but he's concerned about the new information on Douglas and your safety."

Charley Ann hated that she was cut off from her sister but knew it was for the best. She asked E.R. to have his grandfather to reach out to her sister and give her an update. She could wait a few more days and hoped that they would find Liam by then and they could put all of this behind them.

CHAPTER 25

Douglas stopped the car. He shifted into reverse and slowly backtracked down the highway. They were traveling at a high speed and were unable to stop abruptly when they saw the truck chasing them catapult into the swamp. Lucas smiled to himself because things couldn't get any better. He wanted Liam to suffer, and what better way than to hurt those he cared about. He was enjoying the chaos he was bringing to so many, but it was time to get serious and implement his grand finale. It was going to be an award-winning finale.

They pulled up next to the area where the truck went off the road. Both men stayed put as their eyes canvassed the area for movement. Lucas did his homework and knew that Tab was not to be underestimated. He was a seasoned detective and equally as good a private investigator. Lucas admired both Tab and Griff and was enjoying the game they were playing. He had to admit that he was glad that Tab was alone, and he didn't have to deal with both of them at the same time.

After an acceptable amount of time passed, Lucas instructed Douglas to get out of the car to get a closer look. He could see the back of the truck from the road and was surprised just how far into the swamp the truck advanced before being stopped by a large cypress tree. Lucas could hardly contain his excitement. He rubbed his hands together as he thought of the complete ecstasy he would feel as he watched the big shot detective take his last breath. He suddenly realized that the impact could've killed Tab and became annoyed that he might not get the chance to do it himself.

Lucas stepped out of the car. "Go get a closer look. I need to know if the man is still alive. Hurry up! Get in there!" He was becoming agitated and less patient with Douglas.

Lucas watched from the edge of the swamp as Douglas inched his way towards the truck. He realized that he received almost as much satisfaction watching Douglas struggle to make his way to the truck through the swamp as he would have when he implements the rest of his plan. He obtained great joy when people were obedient to him - a fetish he'd inherited from his controlling father. He would swear that his father got great satisfaction every time he beat his sons into submission. Unlike his father, Lucas didn't beat someone to feel power, he moved on to bigger and better ways to get satisfaction. And his father was the first to experience just how powerful he could be. The look of utter shock on his father's face that fatal night when Lucas fought back was forever etched into his mind. To his delight he would revisit that unthinkable plot whenever he pleased.

Lucas was thankful that the road was deserted because Douglas was taking forever to reach the truck that was only about fifteen yards from the road. With the heavy brush and trees behind the truck, it was almost impossible to see unless you were looking for it. As Douglas approached the driver's side of the truck he looked back towards Lucas for instructions.

Lucas yelled, "Well, can you see anything?"

Douglas leaned into the window and noticed Tab's body leaning forward against the steering wheel. He appeared to be unconscious. He reached for the handle and slowly opened the door. He saw that his seatbelt was still secure, and his cell phone had apparently flown on impact and rested on the floor. He reached into the truck and put his fingers onto Tab's neck to check for a pulse.

Douglas turned to Lucas and yelled, "He's still breathing but he's unconscious."

He turned his focus back to the truck and was greeted with a fist to his face. Douglas flew backwards and landed in knee deep water and mud. He wrestled with the palmettos and sloppy mud as he tried to get up. Tab unlocked his seat belt and bolted from the truck. He grabbed his leg that was struck earlier and grimaced in pain as he continued to run. When he felt like he was far enough in, he slowed down and waded through the water trying to be quiet. He made his way deeper into the swamp and found an old oak tree that had toppled from the last hurricane. Tab moved to the back of the stump and sat down. He was lightheaded and slightly disoriented, but alert enough to know that his life was in danger, and he needed to stay hidden. He leaned back and rested his head against the tree. He looked around and was saddened to see all of the beautiful trees that had been destroyed by the heavy winds of past hurricanes, but he was grateful for that one.

As the wind blew through the trees, Tab strained to listen for voices or sounds that would indicate someone was approaching. He could hear two voices arguing which confirmed that there were two people in the car he was following. He guessed that the two men were Douglas and Lucas. If his assumption was correct, he would have to be careful and probably venture deeper into the swamp. Tab wasn't fond of that idea and jumped at every slight movement around him. Among the wildlife that lived there, alligators and snakes concerned him the most. He decided to stay put by the tree and wait for their next move. He reached in his pocket for his phone and realized that it was still in the truck. Disappointed, he leaned back again and waited.

Douglas was soaking wet and full of mud when he made his way back to the road. He dreaded the walk back to Lucas because he knew he was going to be furious. Douglas had robbed Lucas of his fun and he was going to pay for that. He did remember to grab the keys to Tab's truck and his cell phone from the floorboard and hoped that it would count for something.

As he approached the car, he held up the items as if they were trophies. He could almost see the steam coming from Lucas's head and as he got closer saw the deadly stare that waited for him. "One good thing, I got his keys and his phone. At least he can't get too far and can't call for help." Douglas was secretly proud of himself even if Lucas wasn't.

"That would be wonderful Douglas if we were hundreds of miles in the desert. We are only a couple of miles either way to get to civilization. He's probably half-way there by now. Give me the phone." Lucas snatched the phone out of Douglas's hand. He opened the back and removed the battery then threw it to the ground and stomped on it. "We don't want anyone tracking the phone and leading them to us. Now go back into the swamp and see if you can locate him. You said he was unconscious so he may be hurt and still in the area."

Lucas walked to the passenger side of the car and got in. The look he shot Douglas dared him to object. Douglas stood still for a few moments and then feeling deflated, turned, and headed back into the swamp. His body was trembling and not from being cold. He needed a fix, and every part of his body knew it. Lucas promised him that he would get what he needed but he didn't understand how being an addict worked. He could feel the need run through his body like a snake seeking its prey. Within a few hours he would lose complete control and would have to surrender to his cravings.

The water was cold and murky. Douglas was afraid to think about what was in the water and instead focused on the trees that towered overhead. He reached the truck and looked around as he recalled which direction Tab ran. He took one step at a time at first but picked up the pace as his cravings began to take over. The quicker he could locate Tab, the quicker he would feel better. Douglas was focused on the job at hand when he felt the first brush against his leg. He leaped straight up out of the water but unfortunately landed back in the same place. He quickened his step and went about thirty feet before he felt the next brush. First, he screamed, then he stopped, squeezed his eyes shut and prayed.

Tab shuddered as the bloodcurdling scream vibrated through the swamp. He'd hoped that the men had left but apparently, they were still searching for him. He'd lost all track of time but could tell that darkness was on the way. He slowly peeked around the stump and saw a man wrestling with something in the water. He inched around the tree to get a better look but was careful not to be seen. Even though Tab had a distaste for shady criminals he had an even stronger distaste for someone that sat back and didn't help someone in need. The man that was with him in the swamp was being attacked by an enormous alligator and unfortunately, he was no match for it.

Tab made a split decision to help the man because he was clearly losing the battle. As he drew closer, the once murky water was tinted red. His head was pounding, his leg throbbing, and even though he knew he had to act quickly, he hesitated to collect himself and gather the strength needed to face a fierce predator. The last thing he wanted to do was get himself killed in the process of trying to save the man.

The alligator had latched onto the man by his right side. His arm and side were inside of its mouth, and it was thrashing around trying to bring him down. The man was able to fight the gator for a while, but Tab noticed that his face was pale, and the light was lifting from his eyes. He'd lost a lot of blood and was unable to keep fighting with enough strength to win. Tab opened the pocket knife his grandfather had left him and launched forward, landing on the back of the gator. He started to stab the gator repeatedly and after what seemed like hours, the gator released the man but continued to thrash around in the water. Tab attempted to jump off the back and ended up beneath the gator. He continued to thrust the knife in and out of the body and hoped that the gator would retreat. The water was only a few feet deep, but Tab was pinned down at the bottom of the muddy swamp unable to catch his breath. He couldn't tell where the man was because of the cloudy water that obscured his vision. Tab kept stabbing the alligator but out of exhaustion his pace slowed, and he was faced with the reality that he may not survive.

Lucas watched with pleasure from the safety of the road. He heard the excruciating screams and wanted to get a better look. He smiled as he witnessed Douglas' struggle with the alligator. So much blood and the poor weakling was still fighting. Lucas gasped in astonishment when he saw Tab race to the rescue. He thought once again that things could not get any better. He'd hoped to take care of Tab himself but death by stupidity worked just as well. Lucas pressed record on his phone so that he could share it with his dear brother. At one point, he thought that Tab might've pulled it off but as he suspected he wasn't strong enough either. Douglas was still screaming like a baby as he laid there bleeding out and Tab went under and hadn't surfaced. *Oh well*. Lucas shook his head, got into the car, and drove away.

CHAPTER 26

Griff sent E.R. a text telling him that there was no one home at Douglas' house. He tried to call Tab again and it went straight to voice mail. He didn't want to worry but somewhere in the corner of his mind he was beginning to panic. Tab was an experienced detective and even under the bizarre circumstances they encountered the last few days, he was more than qualified to handle them with caution. Griff sat on his sofa and rolled the recent events over in his mind. He felt like he was caught up in a web of chaos and attempted to make connections. He leaned back, closed his eyes and due to his sheer exhaustion, went to sleep.

****

E.R. and Charley Ann finished eating dinner and were sitting on the sofa talking. Charley Ann had so many questions that she wanted to bounce off E.R. but he looked beat. They were both tired and running on fumes but the need to find Liam drove them forward. She decided to talk about herself and hoped that he would do the same. They only met three days ago but it felt like they had known each other forever. She knew all the important things that she needed to know about someone. He was kind, generous, honest, dependable, and handsome. She squirmed as it registered that she was falling in love with a man she hardly knew.

"I was born and raised in Houma. Well, I was raised by my parents until I was fourteen then my sister stepped in after that. She was only seventeen and she gave up her life to keep us together. Thankfully, my parents had an insurance policy that paid off the house upon their death and left us enough savings to live on and pay for college. I was still in high school, and Chelsea had just graduated. She passed up the idea of going away for college and took night classes so she could be there for me. I owe her everything and when Brian started to make threats, I knew that I had to get him away from her one way or another." Charley Ann saw the expression on E.R.'s face turn from interest to concern as she spoke those last words. *Oh my God! I said that out load. I have to be more careful!* She looked away and continued to speak, hoping that she read his expression wrong, and he hadn't caught what she said.

"I finally graduated and began taking classes at Nicholls. I had a hard time when my parents first died but my sister did everything she could to keep life normal for me and made sure I was happy. And I was happy. I went on the occasional date but nothing serious until Brian and you see how that worked out for me. I participated in school events when I could. Funny how life goes on even..."

"How did your parents die?"

"A car accident. The roads were icy, and my father lost control of the car. They slid off the road and into the bayou. They were so young. My mom had a sister that lived in Maine, but she died not long after my mother. My father was an only child, and both sets of my grandparents were already deceased. Chelsea is all I have. Are all of your grandparents still alive?" Charley Ann pushed on as E.R. listened with interest again. It was working. "Do you have any sisters or brothers?"

"All of my grandparents are still alive. You met my grandfather Griff, and I told you about my grandmother Honey. My other grandparents live in Tennessee, but we see them often. I have a little sister Gabrielle." E.R. yawned. "Today seemed like it would never end. My grandfather sent a text saying that no one was home at Douglas' house. I guess he evacuated ahead of the hurricane. If the weather isn't too bad in the morning we can go back out and maybe he'll be there. A lot of people stay and ride out the storm." E.R. yawned again. He leaned back to get comfortable and went on talking. "I was blessed to have both my parents and grandparents around to raise me. I am very close to my grandfather, and he has always been there for me. He's my best friend. I'm sorry you lost your parents when you were so young." E.R. reached out and touched the end of Charley Ann's hair. She was so beautiful. Charley Ann moved closer to E.R. and leaned her head on his shoulder. They sat there in silence as they both enjoyed a little comfort and security.

E.R. jumped off the sofa and felt a cool sensation that ran up his leg. He lifted one leg and then the other. His pants were soaking wet and as he stepped down the ground squished from beneath him. Where am I? He looked around but found it tough to see anything. The darkness surrounded him and wore heavy on his eyes. The force of the wind threatened to topple him over, so he reached out to steady himself. He grabbed onto what appeared to be a cypress tree branch. He panicked. Charley Ann, where are you? He still felt the warmth of her body next to his. The smell of her hair lingered in the air but soon was replaced by the salty fragrance of rain that was steadily falling down. He adjusted his eyes several times, but his vision was still obstructed. He heard a scream and stiffened as he tried to make sense of what was happening. I must be dreaming again. He pinched himself to wake up, but nothing happened.

E.R. inhaled and attempted to slow down the thumping in his chest. He squinched his eyes and assessed the area. It looked like he was in the swamp somewhere in the Jean Lafitte National Reserve, but he didn't know exactly where since it covered a vast amount of area. He was disoriented and didn't know which way to turn. He closed his eyes again and willed himself to breath and calm down. When he opened his eyes, she was there. She extended her hands forward and reached for E.R., but he backed up against the tree out of her reach. She moved backwards away from him. Wait! Don't go. Why am I here. She stopped for a second and then burst forward drifting right past him. Her body was illuminating and cast light as she moved behind him. While still holding on to a branch, E.R. circled the tree and kept his gaze on her as she went deeper into the swamp. He could hear a slight whimpering in the direction she went and wondered if it were her voice that he heard scream. He wanted to follow her but wasn't sure that he should. She had never attempted to hurt him before, but he was still weary of her. Before he could decide, she swooped back to him, grabbed his hand and they both projected forward. He felt his feet lift off the ground as they continued towards the sounds of whimpering. Wait! Stop! Who are you? E.R. hated to admit it, but he was more frightened than he'd ever been, and that was a feeling that he was not used to.

Her hand which lacked warmth, released E.R. and he found himself on top of a toppled cypress tree next to the body of a man facing down. No! No! No! No! What is this? Why am I here? E.R. closed his eyes again and wished he would wake up. After he accepted that he was not in control and unable to wake himself up he looked down at the man next to him. He watched his back carefully to see if he was breathing and even though it was a slight movement, it provided E.R. with an answer. He's still alive. E.R. squatted down next to the man and put his hand on his shoulder but was distracted by a whimper a few yards away. He jumped back up and tried to focus his eyes. Hello? E.R. waited but there was no response. He turned his focus back to the man by his feet and noticed his hand twitch. He stepped over the body and knelt by his side. From that angle he had a perfect view of the man's face and was stunned. Tab! Can you hear me? Tab are you okay? E.R. put his hands on his shoulder and attempted to turn him over, but he didn't budge. Tab opened his eyes and stared straight through E.R. without acknowledging his presence. He can't see or hear me. What am I supposed to do? He looked up at the woman for answers, but she stood motionless above it all. Help me! Help him! Tell me what to do! He shouted in frustration at the woman. E.R. wrapped his arms around Tab and tried to shelter him from the rain. Again, but this time in a whisper he said, Please help me. Please.

CHAPTER 27

Liam had lost track of the days, but he could tell by the sound of fierce wind blowing that it had to be close to Sunday and that Hurricane Ida was having an impact already. He wished he knew where he was and why he was there. The last thing he remembered was calling E.R. and telling him he was on the way to his house. He recalled taking an Uber to the cemetery to pick up his truck and that's it. *I know I reached the cemetery and opened the door to my truck to get in then the rest is blank. God, I hope Charley Ann's alright. E.R. too because he didn't look so good when I dragged him out of the grave and got him home.* Liam continued to try and piece together the chain of events that led him to his current position. *Brian. Could Charley Ann's boyfriend be responsible for all of this? She thought he was following us, and I do remember noticing a truck that was trailing us closely. But if it were him, why would he wait until I came back to the cemetery alone to attack? Unless he had followed us back to my house and then back here to get rid of me. Oh my God! He must have her. I gotta get out of here!*

Liam started pushing on the large white stone that had him imprisoned. There were cracks throughout the stone, but it remained mostly solid. He was grateful for the cracks because they allowed some air to come in and he hoped they would eventually break if he pushed long enough. Liam pushed and kicked until he was completely exhausted then sat back to regroup. While he waited to refuel, he used the daylight that was peeking through the cracks to look around. It hadn't been long that the light was shining through so he figured that it must be early dawn. When he first woke up in this nightmare, he was groggy and went in and out of consciousness for a while. It wasn't until late yesterday that he started to become more clear-headed and aware of his surroundings. He must've been drugged or something. He decided that someone went to a great deal of trouble planning this out because there were water bottles and enough food to keep someone alive for weeks. This was definitely a well thought out plan and not the work of some jealous boyfriend who reacted at the last minute.

Liam grew anxious and started to rub his hands up and down his legs. He felt like the walls were closing in on him and he wanted desperately to get out of there. He felt his phone in his pocket and pulled it out, hoping that the battery wasn't dead. He kept it turned it off to try and save what little battery was left so that he could try to contact E.R. again. He knew that E.R. would be searching for him, especially since he was able to get a couple of calls out to him. Unfortunately, each time he called E.R., the call would drop but he prayed that he relayed the message that he was alive and somewhere without good phone service. He turned the phone on and waited for the Verizon logo to pop up.

Liam said a quick prayer and dialed E.R.'s number. His heart sank when the call went straight to voicemail. He stared at the phone as he waited for the beep. *Hey E.R. it's me. I don't know where I am, but it looks like some sort of cement room that has cracks in the ceiling. Last thing I can remember before waking up here was going back to Fleming Cemetery to get my truck. Oddly enough, I do have some food and two bottles of water, but I really need you to call me back. My phone is about to die and...* Liam didn't have to look at the phone to know that the call dropped. He hoped that the message went through, and that E.R. would dial him right back. He couldn't leave the phone on too long. He rested his head against the wall and smiled as he thought of E.R. and how lucky he was to have him in his life. *If anyone's gonna find me, it's gonna be him.*

****

E.R. felt his arm tingle and opened his eyes to find Charley Ann leaning against him sound asleep. The morning light pushed through the shades announcing that morning had arrived. E.R. couldn't remember the last time he slept that well and was surprised considering they slept sitting up on the sofa. He wanted to close his eyes and go back to sleep but he knew he wouldn't because he was anxious to call his grandfather to get an update. He closed his eyes and just enjoyed the warm comfortable feeling he was experiencing from sitting next to Charley Ann. After a brief time, he slowly lifted her head from his shoulder careful not to wake her. Once free, he headed to the kitchen to make coffee to get the day started. He noticed that it was 7:30 am and wondered why he hadn't heard from anyone yet. His grandfather was not only an early riser but expected everyone else to be.

E.R. went back to the living room to look for his phone. He thought he left it on the coffee table, but it wasn't there. He searched the room and his pockets but came up empty. He went to the sofa and stuck his hands into the cushion's feeling for the phone. At last, he found it between the cushions where he slept and pulled it out. It was dead. He ran to grab his charger and plugged it in waiting for it to load up. His attempts to stay quiet and not wake Charley Ann failed and while he was sorry that he disturbed her sleep, he was happy to see her beautiful smile. Her hair was tousled and cascaded down her face. Ignoring the desire to sit back down with her was difficult and he was still struggling with the fantasy when his phone rang making the decision for him.

"Good morning sunshine. Too busy to charge your phone. Did you get any sleep last night?" Griff loved getting under his grandson's skin.

"Surprisingly, we did. We fell asleep on the sofa and stayed there all night. We just woke up not long ago. I just realized that my phone had died when I tried to call you. What's up?"

"I slept well also in case you were wondering. I'm a little concerned because I can't get in touch with Mr. Tab either. His…"

"Oh My God Paw!" The blood drained from E.R.'s face at the mention of Tab's name. "I had a dream last night. Well I think it was a dream but I'm not sure. I was in the Jean Lafitte Swamp and the lady in white was there. She led me to Mr. Tab who was lying unconscious on the stump of a cypress tree that had fallen from a storm. He opened his eyes but couldn't see or hear me. I also heard screams and moaning not too far away. It was dark and raining so I couldn't see where it was coming from. I think Mr. Tab is in trouble. I pleaded with the lady to help me but that's the last thing I remember. We gotta go see if we can find him before it's too late." E.R. was walking in circles and spoke louder and louder as he went on.

"Wait. E.R. calm down. What are you talking about? Who is the lady in white and how do you know Jean Lafitte Park was where you were? Let's back up and slow down this time."

"I wanted to tell you, but I didn't know how. Ever since I fell into that grave at the cemetery, I've had visions of a lady in a white dress. I know it sounds crazy and at first, I thought I was just hallucinating from hitting my head but then I thought maybe I was dreaming. I'll fill you in more when we are on our way to the park. I'm telling you Paw, Mr. Tab is in trouble, you just have to trust me." A drop of sweat rolled down his forehead and landed on his nose. E.R. never intended on telling his grandfather about his visions but now that he had, he felt the weight of it all lift away.

"Man, I hope you're wrong. I'll pick you up in ten minutes." Griff ended the call and headed for the door. Concern started to creep into Griff's thoughts, but he held them at bay because he knew E.R. well and if he believed that he was having visions then he probably was. He just hoped that they could locate Tab and that he was alright. He was concerned last night when Tab hadn't answered but he just figured that he was busy and would call him back. He fell asleep and when he woke, he checked his phone for a response that wasn't there. His stomach churned as he drove to E.R. 's house. *God, please help us find Tab alive and well and before the hurricane gets here.*

When Griff arrived at E.R. 's house he found them outside and ready to go. Charley Ann climbed in the back seat and E.R. got in the passenger side. E.R. was wearing his white shrimp boots and Charley Ann had white garbage bags and rubber bands in her hands. Griff raised an eyebrow when he noticed, and she held up her hands.

"This is the only pair of shoes I have with me and I'm not staying in the truck. I want to help search for Mr. Tab."

Griff smiled then turned his focus on E.R. and the task at hand. He wanted to ask him about the lady in white but hesitated because he wasn't sure if he shared any of that with Charley Ann yet. He made eye contact with E.R. and shrugged hoping he understood what he was asking.

"It's okay. I just told Charley Ann about the vision but waited until you arrived to address it with both of you at the same time. Ever since I hit my head I've had dreams, visions, or maybe even hallucinations of a lady in a white dress. She's unmistakably dead so I guess we can say she's a ghost. The first time I saw her was after I hit my head right before I passed out. Or after I passed out, I don't know for sure. All I know for sure is that she is appearing to me when I need help. Paw, when you came over to help me that first night she appeared for a moment. When we went to Liam's house and were about to leave, she directed my attention towards the bathroom where Charley Ann was hiding. Then, in Grand Isle, she guided me to the container that Charley Ann was in. At first, she scared me, but I don't think she wants to hurt me but instead is trying to help me. She appeared when Charley Ann screamed, I mean called out for help when the snakes were in the house. Each time she showed up only for a moment. Then yesterday at the Verizon store, I fell asleep, and I dreamed I was back in that grave and she was there. I asked her if she knew where Liam was but before she answered, Charley Ann woke me up. Finally last night I dreamed that I was in the swamp, she appeared, took me by the hand and showed me where Tab was. He was hurt but I couldn't help him because it was like I wasn't there."

Griff listened to his grandson as he described his new-found gift. After his wife's involvement with the supernatural a few years ago, he'd come to terms with the idea of unexplained encounters. Seeing ghosts was a new one but he believed that E.R. was experiencing something supernatural and that it was very real. He was still very uncomfortable with the whole supernatural concept, but he had learned to keep an open mind and not just dismiss the idea.

"I'm not positive about the location but my gut tells me Tab's in the Jean Lafitte Preserve and he's not alone."

Griff slowed down as he approached each turn of the road while Charley Ann and E.R. searched for any sign of Tab. The Preserve encompassed thousands of acres but the part that the road ran through went on for about 3 miles.

"Man, this is gonna be tough. Do you remember any-thing about the area you were in that would narrow the search?" Griff was looking out his side window hoping to see something that would lead them to Tab.

"Look Out!"

Griff jerked his head forward and at the same time slammed on his breaks. "What happened? Did you see something?"

"This is the spot." E.R. jumped out of the truck and crossed the road. They were close to Bayou Coquille when they stopped. "I saw her! She was right in front of the truck. She was right there." E.R. pointed. "This has to be where Tab is."

Griff and Charley Ann exited the truck and caught up to E.R. who was frantically searching the area. The area was isolated so they walked along the road praying that they would find Tab soon. Both Griff and E.R. were familiar with the area and knew well that while some of the swamp appeared high and dry, most parts were wet and soggy. E.R. edged farther and farther off the road so that he could see into the swamp.

"Stop! What's that?" He ran forward as he spoke. "Look! That's a truck." Before Griff could respond, E.R. was in the swamp, knee deep in water and headed to a truck that was partially submerged in the mud. "It's his truck! It's Mr. Tab's truck but it's empty."

Griff noticed tire tracks that indicated exactly where the truck went off the road. The tracks were light and would've probably been overlooked had E.R. not stopped them when he did. The back of the truck was barely visible from the road even though it was only about fifteen yards into the swamp. A shiver ran up Griff's spine and his body shook slightly. Just because he was willing to admit that the supernatural existed didn't mean he was comfortable with it. He didn't see anything because he was looking out the side window, but it couldn't be a coincidence that they picked that exact spot to stop. Griff shook it off and called out to E.R. for more information.

"I remember that in my dream I was standing by the truck, and she took my hand and brought me to Mr. Tab." E.R. crossed in front of the truck and pointed into the swamp. "It was this way. Should we call out for him? There was someone else in the swamp with him, but I didn't see who it was."

"E.R. please be careful. Maybe I should come with you." Griff's voice was shaky.

"I got this. I have my weapon and I will take it slow. Don't come in. I'll call back if I need you. And I'll keep talking so you know I'm okay." E.R. moved slowly, partly because he was being cautious and partly because he was walking through the muddy swamp. There were large palmettos all over the place. The water rippled from time to time suggesting that something was getting too close, and he should run for safety. E.R. had been in that swamp hundreds of times before and as much as he loved the beauty and freedom of the outdoors, he cringed at what was lurking just below the surface of the water or under the brush that covered the land. He inhaled deeply and edged farther into the swamp.

"I'm not sure if this is the right direction. I don't see anything yet but I'm gonna keep going." E.R. inched forward, stopping every so often. The weight of the mud was taxing so he took his time. "I think I see that toppled tree from my dream." E.R. was looking forward as he waded through praying that he was going the right way.

"E.R. can you still hear me?" Griff was getting nervous. He glanced back at Charley Ann who looked just as anxious as they waited for a response. "E.R.!"

"Sorry. I'm here." E.R. stopped for a minute to catch his breath. He placed his hands on his thighs and leaned forward to take a deep breath. He glared down at the water and noticed that it was a different color. "Hey! Something's different about the water here!" E. R stood up and started to move forward when he kicked something with his right foot. He froze and waited to see if anything moved. Again, he inched forward and hit something with his foot but this time it floated to the top. "Whoa!" E.R. backed up quickly.

"What's wrong? E.R. are you okay?" Griff heard some splashing and grew concerned. He was just about to run into the swamp when E.R. answered him.

E.R. managed to squeak out, "I'm okay." His stomach turned and he felt queasy. Before he could register exactly what it was that he was seeing, a foul smell tickled his nose. He held his breath in an attempt to block the odor and looked away. He straightened up and gathered himself before continuing. "I think I'm in the right area." E.R. yelled to Griff as he watched a human arm that had been severed float on top of the water. He wasn't far from the tree that he saw in his dream and as he looked in that direction, he discovered where the odor was coming from. There was a huge dead alligator laying on the edge of the toppled tree.

"Oh my God!" E.R. noticed that the area was covered in blood and panicked as he thought about Mr. Tab. "Paw I found the tree. I don't see Mr. Tab but there's a dead gator and a lot of blood here." E.R. didn't mention the severed arm because he didn't want his grandfather to rush into danger.

"Be careful! Stay where you are, I'm coming in." Griff looked at Charley Ann. "Will you be okay by yourself?" He was already running towards the swamp when she shook her head yes. Griff ran towards the sound of E R.'s voice and when he reached him, E.R. was sitting on the bottom of the tree stump with Tab laying in his arms. E.R. looked up at Griff with his eyes misted over and his face etched in sadness. He attempted to speak but with his throat thickened with grief the words faded before they could reach his lips.

CHAPTER 28

Two Weeks Earlier

Still today, Lucas could remember his mother crying all the time before she left, and he often wondered if he was the reason. He was just a little boy, but that image still haunted him at night. He grew up with an abusive father and even though it was a continuous nightmare, deep down he thought he deserved to be punished for driving his mother away. He didn't deserve to be happy, and he blamed himself for his father's unhappiness.

Lucas was happy that his brother had escaped with his mother. She did try to take both of her sons, but Lorenzo found out and tried to stop her. Lucas was the one that was ripped from his mother's arms not his brother. He was the one that watched the only security he'd ever had jump into a car, drive away, and never look back. For years he'd wondered about the two of them and for years he'd waited for his mother to come back for him. She never did.

His father hired one private investigator after another to find his estranged wife and son but to no avail. Lucas watched as his father's moods grew darker and darker and his wrath became more severe. Looking back, he realized that his father's hatred and abuse towards him was fueled by the loss of his wife and the control he had over her. His father wasn't satisfied with just one son he wanted his wife back. His father never did remarry which was unfortunate for Lucas because it deprived him of any kind of love and affection. He was the casualty of a dysfunctional family, and he accepted his role like a champ.

As he grew older and into his teenage years, he started to realize that he was a lot like his father. At least that's what the teachers and counselors at school pointed out every day. His father was a local and well known for his bad habits and rough demeanor. Lorenzo's callousness and detachment from family and affection of any kind showed in his disregard for his son, a son who tried every day to gain his father's love and affection. Throughout the years, countless people had attempted to intervene on Lucas's behalf but were unsuccessful. It wasn't until years after he graduated from high school that reality set in and he realized that he wasn't the reason his mother left. All those guilty feelings he held on to through the years instantly turned into intense anger that he now directed towards his mother and brother. He felt abandoned by the two people he loved most in the world and that realization started him on his journey to find them both and make them pay.

The beauty of it all was that they had no idea that he was coming for them. He wasn't sure where to begin to look and he knew his father wouldn't give him any information. He remembered his father had private investigators looking for them and decided he needed those facts to begin. That's when he knew he was going to kill his father. He deserved to die because after all, he tried to kill Lucas many times but failed. The only difference was that Lucas did not fail and actually reveled in the deed.

Disposing of his father was a necessary start to his plan that would play out completely very soon thanks to his persistence and determination. Lucas spent his whole life lonely and feeling inadequate while he dreamed of the life he could've had with his mother and brother. The need for motherly love had passed and was replaced with the need for sweet revenge.

CHAPTER 29

E. R. was distraught with grief but wasn't afforded the opportunity to take time off because Trey called with information about Liam's foster care years. He'd located the last foster care home where Liam lived until he left at the age of seventeen. It was located in a small town called Grand Bay, Alabama just on the other side of the Mississippi state line. Trey spoke to the Morgan family, and they said that they would be willing to speak to E.R. if he needed to contact them.

E.R. decided that he could use a distraction and invited Charley Ann to go with him to speak to the family face to face. He needed to gather as much information as he could about Liam's childhood and time in foster care and hoped that the family could shed some light on that. Grand Bay was about two and a half hours away and with the hurricane quickly approaching they were running out of time. The interstates were probably still congested with evacuees but since the hurricane was due to hit soon most people were already where they needed to be and hunkered down. He would take Highway 90 just in case and hoped to bypass some of the traffic. He felt like he didn't have much choice because they needed to find Liam before the storm hit and they were out of leads.

Charley Ann jumped at the chance to go with E.R. because sitting around waiting was making her feel crazy and she felt responsible for Liam's disappearance. She still didn't believe that Brian could've killed Liam or anyone but felt like he was probably involved with someone who could, and Liam got in the way. She prayed that they would find him soon because the longer it took the worse the odds were that he would be alive. She looked at E.R. with admiration as he drove in bad weather, through traffic, determined to help his friend. She'd had several good friends but wasn't sure that any of them would've been as driven as he was if she were missing. In fact, when she took off from Houma a few days ago, no one called to check on her except her sister. In all fairness, she'd gotten rid of her phone to keep Brian from finding her, but they could've contacted her sister. E.R. was a true and loyal friend and she loved that about him. She felt safe and secure when she was with him, a feeling she'd never experienced with Brian.

"What do you think we'll find at the Morgan's house? Did Trey indicate that they had useful information about Liam?"

E.R. thought carefully before answering. "I don't know but I pray they can point us in the direction we need to go to find Liam. Trey said that they weren't sure what information would be helpful but offered to share everything they knew about him with us. Sometimes the smallest thing is important and often overlooked. I wanted to speak to them in person just in case, I don't know, that I will recognize that small thing." E.R.'s voice cracked as he searched for his words. "He has to be alive. He called me and needed my help because he knew he could count on me. I won't let him down."

Charley Ann recognized the agony E.R. was in and wished she could find the words he needed to hear. She reached over and touched his shoulder to let him know that she cared and was there for him. As if on cue, Charley Ann turned on the radio and "You've Got A Friend" by Carole King hijacked the silence that surrounded them, reinforcing her gesture and comforting E.R. in a way that only music can do. Out of the corner of her eye she saw the edges of his lips curl up and form the most beautiful smile and her heart tingled with joy.

The ride went quicker than they expected so E.R. elected to pull into a little mom and pop diner to get a bite to eat. His stomach started to growl. It was still early enough to beat the lunch crowd and neither of them had eaten all day. They placed their orders and while waiting they went over their plan of action for their meeting with the Morgan's. E.R. seemed distracted by the constant flow back and forth from the kitchen and Charley Ann wondered what caught his attention. She followed his gaze and found herself staring at a man washing dishes who from the back resembled Liam. He had the same dark curly hair and stood about the same height. She continued to observe E.R. and his reaction to the stranger to see if that was what had occupied his attention, and it was.

Nervously, Charley Ann shifted in her seat riddled with anticipation waiting for the man to turn around. E.R. didn't wait but instead stood up giving into his curiosity and rushed into the kitchen. Everyone turned to look except, the man in question, the dishwasher who was concentrating on the mounds of dishes that needed his attention. E.R. stood behind him and said, "Liam." There was no response. Again he said, "Hey Liam" and for a second time the man continued performing the task at hand. He was meticulous as he washed each dish and then rinsed with the same special attention. E.R.'s enthusiasm deflated and with his head hung forward, walked back to the table.

"I don't know what I was thinking. I guess the idea that Liam grew up here made me think that maybe he came back but that wouldn't make sense. He wouldn't just leave without a word, I know him."

"I noticed the resemblance too and was hoping that it was him. But I agree with you. I don't think Liam would just take off."

They finished eating and paid the check.

E.R. got back on the highway and headed east towards the Morgan's house. The GPS was right on point and brought them to a small blue house in the middle of a quiet neighborhood street. The house was only a few miles from the restaurant and that fact made E.R. wonder again about the dishwasher and his uncanny resemblance to

Liam. Charley Ann had noticed the same thing even though she hadn't known Liam for long. E.R. thought about the man that his grandfather and Tab found at Liam's house and remembered that he supposedly looked just like Liam. He regretted that he hadn't introduced himself to the dishwasher and gotten a better look, but he let his disappointment dictate his actions and just walked away.

E.R. inhaled deeply and opened his door. Charley Ann did the same and they anxiously stood on the sidewalk in front of the Morgan's home. From the outside, the house looked like a typical family home with a fenced yard, swing set, front porch with a swing and an above the ground pool to enjoy during the summer heat. There were several children playing in the yard and an elderly woman sat in one of the several rocking chairs. The house was modest in size and to E.R.'s surprise, like the yard, well kept. He'd only known one family that fostered children and that was only because his grandfather was hired to investigate an abuse case that turned out to be false, but he remembered that the house was in serious disrepair and the children looked to be neglected. As it turned out, the family was just falling on hard times and struggled to make ends meet. The children were well taken care of, and a few had even been adopted and became a perma-nent member of the family.

E.R. wondered about Liam and his time in foster care because Liam was so kind and down to earth and showed no signs of being abused or mistreated. E.R. was surprised to learn that he grew up in foster care instead of with a loving family. He was saddened as he watched the children in the yard. He was so blessed to have both of his parents and grateful for his upbringing.

E.R. walked up to the porch and introduced himself to the woman.

"Hi, I'm Evan and this is Charley Ann. We're here to speak to Mr. and Mrs. Morgan. I believe they are expecting us."

The woman stood up and E.R. noticed right away that she was a lot younger than he thought. Her hair was a stunning silver color that was pulled back into a ponytail and sat high on top of her head.

"Hello. Evan, is it? I was told that someone called E.R. would be coming by. Is that you?"

"Sorry, Yes. My name is Evan Robert, but they call me E.R. for short." E.R. extended his hand and was soon at ease by the warmth of her smile. She had beautiful white teeth and a perfect smooth complexion. She was actually a beautiful woman and she reminded him of an older Audrey Hepburn. His grandmother's favorite movie was Sabrina, starring Hepburn and he would watch it with her when he was young. He'd had a huge crush on Hepburn and his grandmother still teased him about it.

"I understand that Liam Barrios was a foster child who was in your care a few years ago. I was hoping you could tell me more about his time here with you."

"Has something happened to him? He was such a good boy." Ms. Morgan seemed genuinely concerned about Liam.

"Liam was my partner and he's been missing for a couple of days. He mentioned to me that he'd grown up in foster care but didn't talk much about it. We met about two years ago and he's like a brother to me. I really need to find him and make sure that he's okay."

"Oh my goodness. I sure hope he's alright. As I said he was such a good boy. He was one of my favorites along with Logan. I sure do miss him. He and Logan came to us when they were about four years old. They…"

"Logan? Who's Logan? Did Liam have a brother?" E.R. was confused.

"Oh no dear. Logan and Liam were just best friends. They were both brought to us by the Catholic Church just a few days apart and they quickly formed a bond. From what we were told, both boys had a rough start to life and came from abusive backgrounds. I was truly amazed at how loving and peaceful those two were considering their past."

"Ms. Morgan, do you have any pictures of Liam or Logan? And when was the last time you heard from either one?"

Ms. Morgan opened the door and instructed them to follow her inside. "I have pictures of all of my kids. Me and Mr. Morgan couldn't have children of our own but we both love kids and felt like this was our calling. Please sit down." She offered them a seat in a lovely family room that was filled with pictures on the wall of all the children that she and her husband had fostered through the years.

There were several couches and chairs situated around the room and bookcases that were filled with books, games, and more pictures and photo albums. The room was modest, but cozy. It spoke of hours and hours of happiness and quality time shared with loved ones.

"Here we go." Ms. Morgan walked over to the couch where E.R. was sitting and sat down beside him. In her hand she carried a thick photo album that was labeled 2004.

"This is the year they came to us. Like I said, they were just four years old." There on the first page was a picture of a young Liam and another boy that was almost the spitting image of him.

"Wow. Is that Logan? They look just alike. Are you positive that they weren't related?" E.R. was studying the pictures.

"I'm positive. The nuns assured me that they were not related, and I believed them. But you're right they did look a lot alike. But I could always tell them apart. "

"Oh my God!" Charley Ann gasped catching their attention. Her back was to them as she looked at the pictures that decorated the room. She turned and walked towards them holding a double frame. She handed it to E.R. waiting for his reaction. He was speechless. When he looked up Charley Ann knew just what he was thinking, and they both said it aloud. "The dishwasher at the diner!"

E.R. took the frame from Charley Ann, sat down, and studied the photos of the two men. On the left side was a picture of Liam in his game warden uniform taken recent-ly, and on the right a picture of a man, about the same age as Liam, standing in front of the Pitre Diner, the mom-and-pop diner they had visited earlier.

"Ms. Morgan, is this Logan?" He leaned the photo so that she could see it.

"Yes. That's Logan. He's such a handsome young man and a hard worker." She gleamed with pride.

"So he still lives here in the area? We saw him earlier at the diner but didn't get a chance to speak to him. Does he still live here at the house?" E.R. wanted answers but proceeded with caution.

"Oh no. He has his own house a few streets over from here. He still comes around every chance he gets to help out with the kids. How did you say you know Liam.?" She was concerned that they were asking too many questions about Logan.

"We work together in Lafitte, Louisiana as game wardens. He'd never mentioned Logan before, but they look like they were close at one time. I'd really like to talk to him if I could. Maybe he can help us locate Liam."

"I'm sure he'll help if he can. He's been pretty busy since he bought that diner, and he was in a pretty bad accident recently. He wasn't seriously hurt but the air bags left some bruises, and his truck was a complete loss. I can call him and see if he has time to speak to y'all."

"This picture of Liam is pretty recent. Did he come by and bring it to you, and does he come often?"

"Sadly, we haven't seen Liam for a couple of years. When Liam and Logan were about sixteen, they went on a hunt to find out about their biological families. They never did talk about what they found out, but we know they were both disturbed by their findings. I'm sure they could tell you more about that. Soon after that they turned seventeen and moved on. Logan went into the marines and Liam moved from place-to-place working odd jobs for a while. Eventually, Logan settled back here and about two years ago, Liam sent a letter telling us that he was in Louisiana and had a job working with the Louisiana Wildlife and Fisheries Department. Not too long after that he sent that picture and promised to get back here soon. He never did. He and Logan kept in touch but ever since they looked into their pasts, they were more cautious about spending time together." There was sadness in Ms. Morgan's eyes that suggested that she missed them deeply.

The back screen door opened and slammed shut. Someone was in the kitchen whistling as they walked around.

"There's Mr. Morgan now. Would you like to meet him? He may be able to shed more light on the subject than I can." Ms. Morgan stood up and walked towards the back of the house where the soft whistling sound was coming from. "Oh, It's you. Hi sweetie. I have some people here that want to meet you."

E.R. and Charley Ann ran to the kitchen just in time to see the back screen door slam shut again.

"Wait! Please! Liam's missing! We need your help!" E.R. followed Logan out the door and across the yard.

"Please Wait!"

CHAPTER 30

One Week Ago

Lucas felt like he was on top of the world. Last week he set in motion a plan to finally take control of his own life. The misery that sucked the life out of him every day was slowly being replaced by an immense gratification and he wasn't finished yet. He was just getting started and his body shuddered at the thought of gaining complete satisfaction because it was almost too much to think about. But he was consumed with his thoughts and was now ready for the next step.

Finding Lorna wasn't that difficult, in fact, the information in his father's files led Lucas right to her. At first, he wasn't sure that it was her because he hadn't seen her in over seventeen years, but the small tattoo on her left shoulder confirmed it. He'd forgotten about that tattoo but when he read it in the file, the memory of a heart that enclosed two tiny hearts intertwined flooded his thoughts. He used to trace it with his finger when his mother held him. She used to tell him that the big heart represented her and the two smaller one's represented Lucas and his brother and that they would always be together and nothing in this world could separate them. Lucas's forehead wrinkled and his mood switched from complete satisfaction to disgust as he thought about the lies that he was fed as a child.

He wasn't surprised that Lorna lived in New Orleans close to the only son she had ever loved. The one she saved from a life of pain and suffering. His heart fluttered a little when he first saw her and that constant yearning to be with his mother that he'd felt most of his life took over. His first reaction was to run up to her and jump into her arms like he used to do when he was young. Lucas continued to watch her through the window until the rage began to build up inside of him again. He noted that she looked peaceful and happy and that she still tilted her head back when she laughed. He did remember that infectious laugh she had and longed to hear it one more time. But he knew that he would probably never hear it again and was positive that the next time he was close enough to his mother, she would not be laughing.

Lucas started the engine and hesitated as he attempted to commit the smile on his mother's face to memory. Too bad things turned out the way they did because he really had hoped to one day be reunited with his family. Now all he lived for was revenge and soon he would be one step closer towards his final act. He drove away one last time.

After Lucas located his mother, he took his time to learn her routine and prepare a plan. He knew exactly how he was going to get his revenge and was careful to pay attention to the details needed to execute it. He wondered how often she got together with Liam. He felt his temperature rise as he pictured them having lunch or going to a movie together. *Did they celebrate each other's birthdays? Did they celebrate on my birthday without me?* With each disturbing thought, Lucas grew angrier until he felt his head would explode.

The time had come for Lorna to be reunited with her son, the one she'd abandoned seventeen years ago. Lucas wondered if she would even recognize him. After he'd located his mother, he set out to find his long-lost brother Liam. It wasn't hard to do considering she used her mother's maiden name Barrios when she left. Lucas chuckled at the incompetence of the private investigators his father had hired. *Did they think she would've used her married name or go back to her maiden name if she didn't want to be found?* He couldn't blame them completely because he almost missed it himself when he read the reports. In the beginning of the first report, at the top, was a list of Lorna's relatives who were alive and deceased and then they were never mentioned again. Lucas did exactly what they did at first and searched for Lorna Ricci and Lorna Theriot before the name Barrios jumped off the page. He looked up Lorna Barrios and there she was. He was delighted when he found out she was living in New Orleans because he'd always wanted to visit the city.

Lucas admired the superdome that was lit up with black and gold lights in support of the New Orleans Saints. As he drove around, he noticed that the streets that were usually slammed with people were empty except for a few people brave enough to chance contracting Covid. He turned onto Julia street and parked in the place he'd used each time he came to observe his mother. Through the window of the gallery he sat and watched her mingle with the one customer inside the store. Usually, the "White Linen Nights" event that was happening on Julia street would be in full bloom but with the city requiring proof of vaccinations to participate the crowd was light. Lucas didn't mind because he hated being in crowds of people that bump into you constantly and make it difficult to get anywhere quickly.

He considered walking into the gallery to see if she would recognize him but as much as that idea tempted him, he opted against it and preferred to wait. If his calculations were correct, she would be leaving soon and then he would make his move. He waited in anticipation for her to walk out so that he could surprise her. His mind began tossing around things that he wanted to say when she first realized who he was. *Surprise! Remember me? Hello Mother! Miss me?* He was having so much fun that he almost hated for it to come to an end.

Lucas reached across the seat and picked up the duffle bag. He set it on his lap and fondled the battered monogram that was worn from years of abuse. LRP. His mother bought him that bag and he'd carried it with him at all times. He opened the top and slowly felt the contents, recognizing each thing as his hand slid across. *Ah, there it is.* He curled his fingers around his favorite item – his father's almighty belt. He closed his eyes and watched as if he were watching television, the look on his father's face when he ripped it from his pants right before he left this world.

Lucas started the car and turned down the side street before getting out and walking towards the gallery careful not to be noticed. He stood, with his head down, against the end of the building that his mother walked towards as she left work. He inhaled long deep breaths and exhaled even longer. He had started to become concerned that his timing was off just when he noticed the door to the gallery open wide. Everything went silent except the little bell over the door that made a tinkling sound. This was it. This was the moment he'd waited for and instead of being completely elated, an inkling of doubt crept into his mind and caused him to pause. He swallowed hard, pushed aside the doubt, and watched her walk by. When she turned the corner, he fell in step behind her until he was close enough to touch her. He extended his hand but hesitated when he heard the faint sound of a song touch his ears. Things couldn't get any better. She was wearing headphones and had no idea that he was even there. *How stupid can you be to wear headphones walking alone at night in this city.*

Lucas was tired of all the distractions. He reached out again, and this time wrapped one arm around her throat and covered her mouth with the handkerchief in his other hand. He wished he could see her face but deep down he was glad he couldn't. She started to fight but was overcome by the chloroform and her body went limp. Lucas shoved his mother in the trunk of his car and drove in silence back to the little motel on Airline Hwy that he rented by the week. He backed his car into the parking spot right in front of his room and turned off the engine. His hands were shaking, and a tear fell from his eye as he battled with himself over what was about to take place. Lucas was used to the battle because the moment he decided that he was going to get his revenge, was the moment that he realized there were two different personalities that lived within his mind and from his experience, the darker one always prevailed. He wiped the tear from his face, looked in the rearview mirror and smiled.

CHAPTER 31

Charley Ann watched as E.R. tried to catch Logan. He pleaded with him to stop and listen, but Logan was unfazed or just didn't understand what E.R. was shouting at him. Logan ran through the back gate and seemed to disappear. Charley Ann turned to Ms. Morgan who was standing next to her as the scene unfolded.

"Ms. Morgan, could you please reach out to Logan and explain to him that we are trying to find Liam, not hurt him. You said they were like brothers when they were younger so maybe he would want to know Liam is missing. Do you have any idea why he reacted that way when he saw us?" Charley Ann hoped that she wanted to help them.

"Dear, I have no idea why he reacted that way. Like I said earlier, those boys found out something disturbing several years back that made them suspicious of new people. I know he still loves Liam like a brother and would want to help him. Should I call him and ask him to come back?" Ms. Morgan appeared worried.

E.R. arrived at the back door breathing heavily from chasing down Logan. He couldn't understand why he ran from them before he even met them. What was he running from? Did he have something to do with Liam's disappearance? E.R. filled with questions, refused to leave Alabama without getting some type of clarification because it was the only lead they had. He went inside and joined in the conversation and thanked Ms. Morgan for all of her help.

E.R. showed Ms. Morgan his badge and handed her a card with his office and cell phone number on it and asked her to call if she thought of anything that would be helpful. He also requested that she pass that information on to Logan and tell him to call the work number to verify his story. He wasn't sure why, but he felt like Logan had all the answers that he needed to find Liam and he was getting desperate to find Liam. They left the foster home and headed towards the diner. It was a longshot, but E.R. thought it was worth the try. They turned into the parking lot and chose a spot towards the back of the diner.

"We really need to get Logan to talk to us. I think you should go in first and see if he's back here. I'm sure Ms. Morgan called him when we left. Hopefully, he called the office and confirmed my identity. What do you think has him so spooked? I'm still trying to accept the fact that Liam had this secret life, and I had no clue."

"I'm sure if Liam didn't want to share his past with you, he had his reasons. Logan ran when he heard our unfamiliar voices talking about Liam and I believe it was because he was scared of something or someone. We need to gather as much information that was shared with them about their past. Something has Logan spooked and I would be willing to bet that Liam would behave in the same manner had he been here. That could be why Liam didn't share his past with you because maybe he felt that it would've put you in some sort of danger." Charley Ann didn't like to see E.R. upset.

"You go in the front door and see if he's there. I'll wait here and make sure he doesn't run out the back. Once you locate him, call my cell."

Charley Ann quietly opened the door and got out. She knew how important it was to talk to Logan and was a little nervous about spooking him. She walked towards the entrance and before she reached the front door, she saw Logan speaking to a customer. She lowered her head and walked in and asked for a table for two. The hostess seated her at a table right next to the kitchen. Charley Ann sat down pretending to review the menu while she called E.R. to inform him that Logan was there.

"Wait till he goes into the kitchen then approach him. I'll be waiting at the back door. See if you can get him to agree to talk to me. Be careful." E.R. waited outside of the kitchen door.

Charley Ann took a minute to gather herself. She thought about what she was going to say to Logan that would convince him to talk to them. She was deep in thought and didn't notice that someone had approached her table. When she looked up, she was staring into lovely dark green eyes, and she jumped.

"Oh, I'm sorry. Did I startle you?" Logan backed up a step as she looked up from the menu.

"Wait! Don't go. Just give me a minute. I just have some questions." Logan turned to go, so she blurted out, "Liam's in trouble!"

Logan froze. He thought of Liam and smiled before the corner of his lips turned down and fear set in. His instinct was to run but what if she was telling the truth. And if she wasn't, it was too late anyway because they know where he worked and had located the Morgan's home. He turned back to Charley Ann and with a soft voice told her that he would meet her outside in five minutes.

Charley Ann was apprehensive at first but the broken, exhausted look on Logan's face convinced her that he wasn't going to run. She waited at the table for a minute then proceeded out the door. Right before she walked out, she noticed pictures on the wall. They were pictures of the grand opening of the Diner and one of them had both Liam and Logan posing together out front. She hurried to look at the rest of the pictures because she didn't want to miss meeting with Logan. She dialed E.R. while she looked and was in the process of telling him the plan when she gasped. "Oh My God! I knew it!" Charley Ann exclaimed, "I gotta go. I'll see you out front in a minute." She hung up the phone and immediately opened her camera app to take a picture. She glanced at the other photos making sure she didn't miss anything, then ran out of the restaurant. When she reached the truck, E.R. was running towards her with fear in his eyes. She realized that she'd terminated the call before explaining what she'd found and that worried him.

Charley Ann threw her hands up and said, "I'm alright. Sorry for scaring you."

When E.R. saw that she was safe, he stopped, put his hands on his thighs and attempted to steady his breath. The sprint from the back door to the truck wasn't that far but his adrenaline hijacked his body and pushed him into panic mode.

Between breaths E.R. asked, "What happened?"

Charley Ann gave E.R. an encouraging glance then pointed behind him to Logan who was walking towards them with that same defeated look on his face. E.R. turned and noticed that he was looking into a face that missed a good chance to be Liam. The similarities were startling, and a slight gasp escaped E.R.'s lips. He composed himself and reached his hand out to Logan.

"Hi Logan, I'm E.R. and this is Charley Ann" As he introduced Charley Ann, E.R. looked into her face and noticed that she was bothered by something, yet he knew that she wasn't ready to reveal anything in front of Logan. E.R. clinched his jaw, sent her a slight smile, and then turned his focus to Logan.

Logan didn't take E.R.'s hand but instead shoved his into his pockets. His mannerisms suggested that he was unsettled about his decision to talk to them and wanted to get right to the point.

"What do you want? How do you know Liam?" Logan didn't look at them and was nervously keeping watch of the area around them.

E.R. leaned against his truck in an attempt to put Logan at ease.

"I work for the Louisiana Wildlife and Fisheries department and Liam is my partner. I understand that you grew up with Liam and I hoped that you could help us. A few days ago Liam went missing." E.R. noticed that Logan's disposition changed, and he seemed to relax momentarily.

Logan looked directly into E.R.'s eyes and without words expressed his deep concern for Liam. The intense look in his eyes softened and his body slouched as he searched for words.

"What happened to him?"

"We're not sure. How long have you been here in Alabama? Have you ever been to Grand Isle?" Charley Ann began firing questions at Logan.

E.R. shot her a look, but she didn't heed his silent warning and continued the inquisition.

"When's the last time you were in Louisiana? Have you been in contact with Liam?" Charley Ann wanted him to answer but didn't allow him time before she went on. "Do you have a girlfriend Logan?"

E.R. lifted his hands to stop Charley Ann's interrogation of Logan. She stopped abruptly and reached for her phone. She scrolled to the last picture she took and held it up for both of them to see.

"The girl directly behind you, is that your girlfriend?"

Logan took the phone and examined the photo. She watched as he looked at the photo to see if she could tell by his expression that he knew the person in question.

After a second, he handed the phone back to Charley Ann and simply and honestly said, "No."

E.R. took the phone and as his eyes scanned the photo, his facial expression changed from confusion to shock because he noticed the girl in the photo. He noticed her because it was Sam, their waitress, and Charley Ann's new best friend from Grand Isle.

"Does someone want to fill me in as to what's going on and who the mysterious person in the photo is?" Logan crossed his arms and waited for answers.

CHAPTER 32

After the disturbing discovery that Sam was in the recent photos from the diner, Logan decided that he would divulge the secret that he and Liam shared and tell them everything he knew about Liam's past. They also agreed that they needed to get back to Louisiana and step up the search for Liam and that Logan was going to join in that search.

"Just so you know, Liam's like a brother to me and I would die for him." Logan blurted that out as he walked away.

E.R. shouted back. "Just so you know, I feel the same way." The two men now had a mutual understanding and with it came a level of trust needed to work together. They shared information and decided to meet back at E.R.'s house to devise a plan to move forward in their search.

With so many people evacuating for the hurricane, they would be driving against traffic. E.R. liked the thought of not being slowed down with bumper-to-bumper traffic and prayed that the New Orleans Police Department had not put roadblocks in place to keep people from entering the city. They needed to get back home as soon as possible.

When E.R. got back into the truck his phone beeped. He removed the phone from his pocket and set it on the console while he secured his seatbelt. He pushed the button to start his truck and waited for his phone information to load. E.R. put the truck in reverse as he hit the button on the screen to play his messages. The first message was short and dated late the night before from his grandfather telling him about Douglas. As the next message started to play, the truck screeched to an abrupt stop and a chilling voice spilled from the speakers asking for help.

E.R. grabbed his phone and dialed Liam's number. Charley Ann started to say something, but he held up his hand. He needed time to process what was happening. *How did he miss that call?* Liam needed him and he wasn't there for him. E.R.'s throat was dry as he attempted to swallow. He looked at the phone and noticed that the message was sent at 6:13 that morning. That's when he was sleeping with Charley Ann in his arms and his phone was lost in the couch with a dead battery.

"He called this morning when we were sleeping but it just came through. That doesn't make sense." E.R. leaned against the steering wheel and let out a long slow breath. "At least we know he's still alive and he sounded like he was okay considering being locked away somewhere for the past few days. I need to call my grandfather to update him. We need to get back home and search for him."

E.R.'s mind was all over the place, and he was an emotional wreck.

E.R. gathered his thoughts as he put the truck in drive. He glanced in his rearview mirror and noticed that Logan was still behind him and hoped that he could help go over everything they already knew with a fresh pair of eyes. Maybe they missed something that would lead them to Liam. He knew that Charley Ann was watching him and that she was also frustrated about missing Liam's call. He wanted to reassure her that he was alright, but he wasn't sure himself and instead focused on the road ahead.

E.R. was confident that the man in the hospital, Lucas Ricci, was deeply involved in the whole mess. He was also positive that Sam was involved, but he wasn't sure about the connection. Douglas must've followed us to Grand Isle, but Sam had a job and was working when they met her. He thought back to their conversation with Sam going over everything she said. She claimed that she'd just started working at the Marina that day which was also convenient for her when she claimed to not know anyone or anything. He wasn't suspicious of Sam until he saw her in the photo with Logan and Liam.

"What did Sam say that caused you to question her the way you did? I noticed that you were asking questions to observe her reaction. Did she say something that triggered your suspicion or were you just being cautious?"

"After everything that happened, I was cautious about trusting anyone. At first, I thought it was just coincidence that we met in the bathroom but then she seemed to come on so strong offering us a ride to Artie's and then asking for my phone number to keep in touch." Charley Ann perked up and grabbed her purse from the floor of the truck. "E.R., I have Sam's phone number! She gave it to me at Artie's after she'd asked for mine and I told her I had lost it. She retrieved the napkin from her purse and stared at it for a moment. "Do you think I should call it?"

"No. I'm gonna call my grandfather to see if we can have it traced. We can't be positive that she's involved with Liam's disappearance, but I believe she is, and I don't want her to know we are on to her." E.R. was optimistic for the first time since this started. This was the first real lead they had, and he didn't want to mess it up. There was a small chance that she was innocent and wasn't involved but he could feel it in his gut that she played a part in it.

E.R. called his grandfather and gave him the information on Sam and asked him to trace the phone number. He checked his mirror again to make sure Logan was still following them. He was still reeling at how much Logan looked like Liam. He wore his hair longer and pulled back in a ponytail and he was a little heavier than Liam, but they sure did look alike. E.R. would swear they were brothers if not twins had Logan not confirmed the opposite.

Before they left Alabama and once Logan decided to trust E.R., he opened up about their past and shared what they had learned from the nun when they were sixteen that changed their lives forever. "We were both dropped off at the convent just a few days apart. The nuns secretly placed us with the Morgan's without proper paperwork purposely avoiding a paper trail. In the beginning, we remembered our past lives but as time rolled on the memories faded - too much for a four-year-old to hold on to." Logan was silent for a moment as he revisited that time in his life.

"After the initial shock of being abandoned by our mothers, we bonded with the Morgan's and each other and grew up in a peaceful and happy home. Through the years, we shared with each other the desire to find our biological parents, but it wasn't until we were sixteen that we actually made the first attempt. Liam was the one that urged me to go to the convent to talk to the nun that placed us in foster care with the Morgan's. I didn't want to admit it to Liam, but I was afraid of being rejected all over again. In reality, we were both abandoned by the one person in the world that was supposed to give love unconditionally and I wasn't sure that they wanted to be found." E.R. could see the sadness and turmoil in Logans eyes as he spoke.

"We went to the convent repeatedly attempting to talk to the nun but were repeatedly turned away. We were told they were unable to share any information with us. Then, one day we were summoned back to the convent by Sister Mary Grace, the 95-year-old nun that placed us with the Morgan's. We dropped everything and hurried to the convent because both of us were excited with anticipation that we were finally going to get answers. We were escorted through the convent and to her bedside. Sister Mary Grace was lying in bed with the rosary in one hand and two envelopes in the other. She looked up at us standing at her bedside as her lips formed into a tender smile. Her eyes glazed over as she attempted to speak." That was many years ago, but he could remember it like it was yesterday.

He recalled the joy on her face when she saw them. "Look at you two. Such beautiful young men. I've watched you flourish through the years and have never regretted my decision. As you can see, my final hours are near, and I'd hoped that I would go to see my Lord and Savior knowing you both were safe." Sister Mary Grace coughed as she tried to continue. Her voice was shallow, and she was struggling to go on, but she knew that they had to be warned. "I want you both to know that your mothers loved you very much and only abandoned you to keep you safe. I can still remember the sadness and desperation that was in their voices as they explained everything to me. It was quite remarkable that you two came to me just days apart from similar situations, and I can assure you that you are not related. I know that you've reached out to us on several occasions for information, but I swore to keep this a secret as long as you were safe." She coughed again and this time took longer to recover. Her hand shook as she reached out and handed them the envelopes. "You'll find all the answers that you seek right here in these envelopes." As Logan extended his hand to receive them, she lifted her head from the pillow, grabbed his hand and with every bit of strength she said, "Liam, you must be careful. He came for you the other day. You must be careful." She laid her head back down on the pillow and struggled to catch her breath. She closed her eyes momentarily then opened them and warned him again. "He's the devil that one. He must not find you. Liam, everything you need to know is in that envelope, so you can stop inquiring about your past. He must not find you. He must not find you." She repeated that same message over and over again until she drifted off to sleep.

Logan continued to explain the details of that day to E.R. and Charley Ann. "We were shaking when we left the convent because we hadn't expected to hear the powerful message that Sister Mary Grace had for us. We didn't know what to do with the information at first and were hesitant to open the envelopes. Again Liam opened his and encouraged me to open mine. The envelopes contained our birth certificates and a letter from our mothers. Sister Mary Grace said she had insisted on the letters because she wanted them to be able to explain in their own words why they felt like leaving us was their only option. After we read the letters and spoke to Sister Mary Grace about the lurking danger that was near, we decided that we needed to leave the Morgan's and get "lost" for a while. Liam and I stayed in touch, but we were very cautious not to leave a trail. We'd hoped that one day this would all be behind us, but I think that was just foolish thinking that we could run from the evil. I just hope it's not too late to save Liam." After Logan went into more details about the letters, they decided they had to get on the road because the weather was getting worse. And if they had to shelter in place, they definitely didn't want to be in another state.

Logan tried to remain calm as he followed E.R. back to Louisiana and back to where one of the most important people in the world to him was missing and probably fighting for his life. He hoped he and Liam would be reunited soon in safety once and for all.

CHAPTER 33

The weather was deteriorating quickly making it difficult to see the roads clearly. E.R.'s truck was fighting against the wind to stay on course as he raced to get back home. He felt hopeful that Sam's phone would lead them to Lucas and help them locate Liam. He thought about Sam's friendly smile and her kind eyes and shuddered at the idea that she fooled them into thinking that she was just a stranger. E.R. still didn't know what her connection was to Liam's disappearance, but he was sure there was one. The fact that she was in Grand Isle along with Douglas caused E.R. to settle on the idea that the two of them were working together. And if that was the case, maybe Sam locked Charley Ann in the container not Douglas who they originally blamed. E.R. wasn't sure about anything but at least now they had someone they could get to and possibly find answers.

Charley Ann leaned her head back and closed her eyes. She and E.R. had been running crazy and were exhausted both physically and mentally. They were only about thirty minutes from home where they would be off to the races again. She tried to imagine what life would be like with E.R. under normal circumstances. From the minute they met, it had been one emergency after another and while they'd managed to spend some down time learning about each other, most of their time together was in the midst of chaos. She was happy that she got to see the type of guy he was under pressure and admired his loyalty and perseverance, but she wanted to know what he would be like on a simple date. She had a difficult time trusting herself after her bad judgment of Brian. He was a monster disguised as sweet and loyal and his perseverance in pursuing her was what she liked about him. She never wanted to misjudge someone like that again and was determined to learn from her mistakes.

The truck came to an abrupt stop and Charley Ann was jolted awake. She looked around and realized they were back at E.R.'s house and Griff's truck was in the driveway. E.R. glanced at Charley Ann and after noticing she was awake jumped out the truck and headed for the door. "Wait for Logan and show him in when he gets here. Thanks." E.R. was anxious to see what his grandfather had discovered about Sam… *Sam who. We don't even know her last name! Thank God Charley Ann got her phone number.*

Griff was sitting at the kitchen table when E.R. walked in. E.R. was taken aback at his worn-down appearance. He had dark circles under his grief-stricken eyes and the weight of tension was reflected in his slouched shoulders. He heard E.R. walk into the house but didn't look up immediately. E.R.'s heart was shattered as he looked at his grandfather who was usually full of energy and life but now seemed broken and defeated.

"Hey Paw. You okay?" E.R. pulled out a chair to sit down. Thunder rumbled and the wind howled outside the window. When Griff heard his grandson's voice he perked up and smiled.

"Yeah, I'm fine." He straightened up in his chair and started to bring E.R. up to speed on his search for Sam.

"Trey just called. He traced the phone number you gave me. It belongs to a Samantha Trahan who lives here in Marrero. He also ran a background check on her and she's clean except for a few traffic violations. He's gonna continue to look deeper into her background but he wanted to let us know of her last known location. You know the storm is really kicking up out there and the water is already coming over the banks." Griff seemed to be leading up to something important. "I'm not sure it's safe to be out on the roads until this thing passes. I know that's not what you want to hear but it's the facts." He knew his grandson was anxious to find Liam and would risk everything to do so.

"Paw, where is Sam?"

Griff tried to dance around the question for as long as he could but knew that eventually he would have to tell E.R. that Sam was at the Fleming Cemetery. And the minute he shared that information E.R. would be out the door ignoring the danger he faced on the roads in the bad weather.

Like on cue the wind rumbled across the windows and thunder roared reminding them the Hurricane was close. Both men jumped as a loud crackling noise sounded then the lights flickered several times before the fierce pounding of rain slammed against the house. More outer bands of the hurricane had arrived which kicked off tense hours of waiting for the danger to pass. E.R. could tell his grandfather didn't want to share the information he had with him because the storm was raging, and it was dangerous to be out, but he felt like it was his own decision to make.

"Paw, tell me Sam's location. You know if we don't find Liam soon, it'll be too late to save him. I need to help him. Please." E.R. pleaded with his grandfather.

"She's at the Fleming Cemetery."

E.R. was speechless. That was the last place he would've thought they would find her. His mind raced as he attempted to figure out what she would be doing at the cemetery, especially during a hurricane. If she was from Marrero like Trey reported, then she was familiar with hurricanes and knew that it would be dangerous to be in a place like Lafitte that was outside the levee protection system. Once they closed the flood gates she would be stuck until the hurricane passed and the water subsided. E.R. saw the concern in his grandfather's eyes and didn't want to upset him, but he had to go.

Griff recognized the look on E.R.'s face and while he was concerned about his decision to go, he knew that it was the right thing to do. After all, Liam was family. The memory of E.R. holding Tab's body in his arms tugged at Griff's heart, but he pushed his feelings aside and prepared himself to help his grandson. He stood, grabbed his jacket, and said, "Let's Roll."

E.R. was stunned but glad to see his grandfather back to his old self. He smiled at Griff, pulled him into an embrace and then the two men headed towards the door where Charley Ann was coming in with Logan. She smiled as the men approached.

"Sam's at the cemetery." E.R. introduced Logan to Griff as they walked by and the confused look on Griff's face told him that he noticed Logan's resemblance to Liam right away.

Charley Ann fell into step behind the men and said, "Let's Roll."

The force from the wind grabbed the screen door and slammed it shut. They ran through the already flooded yard to the truck shielding themselves from the stinging rain. A trash can came barreling towards the truck, bounced off the side and disappeared down the street. Normally E.R. was not a fan of hurricanes, but his adrenaline was pumping at the thought of finding Liam, so he was able to override his anxiety with optimism.

E.R. headed to the Leo Kerner Parkway and turned towards Lafitte. The flood gates would already be closed on the old highway and even though there would be a check point at the levee in Crown Point, he prayed they would let him pass. When they reached the levee, E.R.'s stomach dropped, and his optimism was crushed. The entire area on the other side of the levee looked like one big open lake. There was no way his truck would make it through the still rising water that the hurricane was pushing in from the Gulf of Mexico.

E.R. got out of the truck, stood on top of the levee, and tried to comprehend what he was seeing. He had never seen the entire area flooded like this before and the site was disturbing to see. Griff walked up beside him and stood speechless. He knew that if there was that much water on the road, there was water in his own house. Lafitte had been prone to flooding but most of Crown Point was usually spared but that was before the new levees and installation of the new pumps in the Intracoastal Canal. They, like Grand Isle, were outside the levee protection system and left to fend on their own.

E.R. snapped back to reality and realized what Griff had already figured out and whispered, "I'm sorry Paw."

Griff knew that there was nothing he could do about his house, so he decided to forge on with the task at hand. "We need a boat." Griff pointed to a few boats that had been launched at the levee and were actually operating on the highway. E.R. recognized a friend of his and flagged him over. They were running rescue missions for people who decided to stay but underestimated the amount of flooding that was rapidly coming. He agreed to run them to Griff's house so that they could get his boat. God willing they would be able to get to the boat and launch it in the driveway. That was the only way they were going to get to the cemetery.

"Do you think that Sam went to the cemetery and got stranded when the water started to rise? And what would she be doing at the cemetery? Liam has to be there. From the description that he gave of the area he was trapped in, it's not waterproof. We have to hurry." E.R. pushed the nagging thoughts that were flooding his mind back and tried to remain optimistic. "That's it! He must be in one of those old, dilapidated gravesites that have been there forever." His heart sank as he thought of all the water that covered the ground. He hoped and prayed that he wasn't too late. "I should've known that he was there. I thought I heard him call my name a few times, but it was so faint that I thought I imagined it, but looking back..." E.R. shook his head. He searched his mind for the memory of that night he went to meet Liam. The gravesite E.R. fell into was at the base of the Indian Mound that was home to a beautiful old oak tree. Liam could be inside one of the gravesites up on top of the hill and they would still have time to get to him, but the water was rising quickly so they had to hurry.

E.R. was having difficulty wrapping his head around the situation. He still didn't know exactly what was going on or who had Liam. The motive was still a mystery unless Logan was right, and it was a family member who wanted to harm Liam. Logan shared with him the dire warning the nun gave them on her death bed. She revealed that they had a lot in common because both Liam's father and Logan's father were very dangerous men and connected to even more dangerous men. She praised their mothers because they made the ultimate sacrifice and put their children's safety above all else when they dropped them off at the convent. Things went well for years but when they were sixteen, Liam's father finally tracked him to the convent and demanded to know where he was. Sister Mary Grace raised her voice enough to make it very clear the man was a devil in disguise and didn't have good intentions towards his son or his ex-wife. Liam's dad was high up in the drug cartel and extremely dangerous. She was worried he would eventually find them, so she summoned the boys to the convent and urged them to move on and stay vigilant.

E.R. wondered if Liam's father finally tracked him down and that's who took him. Logan was eager to help and tried to explain everything he could about their past, but E.R. had a gut feeling like he was holding something back. He believed that Logan loved Liam and wanted to help find him, but knew he was still keeping a secret. He pushed that thought back and would worry about it later. They were at his grandfather's house and needed to get to the boat.

Griff jumped out of the rescue boat into thigh deep water. He stood for a moment as he digested the severity of the situation. A small wave formed in front of him, and he noticed a redfish swim by. He looked around to his neighbors' houses and they were all flooded. The mailbox that was usually about four feet above the road was now barely above the water. The site of all the destruction took

Griff's breath away. Again he shoved all of his emotions away and focused on getting to the boat.

Griff opened the garage door and was stunned to see that everything was turned upside down and floating. They were able to open the overhead door and drag the trailer that housed the boat out onto the carport. They positioned the trailer so they could push the boat off into the deepest water that was on side of the carport. Thankfully, the weather had calmed because they were in between the early rain bands which arrived before the hurricane. They all got into the boat, located the life jackets and were growing anxious by the minute. Griff trimmed up the motor before he started it just in case the water was too shallow in places. They were finally on their way.

C H A P T E R   3 4

Under normal circumstances it would take Griff about ten minutes to get to the Fleming Cemetery, but the current bad conditions would probably add to that time. He was baffled at the idea that he was driving the boat on the highway that he usually traveled in his truck. He drove slowly so that he didn't cause a wake and push more water into someone's house. Crown Point looked like a ghost town under water. There were a few homes that had been raised over the years to protect against the floods, but it was devasting to see that most of the other homes took on water. He wondered about all of the wildlife in the area and was sick to think that they had no way of getting out of the water unless they got into a tree or found high ground, but Griff doubted there was too much high ground left. Griff thought about his own house and how heartbroken Abby would be when she sees their home in that condition. At the same time he was grateful she was out of harm's way. Everyone in the boat rode in silence trying to absorb the chaos they were witnessing as Griff continued on towards the Intracoastal Canal. From the time they got into the boat, all sorts of unusual things had floated by, the latest being a huge log the length of Griff's boat.

They were close to the launch when they heard the sound of a dog yelping. Charley Ann noticed a dog on top of his doghouse surrounded by water. She stood up and yelled for them to stop before she jumped out of the boat and waded towards the dog.

"Wait Charley Ann, he might be mean. Be careful!" E.R. attempted to jump out of the boat and go after her, but Griff grabbed his arm.

"Give her a minute." Griff met E.R.'s eyes and calmed him down.

E.R. remained standing ready to jump in after her if needed and waited to see the dog's response as she approached it. The poor thing was soaking wet and looked scared to death. As Charley Ann got closer, the dog wagged its tail. Before she knew it, he leaped into her arms knocking her down and under the water. She jumped up, cradling the dog, and turned to reassure everyone she was alright. She looked around to see if anyone was home as she walked up to the house and onto the front porch. The house seemed to be deserted. She let the dog, which turned out to be a small Lab puppy, down and waited as Griff maneuvered the boat closer to her. E.R. jumped onto the porch and looked for a collar, but he didn't have one. They had assumed he belonged to the house where they found him but couldn't be sure.

"We can't leave him here alone without making sure these people are coming home and we have no way of knowing that." E.R. looked down at the soaking wet puppy and then over at Charley Ann who was also soaking wet and said, "The dog can sit on your lap."

Charley Ann smiled and without saying a word stepped into the boat with the dog in one hand and E.R. holding the other. She could hardly keep the puppy in her arms because he was so relieved to have been rescued that he was showering Charley Ann and anyone that came close to him with a kiss. They all shared a much-needed laugh before moving on to the more serious issue of finding Liam.

Once they made it to the Intercoastal Canal Griff trimmed down the motor and put the pedal to the medal. The conditions were worsening by the minute and Griff knew they were in for a rough ride. He wasn't sure how Charley Ann and Logan would handle the boat ride, but he couldn't worry about that now. Going out in the boat during a hurricane was definitely uncharted territory for all of them. He was grateful E.R. was with him because he knew what to watch for as they headed to Lafitte in the rising water. Usual landmarks disappeared when the water was high and could prove to be dangerous. Luckily there wasn't any boat traffic because everyone was hunkered down and waiting on the hurricane. If circumstances were different, they would be doing the same. The situation was treacherous and both Griff and E.R. knew they had a small window of opportunity before this could turn into a catastrophe. Griff said a prayer and tried not to think how ridiculous and dangerous it was to drive a boat to Lafitte as a hurricane approached.

Another squall was passing through causing the winds to whip up again and drive the heavy rain sideways making it difficult to see. Griff pointed, alerting them they were almost there. The boat rocked back and forth, and the stinging rain had no mercy. E.R. stood to scope out a place that would be safe to tie off the boat once they reached the cemetery. There was a Barrier put up a few years ago to protect against flooding but the rising water had toppled over that already. Griff was able to kill the motor, glide right over the wall, and coast all the way to the back of the Indian Mound. He felt like his stomach was in his throat as he surveilled the area and noticed that most of the graves at the bottom of the hill had already succumbed to the rising water.

E.R. hopped out of the front of the boat and found an old tombstone to tie the boat off to while the others were getting ready to get out. Logan jumped out next to E.R. and before anyone else exited the boat E.R. put up his hands to speak. Before he even got a word out, they heard a low whimpering sound coming from the other side of the mound. They were all motionless as they strained to recognize the sound between the howl of the wind and the noise of pounding rain.

"Stop! Why are you doing this? Are you crazy? I didn't agree to any of this! Where is Douglas? I want to go home now!" The voice was mumbled and mixed with whimpering but without a doubt, it belonged to Sam.

E.R. and Logan crouched down, and Griff and Charley Ann sat back down in the boat. Thankfully, the puppy was exhausted and had fallen asleep in a nice warm blanket underneath the console of the boat. E.R. got down on the ground and crawled towards the top to see if he could see exactly what was happening. All he saw was the top of someone's head and Sam who had been crying and looked frightened of the person she was with. E.R. crawled back to the group and reported what he saw, and suggested Griff stay in the boat with Charley Ann and he and Logan each take a side to flank them in. Griff started to object but E.R. quickly reminded him they were the only two people who could operate the boat in case they needed a quick getaway.

Griff lifted his hands in surrender and whispered, "Be careful." He reached into the side of his jacket, unholstered his weapon and extended it to Logan with a look that asked if he knew how to use it. Logan nodded with a yes and took the gun from Griff. They all sat there waiting to see if they would hear more from Sam and whoever was with her. There was more whimpering that turned into sobs every so often which indicated that Sam was terrified of something or someone.

"What are you going to do with him? Oh my God! You are crazy!" Sam had started to scream but her screams were quickly muffled. It sounded like a struggle was happening. Then it went quiet again. The frogs and the crickets continued to chirp, and E.R. was reminded of the night he came to the cemetery looking for Liam. A shiver ran through his body, and he began to shake. He took a few deep breaths to slow his heart rate down enough to hear another voice.

"Shut up before I put you down there with him!" Sam continued to sob but stopped screaming.

"Did y'all hear that. He must be talking about Liam." E.R. had a wild look in his eyes and wanted to rush in to get Liam.

"Wait. Slow down. He might have a gun or a weapon. Go slow and follow the plan. Let Logan go around to the left and you go right. E.R., I know you are anxious to find Liam but let's not force the hand of a crazy man if we don't have to. Be smart and try to assess the situation before he sees you, then you could possibly try to negotiate with him. E.R. did you hear me?" Griff was concerned that his grandson was too anxious and that maybe he should go instead of him, but he knew that would never happen.

E.R. and Logan went over the plan to make sure they were on the same page. After assessing the situation, E.R. was going to approach first, and Logan would be back up if needed. E.R. noticed a strange look in Logan's eyes but chalked it up to the stress of the situation. Their eyes met one last time and E.R. prayed that he could trust Logan and that he could be counted on to help save Liam.

As the two men got into their positions, Logan waited for E.R. to make his move. He knew that E.R. had doubts about his loyalty to Liam, but they were unfounded. He loved Liam like a brother and Liam loved him the same.

They had been together since they were young and had made sacrifices for each other without even realizing it. It wasn't until Sister Mary Grace agreed to tell them the truth that they both realized the actual extent of the sacrifice that was made and the danger they were in. Both men maintained that they would die for each other, but Logan refused to let Liam die for him. He was going to set things right once and for all.

Lucas leaned back against the tomb that imprisoned Liam and glared at Sam. The veins in his neck were so pronounced that they looked like they would pop at any moment. His red shirt matched the color of his face and even though he was soaking wet, his adrenaline made him feel as though his temperature was boiling hot. He couldn't comprehend how he always ended up surrounded by incompetent people. Both Douglas and Sam seemed to be smart skilled people when he first met them. Sure, Douglas was a drug addict, but Lucas felt like that was all the more reason for him to be loyal to the one person supplying him with his drugs. And he was loyal to the end, just not as capable as Lucas had hoped.

Lucas thought he could rely on Douglas to carry out the dirty work, but it quickly became apparent that his help was inadequate. When they followed Liam and the girl from Bourbon Heat to that cemetery, he instructed Douglas to separate the two so that Lucas could kidnap Liam, but he failed. They hadn't expected that another guy would show up and almost ruin the plan. The deviation from the plan rattled Douglas causing Lucas to step up and get his own hands dirty. He apologized to the man as he strangled the breath out of him and explained that it wasn't personal. He just couldn't let anything, or anyone get in the way. After the man stopped fighting and became unconscious, he simply disposed of the body by pushing him into the bayou and figured the gators would take it from there.

Unfortunately, Liam and the girl rescued the other guy from the grave and left the cemetery. Lucas was furious that his plan was foiled but decided he would wait at the cemetery for Liam to come back and retrieve his truck. Lucas and Douglas waited, and just as suspected Liam returned, and the game was back on. Now it was time to finish the job and enjoy the satisfaction he waited so long for.

Lucas shifted his weight and noticed Sam flinch. He could smell the fear in the air and grew more excited with each passing moment. When he met Sam, he was quite taken by her because she came off as not only tough and self-confident but compassionate too. Under any other circumstances he would've considered dating her but currently he needed someone to help carry out his plan for vengeance and it had to be someone who couldn't be traced back to him. Her genuine concern and desire to help her longtime friend Douglas made her the perfect pawn. Not long after he befriended Lucas, he met Sam and convinced her he was the victim of an overpowering abusive wife. He declared that she cheated on him with his estranged brother, and she was trying to take everything from him. He pleaded with her to help him get enough dirt on them to help his case and she fell for it. What Lucas really wanted was to kidnap the two people that were most important to his long-lost brother and make him watch as he killed them slowly.

When Douglas followed Charley Ann and E.R. to Grand Isle, and to the Bridge Side Marina, he tried to call Lucas, but there was no answer. He wasn't sure what to do next but remembered that Sam just so happened to be there visiting her cousin. Lucas had given Douglas instructions to follow Charley Ann and E.R. and at the first opportunity, bring them to him unharmed. Douglas hated to lie to Sam, but he knew that Lucas had fed her this sob story and had no choice but to go along with it. Douglas hadn't known Lucas for very long, but he knew in his gut not to cross him. Sam had promised to help poor Lucas in any way she could, so Douglas played along and talked her into befriending Charley Ann.

Lucas had hoped Douglas and Sam would've been able to secure E.R. and Charley Ann for him in Grand Isle, but of course Douglas was high, and paranoid. Sam refused to play along when she realized Lucas wanted her to do more than just get information for him. Lucas realized that he would have to be more involved if he were to carry out his plans which he fully intended to do.

Lucas hadn't counted on the shed at Liam's house collapsing down on him. He was almost exposed, and his plans ruined, but as usual incompetency is everywhere, so he was able to slip out of the hospital unnoticed. When he finally reached Douglas and found out that he and Sam failed to secure Charley Ann and E.R. he was furious. He ordered Douglas to get back to Marrero and to take Sam with him. They attempted to scope out E.R.'s house and wait for another opportunity to come along but ran out of time because the hurricane was coming in fast, and he had to get to Liam before the rising water flooded the tomb and drowned him.

Lucas looked down into the tomb and was grateful that he chose one that was close to the top of the mound. If he'd chosen differently, Liam would already be dead and would've robbed him of the opportunity to watch him suffer as Lucas killed him himself. When they arrived, his dear brother was frantically trying to plead his case, but Lucas didn't want to hear any of his excuses. He'd carried Sam from her car to the tomb because she was still unconscious from the chloroform. She'd threatened to call the police and left him no choice because leaving loose ends was not an option. Lucas drove away from the swamp after an alligator had taken care of poor Douglas, so he no longer had to worry about him.

By the time Sam regained consciousness, Liam had worn himself out and was lying silently on the floor of the tomb. She woke up and immediately started to demand that he let her go. Sam was a feisty one. That pleased Lucas but at the same time saddened him. He wasn't ready to get rid of her just yet but wanted her to shut up. Sam's rantings caught Liam's attention and he was back up and this time pleading with her.

"Leave her alone! What do you want? Who are you?" Liam was confused and had no idea who the girl was, but she was clearly scared and that tugged on his emotions.

"Well hello again" Lucas smiled down at Liam. "I see you still haven't accepted the situation you're in. I am in control, not you." Lucas laughed and grabbed Sam by the hair. "You don't even know this girl and you want to help her. You fool." Lucas shoved Sam to the ground.

"Wait! Please tell me who you are. What do you want? Let's talk please. I can help you."

"Help me. You don't even know who I am. How can you help me?" Lucas was entertained by Liam's frustration. He sat down on the ground next to the top of the tomb he'd pushed open earlier and stared down at his brother. "You have no idea who I am do you. Look at me! How do you not know who I am?" Lucas yelled as he spoke.

"I know who you are!"

Lucas jumped up just as E.R. rounded the mound and lunged towards him. He attempted to stand but E.R. was on top of him before he could get up, so he reached for his gun. The two wrestled back and forth before Lucas was able to break free and raise his gun, daring E.R. to come at him again. Lucas laughed as he tried to calm down and think. "This is even better than I thought. I have been trying to get to you for some time now." Lucas was still pointing his gun at E.R. and motioned for Sam to stand next to him. "Now, please give me a minute to think things out."

"You are a monster!" Sam leaped towards Lucas, but before she reached him, E.R. grabbed her and shoved her behind him. He held up his hands assuring Lucas he wasn't going to attack. E.R. looked down in the tomb and was relieved to see Liam alive and the woman in white standing over him like a shield. He quickly brought his gaze back to Lucas, trying to buy some time because he knew Logan was watching and would be waiting for an opportunity to make his move.

"I'm here now. Can we please talk." A loud cracking sound forced them all to look up just in time to see a large branch tumble to the ground right below them. The intense winds were bending the trees like they were made of rubber.

Lucas wiped the rain from his face and moved closer to the opening of the tomb. He smiled at Liam as he raised his gun at E.R. and ordered him to come closer. He wanted to make sure that Liam could watch his friend die otherwise he wouldn't suffer like Lucas wanted him to.

Liam became frantic again and scratched at the walls in at an attempt to climb out of the tomb. Sam noticed the look in Lucas' eyes and knew that he was going to pull the trigger. She leaped forward again just as Logan came around from the other side of the mound and caught Lucas' attention. The distraction caused him to fire the gun, but it missed his target. E.R. watched as the woman in white appeared and was standing over Lucas. The grief she had endured was written all over her face. All of a sudden, she was right in front of his face with her mouth open wide and her arms waving in the air. Lucas stumbled backwards at the sight of her and lost his balance.

Sam tackled Lucas to the ground and E.R. jumped on top this time subduing him.

"Hello brother." Logan walked up and looked down at Lucas with pity.

"What! No! Who are you? You are not my brother! Liam's my brother!" Lucas was screaming uncontrollably as E.R. restrained him.

Charley Ann and Griff heard the gunfire and came running around the mound to find Lucas being restrained by E.R., Sam holding a gun and Logan hanging over the top of the tomb talking to Liam. Charley Ann headed straight for Sam, but E.R. warned her off. "Charley Ann no! She's on our side." Charley Ann stopped abruptly and looked at Sam who lowered the gun and began sobbing uncontrollably.

Griff helped E.R. with Lucas who was still screaming at Logan and then they helped get Liam out of the tomb. Aside from being waterlogged from all of the rain that had gathered at the bottom of the tomb, he was in good shape. Logan pulled off his raincoat and wrapped it around Liam. "Thank God you're alright. He almost killed you." Logan was visibly upset.

"I can't believe you're here. How did y'all find me?" Liam was struggling to stand.

Logan helped him up and let him lean on him as they both walked over to Lucas who was screaming, laughing, and crying all at the same time. "Let me go! Get off of me! You think you won!"

As the two men got closer, Lucas became very still, and his eyes jumped from Logan to Liam and back to Logan. His mind was struggling to comprehend what was happening and then as if a light bulb went off, he understood.

Logan looked at Lucas and was disgusted by what he saw. "What happened to you was not my fault. I had no idea where you were just like you didn't know where I was. Why do you hate me so much that you wanted me dead?" Logan searched for some familiar look on Lucas' face but couldn't find one.

E.R. watched in awe as the woman in white was still hovering over Lucas. He looked around and determined that he was the only one who could see her, so he remained silent. They all listened as Logan explained that he and Liam's identities were switched when they were dropped off at the convent and when Sister Mary Grace summoned them, she warned them that Lucas and his father were searching for Liam and that they were in danger. Logan immediately wanted to switch back to his proper identity because he didn't want anything to happen to Liam, but Liam refused and was determined to protect Logan.

"Our father was a joke. He tried to find you and mother for years but failed. I was the one who found the convent and I was the one who found you! He was a horrible man, and I was the one who was beaten every day because he couldn't find y'all. And y'all left me there! How could a mother leave her child with a monster like that?" Lucas was enraged and before they knew it, he broke free, ran to Sam, and grabbed onto the gun. They struggled and the gun fired. Lucas fell to his knees and then ironically toppled into the open tomb that recently held Liam. They all rushed to the tomb and saw that Lu-cas was still conscious lying on the ground.

"Well brother, I assure you that you don't have to wor-ry about those monsters anymore. I killed our father and then tracked down our mother. You should've seen the look of disbelief and shock on her face when I drove that knife deep into her belly where she once nurtured me. She begged and pleaded and tried to convince me that she loved me, but I knew it was all lies. It was way too late to make amends. She had to pay for abandoning me." Lucas choked before he teared up again. "Why did y'all leave me with a monster brother? Why?" Lucas choked again as he drew his last breath.

E.R. watched as the woman in white wrapped herself around Lucas and looked up at Logan with soft, tearful eyes. That's when E.R. realized that the lady in white was the ghost of their mother and he prayed that she was final-ly at peace.

Griff called the local sheriff and waited for them to come out to the cemetery to retrieve Lucas' body. Griff and the sheriff were personal friends and agreed it was in everyone's best interest to get out of Lafitte quickly and meet at the hospital for questioning because the water was rising at an alarming rate. Liam was strong enough to get to Griff's boat where they all piled in and headed back to higher ground. Griff radioed ahead and had an ambulance meet them at the V shape levee to transport Liam to the hospital. The rest of them piled into E.R.'s truck. They rode in silence absorbing the bizarre chain of events that had unfolded before their eyes.

The ambulance reached the hospital before they did and took Liam into the emergency room. Griff hopped out of the truck and ran straight to the elevators. He got in and pressed the button for the third floor. His mind was running in several directions as he rode the elevator up. He was shocked to learn that Liam and Logan had swapped identities and were willing to die for each other. He found comfort in knowing that E.R. had such a great guy for a best friend. Griff thought about Tab and goose bumps covered his body. *I can't imagine life without Tab.* The elevator door opened, and he sprinted passed the nurses station and burst into room 318 to find Tab sitting up in the bed. He ran, wrapped his arms around him and almost knocked the wind out of him.

"It's good to see you too buddy!" Tab returned the embrace. He thought he was going to die out there in the swamp and while he doesn't know how they found him, he is eternally grateful they did.

When Griff finally released Tab, he gave him a lecture. "Don't you ever go off without backup again. You could've died out there. How did you end up in the swamp?"

"When I dropped you off at E.R.'s house, I ran back over to Liam's to take one last look around. Something didn't sit right with me when we had left earlier so I decided since I was close, I would go back and satisfy that nagging gut feeling. When I walked around the back of the shed, someone hit me with a 2 X 4 and ran. I chased him until he jumped into a black sedan. I ran back to my truck and followed them through the neighborhood and onto the old highway headed towards Lafitte. Believe it or not, a deer ran out by the big curve and hit the front of my truck causing me to jerk to the right and to lose control. The car that I was chasing backed up to where I went off the road, so I ran deeper into the swamp hoping they would give up and go away. Lucas forced Douglas to come after me and as you know, he had an unfortunate encounter with a big gator. Griff that thing was huge. I don't know how I missed it because I had to run right past the thing."

Tab's happy expression faded, and he thought of the guy that was with him in the swamp. He looked up at Griff and before he could ask, Griff explained that Douglas was near death when the paramedics arrived but because of Tab's intervention and a miraculous miracle, he survived to see another day. He lost his arm, but the doctors think he'll make a complete recovery. Lucas was not so lucky.

E.R., Charley Ann, Logan, and Sam waited in the E.R. to make sure that Liam was going to be alright. The emergency room doctors checked out Liam and aside from being a little dehydrated, determined he was in good shape, and he could go home. They all joined Griff in Tab's room and realized they had formed a new bond that would never be broken.

While they waited to be questioned by the sheriff, E.R. was able to talk to Liam privately to find out where his head was in all of this. He wanted to know if he had feelings for Charley Ann because E.R. had grown fond of her over the past few days and really wanted to see where things would lead to. He would never move in on Charley Ann if Liam was interested in her.

"So what do you think about Charley Ann? She was a big help over the last few days. She's a tough one too. She really knows how to handle herself." Liam was smiling as E.R. talked about Charley Ann.

"Look at you all flustered over a girl." Liam smiled and continued to tease E.R. about his apparent feelings. "I thought you swore off women a long time ago."

"Hey man. If you like her just say the word and I'll back off. I know you were interested in her at Bourbon Heat and the two of you spent time together afterwards." E.R. was anxiously waiting for a response.

"You got it all wrong, brother. Sure I noticed she was gorgeous, and I considered making a move but as we talked and spent some time together trying to keep her safe, I felt more of a little sister vibe than a girlfriend vibe, you know what I mean? If it's my blessing you're looking for, you got it. I don't know how I will ever repay you for not giving up on me." Liam reached out to E.R. and pulled him into a warm embrace. "You are my brother and I thank God for you."

E.R. wiped his eyes as he backed from the embrace. He felt the same way about Liam, and it didn't matter that they weren't blood related. They were brothers in every other way that counted. Now he felt like he had two brothers because in the short period that he'd known Logan, he had grown very fond of him as well. He was a lot like Liam and E.R. appreciated him stepping up to help when they needed him.

Charley Ann passed by on her way back to the waiting room. Liam noticed that he'd lost E.R.'s attention because he was anxious to talk to Charley Ann. Logan walked up and Liam signaled to E.R. to go and follow Charley Ann. He wasn't sure that E.R. wanted anyone to know that he was interested in Charley Ann, so out of respect for his friend, he kept that information to himself. Liam turned his focus onto Logan and the two sat down to catch up.

"I'm sorry about your mom. I know you hoped that one day you would be reunited with her. If there's anything you need, don't hesitate to ask. I know that we have some distance between us but I'm just a phone call away."

"Speaking of that, I was thinking about staying around for a while." He waited for Liam's response.

"That would be great man. You can stay with me. Hey, do you think we should switch back to our true identities since there's no longer a threat?" Liam held his breath as he waited for Logan's answer.

"I've been Logan since I was four years old. Unless you disagree, I think we should just leave things the way they are. Besides, don't forget that your father is still out there, and Sister Mary Grace said they were both monsters." Logan observed Liam flinch at that thought.

E.R. noticed Charley Ann sitting in one of the many matching waiting room chairs and asked her if she would take a walk with him. He was pleased to see the tender way she looked at him. He wasn't sure what he was going to say, but he needed to let her know how he felt. They walked out into the quiet courtyard and found an iron bench in the corner to sit and talk. Charley Ann sat but E.R. remained standing. His hands were sweating so he shoved them into his pants pocket before starting the conversation.

"How are you doing?" He didn't wait for her response. "These past few days felt like we were on a never-ending roller coaster. I'm so relieved that we finally found Liam, I was really scared that we had lost him." E.R. tried to relax but his efforts failed. Before he went on Charley Ann spoke up.

"E.R., I want to thank you for your kindness towards me even when you thought my ex-boyfriend was responsible for Liam's disappearance. You went above and beyond to protect me, and I really appreciate it." Charley Ann was scared that he was trying to tell her goodbye and she didn't want that to happen. She was awestruck with his selflessness and dedication to his friend Liam and had never encountered anyone with such conviction She stood up so that she was eye level with him.

E.R. stepped back to give her space. He couldn't believe she was going to just get up and walk away after all they had been through. He had to say something. He opened his mouth to speak, but she placed her finger over his lips to stop him. She stared into those beautiful, tender eyes and suddenly wanted to get lost in them forever.

E.R. took her hand into his and gazed back at her.

"I don't want you to leave. I know it's only been a few days, but I can't imagine life without you in it. You've turned my world upside down and I was hoping that you would stay here for a while and see where this goes." Before he could continue, Charley Ann leaped into his arms and answered him with a kiss.

Liam, who watched the whole thing unfold through a glass entrance to the courtyard, grinned and then he and the others joined them.

"I hope we're not interrupting anything here. The sheriff said we were all free to go home now. The doctors advised Tab to spend another night in the hospital but he's not having it. He's already dressed and ready to leave." Liam was all smiles, because aside from losing Lucas, everyone he cared about was safe and together. His smile faded as the lights flickered right before he heard the loudest boom of thunder followed by the sky opening up and heavy rain falling to the ground. They all ran for cover inside the hospital and were reminded that there was a Hurricane knocking at the door.

"Well. I guess that means we're not leaving anytime soon. Let's find my grandfather and Mr. Tab and hunker down for the night." E.R. turned around and looked at each person standing in front of him. "I just want to say that there's no one else I'd rather be with at a time like this than each of you."

Liam spoke up to lighten the mood. "Tell me that again after this thing blows over."

They all laughed, and then they heard a sharp piercing scream echo from down the hall as the lights went out and they were thrust into darkness.

"Here we go again! It's going to be a long night!"

While sitting in the dark refuge of the hospital waiting for the hurricane to pass, E.R. began to reflect on the recent events. This was the first time in some time that he was alone with his thoughts. He was happy that he and Charley Ann were going to have time to get to know each other because he was certain he was deeply in love and wanted to spend his life with her. His mind jumped to Liam as he was still trying to piece together all the new information about Liam, Logan, and Lucas and how their worlds collided so many years later. He smiled when he thought of Logan and hoped they would remain in contact.

E.R. was still baffled when he thought of the connection between Sam, Douglas, and Lucas. He understood that Lucas manipulated them into helping him with his plans of revenge, but he was disappointed that Sam fell for it. However things turn out, E.R. was grateful that Sam came through in the end and wouldn't be surprised if she and Charley Ann remained friends. He understood how Lucas was able to use Douglas because he was at rock bottom with his drug addiction. E.R. said a prayer for Douglas and hoped he would straighten out his life one day.

E.R.'s mind finally stopped on the Woman in white. He still needed to spend some time understanding exactly what that was about. Once he realized that she was not just a dream, he accepted the fact that she wanted something from him. He didn't know why he started to have visions of the woman but was grateful for her help. As he reflected on the times she had appeared, the one thing that was apparent was that she was trying to help him find

Liam. He didn't understand why until it became certain she was Lorna Theriot Ricci, Lucas, and Liam's mother. He had to admit, in the beginning he was afraid she was the woman from the Legend of Coquille but was glad he was wrong. In a time of misguided revenge and dark deceptions, the woman in white turned out to be a guiding vision of light.

CHAPTER 34

Under normal circumstances it would take Griff about ten minutes to get to the Fleming Cemetery, but the current bad conditions would probably add to that time. He was baffled at the idea that he was driving the boat on the highway that he usually traveled in his truck. He drove slowly so that he didn't cause a wake and push more water into someone's house. Crown Point looked like a ghost town under water. There were a few homes that had been raised over the years to protect against the floods, but it was devasting to see that most of the other homes took on water. He wondered about all of the wildlife in the area and was sick to think that they had no way of getting out of the water unless they got into a tree or found high ground, but Griff doubted there was too much high ground left. Griff thought about his own house and how heartbroken Abby would be when she sees their home in that condition. At the same time he was grateful that she was out of harm's way. Everyone in the boat rode in silence trying to absorb the chaos they were witnessing as Griff continued on towards the Intracoastal Canal. From the time they got into the boat, all sorts of unusual things had floated by, the latest being a huge log the length of Griff's boat.

They were close to the launch when they heard the sound of a dog yelping. Charley Ann noticed a dog on top of his doghouse surrounded by water. She stood up and yelled for them to stop before she jumped out of the boat and waded towards the dog.

"Wait Charley Ann, he might be mean. Be careful!" E.R. attempted to jump out of the boat and go after her, but Griff grabbed his arm.

"Give her a minute." Griff met E.R.'s eyes and calmed him down.

E.R. remained standing ready to jump in after her if needed and waited to see the dog's response as she approached it. The poor thing was soaking wet and looked scared to death. As Charley Ann got closer the dog wagged its tail and before she knew it, he leaped into her arms knocking her down and under the water. She jumped up, cradling the dog, and turned to reassure everyone that she was alright. She looked around to see if anyone was home as she walked up to the house and onto the front porch. The house seemed to be deserted. She let the dog, which turned out to be a small Lab puppy, down and waited as Griff maneuvered the boat closer to her. E.R. jumped onto the porch and looked for a collar, but he didn't have one. They had assumed that he belonged to the house where they found him but couldn't be sure.

"We can't leave him here alone without making sure these people are coming home and we have no way of knowing that." E.R. looked down at the soaking wet puppy and then over at Charley Ann who was also soaking wet and said, "The dog can sit on your lap."

Charley Ann smiled and without saying a word stepped into the boat with the dog in one hand and E.R. holding the other. She could hardly keep the puppy in her arms because he was so relieved to have been rescued that he was showering Charley Ann and anyone that came close to him with a kiss. They all shared a much-needed laugh before moving on to the more serious issue of finding Liam.

Once they made it to the Intercoastal Canal Griff trimmed down the motor and put the pedal to the medal. The conditions were worsening by the minute and Griff knew that they were in for a rough ride. He wasn't sure how Charley Ann and Logan would handle the boat ride, but he couldn't worry about that now. Going out in the boat during a hurricane was definitely uncharted territory for all of us. He was grateful E.R. was with him and knew what to watch for as they headed to Lafitte in the rising water. Usual landmarks disappeared when the water was high and could prove to be dangerous. Luckily there wasn't' any boat traffic because everyone was hunkered down and waiting on the hurricane and if circumstances were different, they would be doing the same. The situation was treacherous and both Griff and E.R. knew they had a small window of opportunity before this could turn into a catastrophe. Griff said a prayer and tried not to think how ridiculous and dangerous it was to drive a boat to Lafitte as a hurricane approached.

Another squall was passing through causing the winds to whip up again and drive the heavy rain sideways making it difficult to see. Griff pointed alerting them that they were almost there. The boat rocked back and forth, and the stinging rain had no mercy. E.R. stood to scope out a place that would be safe to tie off the boat once they reached the cemetery. There was a Barrier put up a few years ago to protect against flooding but the rising water had toppled over that already. Griff was able to kill the motor, glide right over the wall, and coast all the way to the Indian Mound. He felt like his stomach was in his throat as he surveilled the area and noticed that most of the graves at the bottom of the hill had already succumbed to the rising water.

E.R. hopped out of the front of the boat and found an old tombstone to tie the boat off to while the others were getting ready to get out. Logan jumped out next to E.R. and before anyone else exited the boat E.R. put up his hands to speak. Before he even got a word out, they heard a low whimpering sound coming from the other side of the mound. They were all motionless as they strained to recognize the sound between the howl of the wind and the noise of pounding rain.

"Stop! Why are you doing this? Are you crazy?" The voice was mumbled and too far away to identify.

E.R. and Logan crouched down, and the Griff and Charley Ann sat back down in the boat. Thankfully, the puppy was exhausted and had fallen asleep in a nice warm blanket underneath the console of the boat. E.R. got down on the ground and crawled towards the top to see if he could see exactly what was happening. All he saw was the top of someone's head and Sam who was arguing with the person she was with. E.R. crawled back to the group and reported what he saw and suggested that Griff stay in the boat with Charley Ann and he and Logan each take a side to flank them in. Griff started to object but E. R quickly reminded him that they were the only two people that could operate the boat in case they needed a quick getaway.

Griff lifted his hands in surrender and whispered, "be careful." He reached into the side of his jacket, unholstered his weapon and extended it to Logan with a look that asked if he knew how to use it. Logan nodded with a yes and took the gun from Griff. They all sat there waiting to see if they would hear more from Sam and whoever was with her.

"What are you going to do with him? Oh my God! You are crazy!" Sam continued to yell at the person with her. It sounded like a struggle was happening then it went quiet again. The frogs and the crickets continued to chirp, and E.R. was reminded of the night he came to the cemetery looking for Liam. A shiver ran through his body, and he began to shake. He took a few deep breaths to slow his heart rate down enough to hear another voice.

"Shut up before I put you down there with him!" The voice was still out of earshot.

"Did y'all hear that. He must be talking about Liam." E.R. had a wild look in his eyes and wanted to rush in to get Liam.

"Wait. Slow down. He might have a gun or a weapon. Go slow and follow the plan. Let Logan go around to the left and you go right. E.R., I know you are anxious to find Liam but let's not force the hand of a crazy man if we don't have to. Be smart and try to assess the situation before he sees you, then possibly you could try to negotiate with him. E.R. did you hear me?" Griff was concerned that his grandson was too anxious and that maybe he should go instead of him, but he knew that would never happen.

E.R. and Logan went over the plan to make sure they were on the same page. After assessing the situation, E.R. was going to approach first, and Logan would be back up if needed. E.R. noticed a strange look in Logan's eyes but chalked it up to the stress of the situation. Their eyes met one last time and E.R. prayed that he could trust Logan and that he could be counted on to help save Liam.

As the two men got into their positions, Logan waited for E.R. to make his move. He knew that E.R. had doubts about his loyalty to Liam, but they were unfounded. He loved Liam like a brother and Liam loved him the same. They had been together since they were young and had made sacrifices for each other without even realizing it. It wasn't until Sister Mary Grace agreed to tell them the truth that they both realized the actual extent of the sacrifice that was made and the danger that they were in. Both men maintained that they would die for each other, but Logan refused to let Liam die for him. He was going to set things right once and for all.

Lucas leaned back against the tomb that imprisoned Liam and glared at Sam. The veins in his
neck were so pronounced that they looked like
they would pop at any moment. His red shirt matched the
color of his face and even though he was soaking wet, his
adrenaline made him feel as though his temperature was
boiling hot. He'd gotten used to controlling things and he
was struggling with Sam taking control. He couldn't
comprehend how he always ended up surrounded by incompetent people. Both Douglas and Sam seemed to be
smart skilled people when he first met them. Sure, Douglas was a drug addict, but Lucas felt like that was all the
more reason for him to be loyal to the one person supplying him with his drugs. And he was loyal to the end, just
not as capable as Lucas had hoped. Lucas thought he
could rely on Douglas to carry out the dirty work, but it
quickly became apparent that his help was inadequate.
When they followed Liam and the girl from Bourbon Heat
to that cemetery, he instructed Douglas to separate the
two so that Lucas could kidnap Liam, but he failed. They
hadn't expected that another guy would show up and almost ruin the plan. The deviation from the plan rattled
Douglas causing Lucas to step up and get his own hands

dirty. He apologized to the man as he strangled the breath out of him and explained that it wasn't personal. He just couldn't let anything, or anyone get in the way. After the man stopped fighting and became unconscious, he simply disposed of the body by pushing him into the bayou and figured the gators would take it from there.

Unfortunately, Liam and the girl rescued the other guy from the grave and left the cemetery. Lucas was furious that his plan was foiled but decided he would wait at the cemetery for Liam to come back and retrieve his truck. Lucas and Douglas waited, and just as suspected Liam returned, and the game was back on. Now it was time to finish the job and enjoy the satisfaction he waited so long for.

Lucas shifted his weight and noticed that Sam didn't flinch. When he met Sam, he was quite taken by her because she came off as not only tough and self-confident but compassionate too. Under any other circumstances he would've considered dating her but currently he needs someone to help carry out his plan for vengeance and it had to be someone that couldn't be traced back to him. Her genuine concern and desire to help her longtime friend Douglas made her the perfect pawn. Not long after he befriended Douglas, he met Sam and convinced her that he was the victim of an overpowering abusive wife. He declared that she cheated on him with his estranged brother, and she was trying to take everything from him. He pleaded with her to help him get enough dirt on them to help his case and she fell for it. What Lucas really wanted was to kidnap the two people that were most important to his long-lost brother and make him suffer as he did.

When Douglas followed Charley Ann and E.R. to Grand Isle, and to the Bridge Side Marina, he tried to call Lucas, but there was no answer. He wasn't sure what to do next but remembered that Sam just so happened to be there visiting her cousin. Lucas had given Douglas instructions to follow Charley Ann and E.R. and at the first opportunity, bring them to him unharmed. Douglas hated to lie to Sam, but he knew that Lucas had fed her this sob story and had no choice but to go along with it. Douglas hadn't known Lucas for very long, but he knew in his gut not to cross him. Sam had promised to help poor Lucas in any way she could, so Douglas played along and talked her into befriending Charley Ann.

Lucas had hoped that Douglas and Sam would've been able to secure E.R. and Charley Ann for him in Grand Isle, but of course Douglas was high, and paranoid and Sam refused to play along when she realized Lucas wanted her to do more than just get information for him. He realized that he would have to be more involved if he were to carry out his plans which he fully intended to do.

Lucas hadn't counted on the shed at Liam's house collapsing down on him. He was almost exposed, and his plans ruined but as usual incompetency is everywhere, so he was able to slip out of the hospital unnoticed. When he finally reached Douglas and found out that he and Sam failed to secure Charley Ann and E.R. he was furious.

He's ordered Douglas to get back to Marrero and to take Sam with him. They attempted to scope out E.R.'s house and wait for another opportunity to come along but ran out of time because the hurricane was coming in fast, and he had to get to Liam before the rising water flooded the tomb and drowned him.

Lucas looked down into the tomb and was grateful that he chose one that was close to the top of the mound. If he'd chosen differently, Liam would already be dead and would've robbed him of the opportunity to watch him suffer. When they arrived, his dear brother was frantically trying to plead his case, but Lucas didn't want to hear any of his excuses. Lucas drove away from the swamp after an alligator had taken care of poor Douglas, so he no longer had to worry about him.

Liam had worn himself out and was laying silently on the floor of the tomb. Sam's rantings caught Liam's attention again and he was back up and this time pleading with him.

"Leave her alone! What do you want? Who are you?" Liam was confused and had no idea who the girl was, but she was clearly scared and that tugged on his emotions.

"Well hello again" Lucas looked down at Liam. "I see you still haven't accepted the situation that you're in." Lucas' voice was low and scratchy and lacked the confidence from before. He was having second thoughts about killing Liam and didn't like that Sam took over the situation.

"Wait! Please tell me who you are. What do you want? Let's talk please. I can help you."

"Help me. You don't even know who I am, how can you help me?" Lucas was entertained by Liam's frustration. He sat down on the ground next to the top of the tomb he'd pushed open earlier and stared down at his brother. "You have no idea who I am do you. Look at me! How do you not know who I am?" Lucas yelled as he spoke.

"I know who you are!"

Lucas jumped up just as he heard E.R. voice and saw that he had rounded the mound and lunged towards him. He attempted to stand but E.R. was on top of him before he could get up. The two wrestled back and forth before Lucas was able to break free and scramble to safety. Lucas laughed as he tried to calm down and think. "This is even better than I thought. I have been trying to get to you for some time now."

E.R.'s focus was still on Lucas when he caught a glimpse of white out of the corner of his eye. He turned his attention towards Sam and noticed that the lady in white was hovering above her. Before he could make sense of the situation, he noticed that Sam was holding the gun. *She must've gotten the gun from Lucas.* Feeling relieved, he held up his hands assuring Lucas that he wasn't going to attack. E.R. looked down in the tomb and was pleased to see Liam alive and the woman in white standing over him like a shield. He quickly brought his gaze back to Lucas, trying to buy some time because he knew

Logan was watching and would be waiting for an opportunity to make his move.

"I'm here now. Can we please talk." A loud cracking sound forced them all to look up just in time to see a large branch tumble to the ground right below them. The intense winds were bending the trees like they were made of rubber.

Lucas wiped the rain from his face and moved closer to the opening of the tomb. He smiled at E.R. as he watched the light bulb go off inside his head and realization of the situation become clear.

Liam became frantic again and scratched at the walls in an attempt to climb out of the tomb. Lucas noticed the look in Sam's eyes and knew that she was going to pull the trigger. E.R. jumped into action and leaped towards Sam just as Logan came around from the other side of the mound and caught her attention. The distraction caused her to fire the gun, but it missed her target. E.R. watched as the woman in white appeared and was standing over Lucas. The grief she had endured was written all over her face. All of a sudden, she was right in front of his face with her mouth open wide and her arms waving in the air. Lucas stumbled backwards at the site of her and lost his balance.

"Hello brother." Logan walked up and looked down at Lucas with pity.

"What! No! Who are you? You are not my brother! Liam's my brother!" Lucas was screaming uncontrollably.

Charley Ann and Griff heard the gunfire and came running around the mound to find Lucas yelling, Sam holding a gun and Logan hanging over the top of the tomb talking to Liam. Charley Ann headed straight for Sam, but E.R. warned her off. "Charley Ann no! She's on our side." Charley Ann stopped abruptly and looked at Sam who was now pointing the gun at her. E.R.'s warning to Charley Ann caught everyone's attention and they all froze.

"What are you doing?" Charley Ann was baffled.

"Hello Charley Ann. It's good to see you again. I'm sorry it's under these unfortunate circumstanced but some things just can't be helped." Sam's eyes were wild with fury. Everyone stood still as they listened to Sam's chilling words. "Dear Lucas here thought that I was just some poor sap that wanted to help him escape his abusive cheating wife." Sam started to laugh uncontrollably. "You are so pathetic! You couldn't even carry out your own plans of revenge."

Sam looked at E.R. and back to Charley Ann. "When we got here, he said that he was going to kill Liam, but he chickened out. He started to weep like a baby and was mumbling that maybe it wasn't Liam's fault." Sam looked towards Lucas with disgust. "Of course it's Liam's fault! He should've searched for you even when mother didn't! That's right mother, our mother! She was pregnant with me when she left our father!"

Lucas looked deflated and simply sat down on the ground.

Sam was fighting back tears as she continued her rant. "We all blame our father, but Lorna was the real monster. How does a mother abandon her children? And why would she only reach out to Liam and not us." Sam looked over at Logan and smiled. "That was a smart move brother. But what kind of a friend would you have been had Lucas killed the person he thought was you in that gravesite? I guess you are the only one living without torment or a desire of revenge. I bounced from one foster care to another and each one was worse than the previous one. When I turned 13, I ran away and have been on my own since then. I tracked down Lorna and Lorenzo and waited for years to get my revenge. Luckily, my dear brother here beat me to it, at least when it came to our parents. Good job big brother."

Sam's face turned ash white as she stared past Lucas. "No! It can't be you! You're dead! I saw him kill you!" Sam was screaming at the lady in white who was floating above Lucas. She lifted the gun and fired emptying the chamber of bullets. Griff moved forward and tackled Sam to the ground. Sam's body went limp, and she stopped struggling with Griff but continued to stare over Lucas' head.

Griff relieved Sam of the gun and handed it back to Charley Ann. Lucas who was still screaming at both Sam and Logan had been hit by some of the bullets and was fading fast from the loss of blood. E.R. and Logan helped get Liam out of the tomb and aside from being water-logged from all of the rain that had gathered at the bottom of the tomb, he was in good shape. Logan pulled off his raincoat and wrapped it around Liam. "Thank God you're alright. They almost killed you." Logan was visibly upset.

"I can't believe you're here. How did y'all find me?" Liam was struggling to stand.

Logan helped him up and let him lean on him as they both walked over to Sam who had begun to scream, laugh, and cry at the same time. "Let me go! Get off of me! You think you won!"

As the two men got closer, Lucas's eyes jumped from Logan to Liam and back to Logan. His mind was struggling to comprehend how they fooled him with the switch.

Logan looked at Lucas and was disgusted by what he saw. "What happened to you was not my fault. I had no idea where you were just like you didn't know where I was. Why do you hate me so much that you wanted me dead?" Logan searched for some familiar look on Lucas' face but couldn't find one.

E.R. watched in awe as the woman in white was still hovering over Lucas. He looked around and determined that he and Sam were the only ones that could see her, so he remained silent. They all listened as Logan explained that he and Liam's identities were switched when they were dropped off at the convent and when Sister Mary Grace summoned them, she warned them that Lucas and his father were searching for Liam and that they were in danger. Logan immediately wanted to switch back to his proper identity because he didn't want anything to happen to Liam, but Liam refused and was determined to protect Logan.

"Our father was a joke. He tried to find you and mother for years but failed. I was the one that found the convent and I was the one that found you! He was a horrible man, and I was the one that was beaten every day because he couldn't find y'all. And ya'll left me there! How could a mother leave her child with a monster like that?" Lucas became enraged and before they knew it, he broke free, ran to Charley Ann, and grabbed onto the gun. They struggled and the gun fired. Lucas fell to his knees and then ironically toppled into the open tomb that recent-ly held Liam. They all rushed to the tomb and saw that Lucas was still conscious lying on the ground.

"Well brother, I assure you that you don't have to wor-ry about those monsters anymore. I killed our father and then tracked down our mother. You should've seen the look of disbelief and shock on her face when I drove that knife deep into her belly where she once nurtured me. She begged and pleaded and tried to convince me that she loved me, but I knew it was all lies. It was way too late to make amends. She had to pay for abandoning me." Lucas choked before he teared up again. "I had no idea about Sam. Why did ya'll leave me with a monster brother? Why?" Lucas choked again as he drew his last breath.

E.R. watched as the woman in white wrapped herself around Lucas and looked up at Liam with soft, tearful eyes. That's when E.R. realized that the lady in white was

the ghost of their mother and he prayed that she was finally at peace.

CHAPTER 36

Griff called the local sheriff and waited for them to come out to the cemetery to retrieve Lucas' body and take Sam into custody. Griff and the sheriff were personal friends and agreed that it was in everyone's best interest to get out of Lafitte quickly and meet at the hospital for questioning because the water was rising at an alarming rate. Liam was strong enough to get to Griff's boat where they all piled in and headed back to higher ground. Griff radioed ahead and had an ambulance meet them at the V shape levee to transport Liam to the hospital and the rest of them piled into Griff's truck. They rode in silence absorbing the bizarre chain of events that had unfolded before their eyes.

The ambulance reached the hospital before they did and took Liam into the emergency room. Griff hopped out of the truck and ran straight to the elevators. He got in and pressed the button for the third floor. His mind was running in several directions as he rode the elevator up. He was shocked to learn that Liam and Logan had swapped identities and were willing to die for each other. He found comfort in knowing that E.R. had such a great guy for a best friend. Griff thought about Tab and goose bumps covered his body. *I can't imagine life without Tab.* The elevator door opened, and he sprinted passed the nurses station and burst into room 318 to find Tab sitting up in the bed. He ran to him, wrapped his arms around him and almost knocked the wind out of him.

"It's good to see you too buddy!" Tab returned the embrace. He thought that he was going to die out there in the swamp and while he doesn't know how they found him, he is eternally grateful that they did.

When Griff finally released Tab, he gave him a lecture. "Don't you ever go off without back up again. You could've died out there. How did you end up in the swamp?"

"When I dropped you off at E.R.'s house, I ran back over to Liam's to take one last look around. Something didn't sit right with me when we had left earlier so I decided since I was close, I would go back and satisfy that nagging gut feeling. When I walked around the back of the shed, someone hit me with a 2 X 4 and ran. I chased him until he jumped into a black sedan. I ran back to my truck and followed them through the neighborhood and onto the old highway headed towards Lafitte. Believe it or not, a deer ran out by the big curve and hit the front of my truck causing me to jerk to the right and lose control. The car that I was chasing backed up to where I went off the road, so I ran deeper into the swamp hoping that they would give up and go away. Lucas forced Douglas to come after me and as you know, he had an unfortunate encounter with a big gator. Griff that thing was huge. I don't know how I missed it because I had to run right past the thing."

Tab's happy expression faded, and he thought of the guy that was with him in the swamp. He looked up at Griff and before he could ask, Griff explained that Douglas was near death when the paramedics arrived but because of Tab's intervention and a miraculous miracle, he survived to see another day. He lost his arm, but the doctors think that he'll make a complete recovery. Lucas was not so lucky.

E.R., Charley Ann, and Logan waited in the emergency room to make sure that Liam was going to be alright. The emergency room doctors checked out Liam and aside from being a little dehydrated, determined that he was in good shape, and he could go home. They all joined Griff in Tab's room and realized that they had formed a new bond that would never be broken.

While they waited to be questioned by the sheriff, E.R. was able to talk to Liam privately to find out where his head was at in all of this. He wanted to know if he had feelings for Charley Ann because E.R. had grown fond of her over the past few days and really wanted to see where things would lead to. He would never move in on Charley Ann if Liam was interested in her.

"So what do you think about Charley Ann? She was a big help over the last few days. She's a tough one too. She really knows how to handle herself." Liam was smiling as he talked about Charley Ann.

"Look at you all flustered over a girl." Liam smiled and continued to tease E.R. about his apparent feelings. "I thought you swore off women a long time ago."

"Hey man. If you like her just say the word and I'll back off. I know you were interested in her at Bourbon Heat and the two of you spent time together afterwards." E.R. was anxiously waiting for a response.

"You got it all wrong brother. Sure I noticed that she was gorgeous, and I considered making a move but as we talked and spent some time together trying to keep her safe, I felt more of a little sister vibe than a girlfriend vibe, you know what I mean? If it's my blessing you're looking for, you got it. I don't know how I will ever repay you for not giving up on me." Liam reached out to E.R. and pulled him into a warm embrace. "You are my brother and I thank God for you."

E.R. wiped his eyes as he backed from the embrace. He felt the same way about Liam, and it didn't matter that they weren't blood related, they were brothers in every other way that counted. And now he felt like he had two brothers because in the short period that he'd known Logan, he had grown very fond of him as well. He was a lot like Liam and E.R. appreciated him stepping up to help when they needed him.

Charley Ann passed by on her way back to the waiting room. Liam noticed that he'd lost E.R.'s attention because he was anxious to talk to Charley Ann. Logan walked up and Liam signaled to E.R. to go and follow Charley Ann. He wasn't sure that E.R. wanted anyone to know that he was interested in Charley Ann, so out of respect for his friend, he kept that information to himself. Liam turned his focus onto Logan and the two sat down to catch up.

"I'm sorry about your mom. I know you hoped that one day you would be reunited with her. If there's anything you need, don't hesitate to ask. I know that we have some distance between us but I'm just a phone call away."

"Speaking of that, I was thinking about staying around for a while." He waited for Liam's response.

"That would be great man. You can stay with me. Hey, do you think we should switch back to our true identities since there's no longer a threat?" Liam held his breath as he waited for Logan's answer.

"I've been Logan since I was four years old. Unless you disagree, I think we should just leave things the way they are. Besides, don't forget that your father is still out there, and Sister Mary Grace said that they were both monsters." Logan observed Liam flinch at that thought.

E.R. noticed Charley Ann sitting in one of the many matching waiting room chairs and asked her if she would take a walk with him. He was pleased to see the tender way she looked at him. He wasn't sure what he was going to say, but he needed to let her know how he felt. They walked out into the quiet courtyard and found an iron bench in the corner to sit and talk. Charley Ann sat but E.R. remained standing. His hands were sweating so he shoved them into his pants pocket before starting the conversation.

"How are you doing?" He didn't wait for her response. "These past few days felt like we were on a never-ending roller coaster. I'm so relieved that we finally found Liam, I was really scared that we had lost him." E.R. tried to relax but his efforts failed. Before he went on Charley Ann spoke up.

"E.R., I want to thank you for your kindness towards me even when you thought my ex-boyfriend was responsible for Liam's disappearance. You went above and beyond to protect me, and I really appreciate it." Charley Ann was scared that he was trying to tell her goodbye and she didn't want that to happen. She was awestruck with his selflessness and dedication to his friend Liam and had never encountered anyone with such conviction She stood up so that she was eye level with him.

E.R. stepped back to give her space. He couldn't believe that she was going to just get up and walk away after all they had been through. He had to say something. He opened his mouth to speak, but she placed her finger over his lips to stop him. She stared into those beautiful, tender eyes and suddenly wanted to get lost in them forever.

E.R. took her hand into his and gazed back at her.

"I don't want you to leave. I know it's only been a few days, but I can't imagine life without you in it. You've turned my world upside down and I was hoping that you would stay here for a while and see where this goes." Before he could continue, Charley Ann leaped into his arms and answered him with a kiss.

Liam, who watched the whole thing unfold through a glass entrance to the courtyard, grinned and then he and the others joined them.

"I hope we're not interrupting anything here. The sheriff said we were all free to go home now. The doctors advised Tab to spend another night in the hospital but he's not having it. He's already dressed and ready to leave." Liam was all smiles, because aside from losing Lucas, everyone he cared about was safe and together. His smile faded as the lights flickered right before he heard the loudest boom of thunder followed by the sky opening up and heavy rain fell to the ground. They all ran for cover inside the hospital and were reminded that there was a hurricane knocking at the door.

"Well. I guess that means we're not leaving anytime soon. Let's find my grandfather and Mr. Tab and hunker down for the night." E.R. turned around and looked at each person standing in front of him. "I just want to say that there's no one else I'd rather be with at a time like this than each of you."

Liam spoke up to lighten the mood. "Tell me that again after this thing blows over."

They all laughed, and then they heard a sharp piercing scream echo from down the hall as the lights went out and they were thrust into darkness.

"Here we go again! It's going to be a long night!"

While sitting in the dark refuge of the hospital waiting for the Hurricane to pass, E.R. began to reflect on the recent events. This was the first time in some time that he was alone with his thoughts. He was happy that he and Charley Ann were going to have time to get to know each other because he was certain that he was deeply in love and wanted to spend his life with her. His mind jumped to Liam as he was still trying to piece together all the new information about Liam, Logan, Lucas, and Sam and how their worlds collided so many years later. He smiled when he thought of Logan and hoped they would remain in contact.

E.R. was still baffled when he thought of the connection between Sam, Douglas, and Lucas. He understood that Lucas manipulated them into helping him with his plans of revenge, but he never dreamed that Sam had her own agenda. He understood how Lucas was able to use Douglas because he was at rock bottom with his drug addiction. E.R. said a prayer for Douglas and hoped that he would straighten out his life one day.

E.R.'s mind finally stopped on the Woman in white. He still needed to spend some time understanding exactly what that was about. Once he realized that she was not just a dream, he accepted the fact that she wanted something from him. He doesn't know why he started to have visions of the woman but was grateful for her help. As he reflected on the times that she had appeared, the one thing that was apparent was that she was trying to help him find Liam. He didn't understand why until it became certain that she was Lorna Theriot Ricci, Lucas, Liam, and Sam's mother. He had to admit, in the beginning he was afraid that she was the woman from the Legend of Coquille but was glad he was wrong. In a time of misguided revenge and dark deceptions the woman in white turned out to be a guiding vision of light.

Acknowledgments

To my family and friends. Thank you for not only supporting me but for being patient and encouraging me to write *Misguided Revenge*. The surprisingly overwhelming response to my first novel, *Slipping Into Darkness,* touched my heart and inspired me to continue to do something I truly love to do.

Misguided Revenge was so much fun to write, and I want to thank the following incredible people for their help: My grandson Davin Ortego for being the inspiration for my amazing main character E.R. (Evan Robert). My Beta readers: Glenn Griffin, Charisse Zanca, Peggy Morgan, Sr. M. Clared, Gilda Bourgeois, Barbara Flowers and Pam Volek.

Thank you to my sister n law Kathy Griffin for always helping with my computer issues. Without you I would have to go back to using a typewriter.

A special thank you to Charisse, for not only reading my book but listening to me talk about it over and over again. You keep me sane.

Another special thank you to Pam, for not only reading my book, but for brainstorming with me throughout and sharing her much needed time, ideas, and "suggestions" as I was editing and deciding on a title.

Without all of their love, support and of course constructive criticism, things would've been so much more difficult.

Thank you to my husband Glenn, for once again encouraging me to follow my dream and always having my back. I love our life and I love you more every day.

Most important of all, I want to give Glory to God. I am truly Blessed and owe everything to him. Through him all things are possible. God's Will Be Done!

You all make life worth living.
Love to all.

Also by
D. M. Bourgeois

ABOUT THE AUTHOR

D. M. Bourgeois was born in New Orleans and now resides in Crown Point, Louisiana with her husband Glenn. She received a B.A from Nicholls State University in Thibodaux, Louisiana. She believes that her life is blessed, and aside from being a mother and grandmother, becoming an author is one of her greatest joys. Her first novel, SLIPPING INTO DARKNESS, was a Silver Falchion Finalists in the Best Supernatural category.

For more information you can visit D. M. Bourgeois @
Website: dmbourgeois.com
Email: dmbourgeois61@gmail.com
Facebook: dmbourgeois61
Instagram: d.m.bourgeois